THE PEOPLE
AND
UNCOLLECTED
STORIES

Books by Bernard Malamud

THE NATURAL

THE ASSISTANT

THE MAGIC BARREL

A NEW LIFE

IDIOTS FIRST

THE FIXER

PICTURES OF FIDELMAN

THE TENANTS

REMBRANDT'S HAT

DUBIN'S LIVES

GOD'S GRACE

THE STORIES OF BERNARD MALAMUD

THE PEOPLE AND UNCOLLECTED STORIES

Bernard Malamud

THE PEOPLE
and
Uncollected Stories

EDITED AND INTRODUCED BY
ROBERT GIROUX

FARRAR · STRAUS · GIROUX
NEW YORK

Copyright © 1989 by Ann Malamud
Introduction copyright © 1989 by Robert Giroux
All rights reserved
First printing, 1989
Printed in the United States of America
Published simultaneously in Canada by Collins Publishers, Toronto
Designed by Jack Harrison

Library of Congress Cataloging-in-Publication Data
Malamud, Bernard.
The people, and uncollected stories / Bernard Malamud;
edited and introduced by Robert Giroux.
p.   cm.
I. Giroux, Robert.   II. Title.
PS3563.A4P4   1990   89-11764
813'.54—dc20

Contents

STORIES

Introduction

BY ROBERT GIROUX

My writing has drawn, out of a reluctant soul, a measure of astonishment at the nature of life.

BERNARD MALAMUD

ONE SUNDAY AFTERNOON in June 1940 a lonely young writer in his twenties walked from his rooming house in Washington, D.C. to a park, haunted by the news that Paris had fallen to the Nazis. He tried to efface the gloom and despair of France's defeat, while "sitting in the Dupont Circle park on this still Sun-. day," by recording the quotidian signs of ordinary life passing before his eyes:

"A little girl in a red dress much too large for her wobbled across the grass after a gray kitten."—"A woman stopped to speak intently to the man she was walking with."—A poor man "in a shabby suit drifted across the cement walk . . . glanced hesitantly, then passed by."—A flock of "pigeons flew down from the housetops to peck at scattered crumbs." The scene's peace and serenity were calming his nerves: "Much of the throb in my brain was gone." But at that moment he heard cries of "Stop, thief!" and saw a fleeing man caught almost in front of him by his pursuer. A small crowd gathered and the robber, his arms pinioned behind, turned to the nearby writer. He "asked me to give him a cigarette. I got one for him and lit it. Then he asked if I thought he looked like a thief. I said no, and he nodded."

The writer wondered why he felt no pity and attributed this to the man's indifferent manner; he had robbed so often that his arrest meant nothing to him. The police arrived and "the crowd broke up and I walked along Connecticut Avenue, wondering if I should be glad that the war had dulled my emotions so that I felt no pity for yet some more human misery."

The young writer was Bernard Malamud. He sent the piece he had written to *The Washington Post*; they published it in July 1940. It has interest as one of the earliest published writings of a man who, in the decades that followed, became one of America's foremost writers. Brief though it is, it is wholly Malamudian in feeling and themes, including the celebration of ordinary life against an unusual or tragic background.

*   *   *

Bernard Malamud had come to Washington in the spring of 1940 to work as a clerk in the Census Bureau. Born in Brooklyn on April 26, 1914, he was the elder of the two sons of Max and Bertha (Fidelman) Malamud, Jewish immigrants from Russia. His parents had worked hard to establish a late-night neighborhood grocery store in Brooklyn, a setting destined to become familiar in his work. The store changed locations over the years, until it settled at 1111 Macdonald Avenue, where the family lived in rooms over the store. Bertha Malamud died in 1929, when Bernard was fifteen, and Max Malamud remarried. ("After the death of my own mother," Bernard wrote,* "I had had a stepmother and a thin family life.")

Eugene Malamud, Bernard's younger brother, was hospitalized twice for schizophrenia; he died of a heart attack at age fifty-five. Bernard's uncle, Charlie Fidelman, a prompter at the Yiddish theater on the Lower East Side, had toured with a repertory company in Buenos Aires. He may have inspired an early story in this book, "Benefit Performance," as well as "Suppose a Wedding," a scene from a play published in *Idiots First*. Bern went to grammar school in Brooklyn at P.S. 181 and, after graduating from Erasmus Hall High School in 1932, entered City College, where he received his B.A. in 1936.

* The autobiographical quotations are from "Long Work, Short Life," the seventh Ben Belitt Lecture, given by Bernard Malamud at Bennington College on October 30, 1984.

"I had hoped to start writing short stories after graduation from City College during the Depression," he wrote, "but they were long in coming. I had ideas and felt I was on the verge of sustained work. But at that time I had no regular means of earning a living; and as the son of a poor man, a poor grocer, I could not stand the thought of living off him, a generous and self-denying person. . . . I registered for a teacher's examination and afterwards worked a year at $4.50 a day as a teacher-in-training in a high school in Brooklyn." He also took civil service exams for postal clerk and letter carrier. "This is mad, I thought, or I am. Yet I told myself the kind of work I might get didn't matter so long as I was working for time to write."

He was offered work in Washington in the spring of 1940. "I accepted at once though I soon realized the 'work' was a laugh. All morning I conscientiously checked estimates of drainage ditch statistics, as they appeared in various counties in the United States. Although the work hardly thrilled me, I worked diligently and was promoted after three months. . . . I had begun to write seriously on company time. No one seemed to care what I was doing so long as the record showed I had finished a full day's work. After lunch I kept my head bent low while I was writing stories at my desk. . . . I wrote a piece for *The Washington Post*, mourning the fall of France after the German Army . . . was obscenely jubilant in conquered Paris. I felt unhappy, as though mourning the death of a civilization I loved; yet somehow I managed to celebrate ongoing life and related acts. . . . Though I was often lonely, I stayed in the rooming house night after night trying to invent stories I needn't be ashamed of." One such story, published in this book for the first time, is "Armistice," a fictional treatment of the fall of France as it affects an American grocer and his son.

Returning to New York in September 1940 for an evening school job, Bernard earned his M.A. in English two years later at Columbia University—he wrote his master's thesis on Hardy's *The Dynasts*—and thought about writing a novel. By 1943 he had finished a dozen stories, a few of which began to appear in little magazines. One of these, "The Place Is Different Now," originally published in *American Prefaces*, he called "the forerunner of *The Assistant*."

A severe critic of his own writing, he burned the manuscript of his first completed novel, *The Light Sleeper*, "one night in Oregon because I felt I could do better." While writing and teaching at night at Erasmus Hall High School in Brooklyn, he met Ann de Chiara and they were married in 1945. ("She had been a Catholic. I defined myself as Jewish.") Their son, Paul, was born in 1947 and their daughter, Janna, in 1952.

When their son was two, the Malamuds moved from New York to Corvallis, Oregon, where Bernard had received an offer to teach at Oregon State College. Also in 1949, *Harper's Bazaar* bought the first story for which he was paid, "The Cost of Living." While at Oregon State he worked on his novel *The Natural*, which he had begun before leaving New York. He also wrote perhaps his most famous story, "The Magic Barrel," in a carrel in the basement of the college library. He was allowed to teach freshman composition but not literature because, he wrote, "I was nakedly without a Ph.D."

As editor in chief of Harcourt, Brace and Company, I first heard of Bernard Malamud's writing from two friends: Alfred Kazin told me Bern had written a novel about baseball; a year later Catharine Carver, who had taken "The Magic Barrel" for *Partisan Review*, sent me a typescript of the story in advance of publication. When Bern and I met, I told him not only how much I admired *The Natural*, into which were woven the myths and realities of America's favorite sport, but "The Magic Barrel" as well. The story was not only wholly unlike *The Natural* in style and content, it was also unlike anyone else's writing anywhere. The two works, as I saw it, added up to genius, and to Bern I expressed the hope that the novel might be followed by a book of stories. When we signed the contract for *The Natural*, I quoted the famous statement "I greet you at the beginning of a great career," to which Bern replied "Emerson to Walt Whitman." I knew I had found a friend as well as a major writer.

Though it seemed unlikely at the time, fate arranged that I was to be the editor of all his books. Having moved to Farrar, Straus and Company in 1955, I regretted that Bern could not move with me. A year later he told me Harcourt had turned down his new book, and I said I couldn't believe they would reject his stories. "No," he said, "it's a novel called *The Assistant*. Would you like to read it?" Roger Straus and I were bowled over by this fine novel, which some readers consider his masterpiece.

In 1957, when *The Assistant* appeared, it won the Rosenthal Award of the National Institute of Arts and Letters. Bern dedicated it to his father, who had died just after the publication of *The Natural*. ("What does a writer need most? When I ask this question, I think of my father.") In 1958 we published *The Magic Barrel*, his first collection of stories, which he dedicated to his brother, Eugene. It won the National Book Award.

In September 1961 he joined the faculty at Bennington College in Vermont, where he remained the rest of his life. "The college, an unusual place to work and learn," he wrote, "soon became a continuing source of education for me." In 1967 he won the Pulitzer Prize, as well as his second National Book Award, for *The Fixer*. In 1979 he received the Governor's Award from the Vermont Council on the Arts. He served as president of the American P.E.N. from 1979 to 1981, and in 1983 he was awarded the Gold Medal for fiction by the American Academy and Institute of Arts and Letters. Having written and published eight novels and four collections of stories, he died of a heart attack in New York on March 18, 1986, one month short of his seventy-second birthday.

*   *   *

This book includes sixteen uncollected stories by Bernard Malamud, and his unfinished novel, *The People*. He left instructions for his literary executors—Timothy Seldes, Daniel Stern, and myself—to decide what unpublished or uncollected work, if any, was to appear posthumously. After consulting with his family, we all agreed that *The People*, even though unfinished, should be made available to readers. This was not an easy decision to arrive at. He had been able to complete drafts of only sixteen of the twenty or so chapters he had projected for the novel, and we were aware of what he had said in his Bennington lecture: "I would write a book, or a short story, at least three times—once to understand it, the second time to improve the prose, and a third to compel it to say what it still must say." *The People* did not have the benefit of his usual painstaking procedure. Though he had worked hard at it during the months preceding his death—indeed, he was at his writing desk working on Chapter 17 on the day he died of a heart attack—his first draft of the novel was unfinished.

In concept *The People* ranks with Malamud's most serious work. It is a comic-tragic narrative of a persecuted and doomed people, a tribe of Indians in America's Northwest in the post-Civil War period who put their hopes for justice in an itinerant peddler and occasional carpenter named Yozip. He resists the honor of chiefdom but finds it thrust upon him anyway, and becomes their chief under the new name of Jozip. In a sense, the genesis of *The People* dated back to the 1940s, when a friend of the Malamuds told a joke about a "Jewish Indian." Bernard was amused, and the idea of such an unlikely character as a hero appealed to his creative imagination. Like much of his work, which often took form only years after the original conception, *The People* had a slow gestation over decades. While living and teaching in the Northwest, for example, he did research on the Nez Percé tribe, also called the Shahaptin or Cho-punnish, whose territory was eastern Oregon, Washington, and central Idaho. The tribe in the novel is simply identified as the People.

It was not until 1983–84 that he began to make notes for his new novel, at a moment in his life—he had reached his seventies—when he was seeking a change of material:

> I may have done as much as I can with the sort of short story I have been writing so long—the somewhat mythological, biblically oriented tales I have been writing. These become more and more difficult to do and I feel I must make a change. What I see as possible is another variation of the comic-mythological—possibly working out the Chief Joseph of the Nez Percé idea—in other words, the Jewish Indian; or the igloo piece of the race to the North Pole. Possibly both, but I must recover the voice I need. I have reached a dangerous place for a writer to be, that means I should search for a new material.

Malamud gave a reading of the opening chapters of *The People*, to standing-room-only, at the Bruno Walter Auditorium in Lincoln Center in 1985. The audience was enthusiastic and he was at ease and showed his usual sense of humor in the question period that followed. In March 1986, the night before his death, the Malamuds were dinner guests of Roger and Dorothea Straus when he revealed that he was within three or four chapters of completing his first draft of *The People*. He thought the final manuscript might be ready in the fall and was sanguine about its prospects.

The People, without the fragment of Chapter 17, ends with these words: "The moaning of the Indians began as the freight cars were moving along the tracks." The U.S. government has expropriated their lands, and despite their bravery, they are powerless to resist a superior force. Are we to conclude that Malamud intended to write a novel of defeat and despair? On the contrary, his notes for the subsequent chapters, which are here appended to the text, show that Jozip, despite his failure as the tribe's chief, has refused to accept defeat. The Jewish peddler returns to his cousin in Chicago determined to become a more effective champion of the rights of the People, and enrolls in night school to study law.

It is a tragedy that Bernard Malamud did not live to give final form to his vision of *The People*. Paul Malamud, his son, expressed it well in words he wrote after reading the manuscript his father left behind:

> Is despair the final meaning of this work, for Malamud and Jozip the carpenter? Far from it. The notes and outline show that Malamud wished to conclude with a vision of hope: Jozip was to plead the cause of the People before a nation rapidly becoming more civilized. Malamud's theme is that words and thoughts can conquer chaos, knowledge can conquer ignorance, ethics and law can conquer barbarism. . . . Malamud believed the universe responds to the human desire for justice.
>
> Because the vision in this work is so clear, the surviving fragment of *The People* is greater than the sum of its parts. For the author and the reader the story—if not the novel—is complete.

*   *   *

Ten of the sixteen stories collected in the second half of this book were published in magazines between 1943 and 1985: "The Literary Life of Laban Goldman," "Benefit Performance," "The Place Is Different Now," "An Apology," "An Exorcism," "A Wig,"

"Zora's Noise," "A Lost Grave," "In Kew Gardens," and "Alma Redeemed." Although the author included none of them in a book, the literary executors agree that they merit being read. They decided this is also true of six of the group of unpublished stories found among Malamud's papers, namely, "Armistice," "Spring Rain," "The Grocery Store," "Riding Pants," "A Confession of Murder," and "The Elevator." Though these stories vary widely in themes, date of composition, locales, and style, they provide evidence of their author's development and growth over a long and brilliant career of more than forty years.

"A Confession of Murder" requires comment because he did not write it as a story. It is the opening section of a novella he wrote in 1952–53, titled *The Man Nobody Could Lift*, which he set aside and finally abandoned. Its central themes—moral responsibility and the difficulty, if not impossibility, of communication—were favorites of Malamud's and found their most unusual expression in *God's Grace* (1982). This self-contained opening chapter is a portrait of a mentally ill young man who confesses to the murder of his father, and concludes with an atypical surprise ending.

The last two stories Malamud wrote, in his search for new forms, were what he called "fictive biographies." While working on *Dubin's Lives* (1979), the novel whose hero is a biographer, he did extensive reading in biographies. In New York he attended meetings of a "psychobiography" group made up largely of psychiatrists and analysts, and presented a paper or two of his own. In 1982, at the time of the publication of *God's Grace*, he was a fellow at the Center for Advanced Study in the Behavioral Sciences at Stanford, when he had to undergo open-heart surgery. On his recovery and return to his home in Bennington, he turned once again to writing stories. This is from his notes in 1983:

> *The biographed stories*—people like D. H. Lawrence, Strindberg, Proust, and other literary characters I have become interested in. Others—Puccini, Verdi, Mahler. [Shall I] use the device I have been working on about Virginia Woolf? [Shall I] do Alma and Mahler? . . .
> Method: start with a scene in one life, explicate that as a fiction,

then go into the biographical element and develop further. You come out, or should, with an *invention forward as a story*, limited but carrying the meaning of the life as a short story.

"In Kew Gardens," the Virginia Woolf story, appeared in *Partisan Review* and the Alma Mahler story, "Alma Redeemed," in *Commentary*—both in 1984. It is worth noting that there are some details in the stories which may seem fanciful, but are based on fact; that is his point. These two stories, by a master of the form, are perhaps the most unusual he wrote and provide a fitting finale to this posthumous book.

*　　*　　*

After Malamud's death in 1986, Saul Bellow wrote a memorial tribute to his friend and fellow writer, which was read by Howard Nemerov, at the American Academy and Institute of Arts and Letters. I quote from the Bellow eulogy:

> Well, we were here, first-generation Americans, our language was English and a language is a spiritual mansion from which no one can evict us. Malamud in his novels and stories discovered a sort of communicative genius in the impoverished, harsh jargon of immigrant New York. He was a myth maker, a fabulist, a writer of exquisite parables. The English novelist Anthony Burgess said of him that he "never forgets that he is an American Jew, and he is at his best when posing the situation of a Jew in urban American society." "A remarkably consistent writer," he goes on, "who has never produced a mediocre novel. . . . He is devoid of either conventional piety or sentimentality . . . always profoundly convincing." Let me add on my own behalf that the accent of hard-won and individual emotional truth is always heard in Malamud's words. He is a rich original of the first rank.

To close on a personal note, I was always aware that Bernard Malamud, like all good writers, had no need of an editor, yet I considered myself fortunate to have been that editor. I was honored when he dedicated in my name *The Stories of Bernard Malamud* (1983), the last book published during his lifetime, but I am prouder of his written inscription, "For Bob, my first and only editor." In his introduction to that book he wrote: "Art celebrates life and gives us our measure." His art has given us his measure, which is great.

*   *   *

I wish to acknowledge the help I have received from friends and associates in preparing this book. The editorial assistance of novelist Robert Dunn, who worked closely with Bernard Malamud while he was writing *The People*, transcribing his handwritten manuscript and notes, has been invaluable. Jill Hays helped with the research and typing during the Malamuds' summers in Bennington. I am grateful to my co-executors, Timothy Seldes and Daniel Stern, for their friendly advice and cooperation. I owe thanks to Saul Bellow and Paul Malamud for quotations from their writings. For editorial and copy-editing help I am grateful to Kerry Fried, Claudia Rattazzi, and Lynn Warshow. Lastly, without the unstinting help of Ann Malamud in tracking down and making available unpublished manuscripts from her husband's papers, in helping to verify dates and references and to decode numerous handwritten notes, it would have been impossible to bring this volume to conclusion.

THE PEOPLE

❧ ONE ❧

Yozip

HERE'S YOZIP rattling around in his rusty wagon.

After escaping military service in the Old Country, he worked a year and bought the vehicle in St. Louis, Missouri. Yozip wore a Polish cap and trimmed his reddish beard every second week. Yet people looked at him as if he had just stepped out of steerage. An officious Jew he met in Wyoming told him he spoke with a Yiddish accent. Yozip was astonished because he now considered himself to be, in effect, a native. He had put in for citizenship the day after he had arrived in the New World, five years ago, and figured he was an American by now. He would know for sure after he had looked through the two or three official documents his cousin was keeping for him for when he got back from wherever he was going. He was going where his horse led him. They were drifting westward, a decent direction. Yozip thought of himself as a traveler who earned his little living on the road.

In Nebraska, he peddled for a peddler who had rented him a wagon full of dry goods. This man had struck it rich in California and now lived on his interest, though he kept his small business going. In Wyoming, they parted for ideological reasons: one hated pacifists, the other considered himself to be one. Yozip bought his fifth wagon and third nag, a beast called Ishmael. He sold a variety of small goods and knickknacks to farmers' wives who lived not too far off the main road. He sold them thread, needles, thimbles, ribbons, pieces of lace, and eventually dresses his cousin Plotnick shipped him from Chicago; he imagined the women who bought them liked to remember the figures they had once had. Some were ecstatic when Yozip appeared with his load of dry goods. He added new stock to his old stores. Now he moved farther west than he and his horse had gone before. Yet he often cursed himself for his restlessness because it added nothing to his life but restlessness.

He tried to recall the names of the states he had passed through. Some were words he could not remember, so when he came to a place with an Indian name he slowly spelled it out, more or less phonetically, and wrote it on a card he kept in his pants pocket. He moved into Idaho, stopping off for a while at Moscow. Nothing in Moscow reminded him of Moscow. Yozip trundled down into the Willamette Valley in Oregon and then tracked up into Washington. It amazed him to discover that he had come at last to the Pacific Ocean. He gave a short hooray and stopped to weep at the water's edge. Yozip removed both boots and tramped on the blue water in the Pacific. It was barely spring; the ocean was freezing but Yozip thoroughly washed and dried both feet before drawing on his leather boots. He soaped Ishmael and washed him down from head to hooves. Yozip cooked vegetables in a tin pot and treated his horse with respect. He spoke to him often, whispering into his good ear.

"You may be a horse to your mother," he said in Yiddish, "but to me nothing less than a friend."

The horse whinnied emotionally.

Now that he had traversed the land, or what was ultimately to be the United States of America—for the time of this story was 1870 and the country was astonishingly young and fertile—Yozip felt the moment had come to invent his fortune. He turned the wagon due north and headed up the Pacific Coast. He felt a hunger to be in a new place but had no idea where the hunger or the place had originated. Night after night he tracked it to the stars. They shone like piercing brilliant pearls. He felt more and more a broad love for nature but wasn't sure why. However it happened, nature made him feel serious and concerned, a sensible way to be. Nature was also in the sky, where many things came together; it was, he felt, something he had guessed out as the oneness of the universe. This thought astounded him because he had never had it before.

He felt in himself a destiny he could not explain, except that when he approached it to claim it as his own it seemed to tear itself out of his hands and spin skyward. Yozip believed he could be somebody if he tried, but he did not know what or how to try. If a man did not know what to do next, could you call that a destiny?

Sometimes clusters of soldiers appeared in a field and quickly disappeared.

One of them fired a shot from a rifle at Yozip, but he fell on his belly and then quickly went his way. Ishmael had jumped two feet into the air. Yozip never saw the soldiers again; and besides he had heard the war was over, for which he cheered the Lord.

In Seattle, in a burst of imagination, he sold his wagon for an unheard song. Only one man would bid a cartwheel for it. So he kissed Ishmael goodbye forever. The horse whinnied briskly, pure morale. Yozip got rid of his dry goods, giving away an oversize housedress for a thin woman to a fat lady who laughed engagingly and plucked a white hair out of his beard. He went assaying in a swift stream for a day and a half and discovered a discolored stone that turned out—when he had licked it with his fuzzy tongue—to be a nugget of pure gold that someone might have lost out of a hole in his pants pocket. Yozip sold the nugget for a horse he mounted, and galloped around to see what there was to see. You can't tell until you get there and look twice. It then occurred to him he still had two mouths to feed; so Yozip headed eastward, looking for an honest day's hard work.

⚜ TWO ⚜

The Marshal

ONE DAY YOZIP, on his sleek black horse, rode into a town fifty miles east of Pocatello. He thought it was time to refresh himself because he was not feeling his best and the horse dawdled. He wasn't sure what he wanted to do next, but that was his state of mind these days. He would look for a room in a boardinghouse and rest a week before moving on. It already seemed to Yozip that something was wrong with his life although he had no idea what. It had occurred to him that the few people visible on the main street regarded him uncomfortably as he passed by on his horse. When he smiled at them they responded by looking away. Here you are peaceably entering a town on a new horse and everyone reacts as if they had known you for years and never liked you.

He sensed he was in the presence of error and wondered what it was. The town seemed to be silently awaiting and appraising him. As he trotted on, several more people appeared. The horse broke into a mild gallop. Yozip observed about a dozen men and a woman in a flowered hat standing at one side of the road, and a crowd of about twenty people gathered together farther up. He was tempted to raise his new cowboy hat to them but didn't like to misrepresent himself. He was surprised by and concerned about his thoughts. Either there is more to life or I am a fool. He had accomplished nothing to speak of. He rode on disheartened.

Yozip thought he would stop at a saloon, water his horse, and gulp down a glass of beer. If he stayed longer than tomorrow his first order of business was to find himself a job. He was looking for work and he was looking for a boardinghouse. He was not looking for, or at, this burly man who faced him with a drawn pistol.

"Git off," the stranger said to Yozip, pointing at his horse.

Yozip dismounted in a hurry.

"I'm Morgan Mahoney," said the man with the drawn gun. He pointed over his shoulder to another man in a slouch hat holding a smaller pistol.

"That there is my brother Bailey. Who the hell are you?"

"Yozip Bloom," he said. He did not like saying his name in public.

"Are you the one that is the new marshal?"

"No. I am a copitner."

"What the hell is that?"

"Yozip pantomimed driving a nail into a block of wood. "A copitner," he said carefully.

Morgan experienced a fit of laughter.

Bailey, his brother, broke into a long grin.

Morgan raised his .45, aimed, and shot Yozip's new hat off his head. The horse whinnied and was about to bolt, but Yozip grabbed him by his mane, drew the animal down, and calmed him by talking in his ear.

He picked up his hat from the dust and placed it on his head. Now Bailey shot the tall hat off his head, and Morgan shot at it again. The hat jumped two feet with three holes in its crown.

Yozip had to grab the reins hard to control his fearful, wildly bucking horse.

"Why do you shoot me in my hat?" he shouted.

Both brothers laughed aloud.

"Are you a greenhound?" Bailey said.

"Greenbug," said his brother.

"My name is not Greenburg. You got the wrong poddy. I come to the saloon for a gless beer. Is this the way somebody treats a strenger?"

He bent for his hat, thought twice, then straightened up quickly, leaving his cowboy hat on the ground in order to spare the horse's nerves.

A crowd of two dozen people, including a single Indian, stood in silence near the two wooden steps ascending to an open saloon door.

"I'm a peaceful man," Yozip explained. "I go now away. Kindly step aside and don't frighten my horse."

Morgan waved his Colt in Yozip's face.

"Dance," he said.

"I don't dance," said Yozip.

"Dance, you bastard Jew."

Morgan shot at his boot. Despite Yozip's wild grab at his reins the horse bucked, reared, kicked, and galloped toward the crowd on the other side of the road. The spectators scattered, but an old Indian wearing braids and a blanket grabbed the animal by the muzzle and slowly steadied him.

To end the comedy Yozip turned to Morgan and punched him severely in the throat. Morgan gazed at him, cross-eyed. He gasped as if his blood had curdled, and sank slowly to his knees as he passed out.

Bailey pointed his pistol at Yozip's head.

Yozip, who had always thought of himself as a man of limited means, tore the gun from his grasp and, before Bailey could figure out what the greenhorn was up to, brought the weapon down hard on his head.

An old sheriff wearing a star on his shirt then appeared at the doorway of the saloon. He descended the stairs in heavy slow steps.

As Yozip watched in disbelief the sheriff pinned a marshal's badge on Yozip's left suspender.

"This is our new marshal," the sheriff announced to the silent crowd. "I guess we kin stop lookin' now." He said to Yozip, "The town of Wilberforce will pay you $3.50 a day and a dollar more to feed your horse. As of right now you are officially on our payroll. All we ask is that you behave yourself and respect the law. I can't figger out why you didn't wire us you wuz comin'."

"You've got the wrong man," Yozip replied. "I am a copitner

who is looking for a job, but not to be a marshal. This is not my line of work."

He handed the sheriff his tin star. But the sheriff refused to accept it, so Yozip pinned it back on his suspender strap. The applause of the crowd astonished him.

✖ THREE ✖

Kidnapped

YOZIP, slightly drunk, walked into a wall.

At once his arms were pinned to his sides by two strong Indians who he knew had been trailing him, and a gag that smelled of horse was thrust into his mouth. Yozip wasn't sure they were Indians until he smelled the sour head of the brave squeezing his hard arm around the former peddler's neck. Yozip fought as best he could, grunting, rumbling, coughing, and though they made no attempt to cut off his breath, he felt himself about to fall unconscious. He heard an aborted groan he assumed was his, and when he was once again sanely aware of life and fate, he found himself seated stiffly on Bessie, his mare, who had been tethered nearby, both arms bound with leather thongs behind his back, the horses trotting crisply in the direction of the high Western half-moon.

For a long while three horses, spread single file, moved swiftly along the shore of a stream, then turned into a forest, Yozip's mare running rhythmically with the others, though her master, blindfolded and dismayed, had no idea where he was. He felt the shadows of trees flit by. Nobody tried to lead his horse, who moved on as if she had been born in the territory. Yozip felt the aftermath of a dyspeptic headache and cursed the beers he had drunk last night in the saloon. His bladder was cutting him and it shamed him to think how it would be if he was to let go his water in his buckskin pants.

The Indians galloped west, then abruptly changed direction and galloped east.

Now when Yozip counted the hoofbeats there was an additional horse and he realized that a third Indian had joined the company. Having no sense of his fate he began to fear it. The riders splashed across another stream, then galloped up a rising hill before descending into a long valley. Yozip sensed dawn risen on his head. When the offensive rag was snatched off his eyes, he counted five braves present, who were his captors and silent companions.

They were approaching an Indian village of large and small tepees decorated with symbols Yozip recognized from nowhere. His arms were unbound. He was allowed to dismount and was delivered into a tall tepee that rose like a mast above the earth. Then a gray-haired, weather-faced chief, in a ragged eagle-feather war bonnet, appeared and claimed his visitor. He pointed to a pit of cinders where Yozip was able to relieve himself without disgrace.

Having been kidnapped, he was already tensely running through his mind various plans of escape from this place he didn't know and couldn't describe.

The old Indian cast off his ceremonial bonnet with a suppressed yawn. He was at least seventy, with furrowed brow, deep eyes, tightly braided long hair, and a bent nose. For a minute he studied Yozip's face with a blank expression, saying nothing. Yozip attempted a short smile, as if to determine if it was still working, but evoked no serious response from the chief.

The old Indian at last spoke. "I had forbid you to be hurt," he said in English. "Did my braves hurt you?"

The ex-peddler, relaxed by the question, replied he hadn't been mistreated.

"They gave me also a gless water."

The chief grunted. He touched a finger to himself, then to Yozip. "We meet equal."

Yozip agreed in principle.

The old Indian admitted that the white man's tongue was not comfortable to him although he had once gone to a missionary school.

"It is a tongue of wind and noise. I do not trust it. But if you speak slow words I will answer to them."

"Slow is slow," Yozip agreed. "Excuse me that I tulk with my eccent. I am not an educated man."

This confession embarrassed him but he felt he must make it.

The chief stared at his mouth as if to discover the source of the accent. Unable to, he grunted, which might mean he took a man's word for what he said about himself.

"But I listen," Yozip said, forgetfully touching his shirt pocket to give his marshal's star a serious rub, though that was from another time and he was no longer a marshal. If anything, he was an unemployed carpenter adrift in a forest among a tribe of Indians. If the chief could use him to repair an old chest, or rebuild some shelves, they were in business. If not, he had no idea what the red men wanted of him.

The old chief, after a tick of silence, told Yozip he had seen him punish two evil men who had twice shot off his hat.

Yozip recalled the Indian who had skillfully caught his horse by the bridle and with a whisper calmed her. He explained to the chief that he was personally a peaceful man. "I am not anymore a town marshal. This is not my business."

"My tribe is of peaceful people," said the chief. "Only one white man has lost his life by an Indian's hand in the time of my life. We do not kill white men, though they bring no good to us. We live in peace."

Yozip, heartened, said it would interest him to know why the braves had kidnapped him last night. "What do you want from me?"

"We seek to do what the Great Spirit told us when this earth fell from the ocean sky. The sun and moon were candles. All men come from the Great Spirit, who made us born as men. His name is Quodish. Man spoke his words. They spoke then in one tongue. Quodish is the sun who is sacred.

"Is it not so?" he asked Yozip.

"To me this is reasonable," Yozip answered. "And if a man tulks to me reasonable I don't say to him no."

"Once red man and white were brothers. What one brother had of two he gave one to the other."

"Of cuss," Yozip said. "Who needs everything?"

The chief nodded seriously. Yozip responded with a nervous laugh.

"You must speak my words to the white man," said the chief. "Many moons past, when we signed the papers to live in peace in this valley, it was promised to us that white people would not interfere with our lives. Now we have been fifteen winters on this land that lives in our heart. But the settlers do what they please and now they push against us on this land we were given for our reservation when we signed your papers with the white man. But when gold was found in our hills they have made bad trouble for us. They cross our land when they wish and interfere with our cattle and horses, and they also brand their letters on the flesh of our animals. When we recognize our stock and claim them, they are quick to reach for their guns. The white men have loud voices and they lie and swear that our tribe does not belong in this valley. When I tell them about the papers I have signed they say these papers were meant to be for an entirely different valley. In disgust I turn away from them. They speak an endless stream of lies but we do not wish to fight with them. The Great Spirit who made us told me to speak these words. He said you would understand."

"Me? Yozip?"

"You, with your name."

"Aha," said Yozip. "I give you my honest word that when I will go among people again, I will tulk to them and say what you told me. If you don't hurt white men why should they steal from you your land?"

"There is further to say," said the old chief. "As the moons change so does the world change. I have told my braves that the old moons are gone, and now is the time for new change, but never of our forests or sky."

The chief nodded and Yozip nodded. They were sitting cross-legged on the ground.

"We are an ancient tribe," said the chief. "Some call us the first of this land. Our ancestors said they were the children of Quodish. We live in his word. We speak his name in our hearts. We touch our heads when we think of him. I say my words to him. Do you understand what I mean?"

"Of cuss," said Yozip, though he did not say what the words might mean.

"We are descended from the first tribe."

"This I understand. From the first comes the second."

"Where do you come from?" asked the chief.

"I come from Russia. I am a socialist."

"What is socialist?"

"We believe in a better world. Not to hurt but to help people."

"These are our words too," said the old chief. "We are the People."

"Amen," said Yozip.

"Aha," said the chief, with a nod of his head. "Now I come to your adventures of last night."

"Please."

The chief said, "I wish you to know it is possible we might ask you to stay with us in our tribe if we think you are worthy. Perhaps you can help us. We will teach you many things we know. When the old ways die we must think and speak in better ways."

Yozip answered almost in fright: "Please, Mr. Chief, I told you I am not educated. Also you hear how I tulk with my eccent. What can such a man do for you?"

"I do not hear this accent. It does not say any words in my ear. I have told my braves and sub-chiefs we must do more than in bygone moons to protect our tribe. They say they understand my words and will preserve them. They know and have agreed with me that if you go through our rites and vigil we may ask you to live with us and speak for us. We will ask you to speak from your heart. You must tell the white men to let us live in peace on our land. We will not be led like animals to another reservation. This is our dear land. My father told me when I was a young man and he was old and dying: 'You may give up anything but you must never give up the land. The bones of your father will soon lie on the land and you must guard these bones forever.' "

The chief then said: "The white men must respect our ways. He must live in peace with us and not kill Indians with bad thoughts and words that burn. You must say this to them with drops of blood in your mouth."

"Naturally," Yozip said. "But how can I be an Indian if I was born in Zbrish, in Russia? This is a different country, far away, where was born my father and mother. I live now in America, and also maybe I am by now a citizen. I will know when I see my cousin Plotnick in Chicago, if you will be so kind to tell me where to buy a ticket for the train."

"If our tribe accepts you," said the chief without moving an eyelash, "you will be a red man of this tribe. The Great Spirit spoke this to me in words of smoke and fire. When you see yourself in a silver glass you will see your true color."

Yozip looked around for something that might resemble the baptismal font he had seen one day when he had peeked into a church in Antwerp, on his way to America. What he saw now at the top of the tepee was a smoke hole through which a shaft of sunlight shone.

"Peace is the word of Quodish," said the chief. "It is the best word."

"Peace comes first," Yozip said, "and after comes business."

He considered wringing his hands for his freedom, but the chief then offered the ex-peddler his peace pipe. The smoke was strong and bitter but Yozip drained the hot pipe to its core, although in the process he felt like vomiting.

"Yah," said the chief.

As Yozip clawed at the flap of the tepee to let in a breath of air and escape the heartburn and sickness he had got from the chief's bitter pipe, he walked into a warrior entering the tent, who beheld him with contempt as he spat into Yozip's eye.

The eye felt as though it had been plucked out of his head. The old chief, trembling with anger, threatened the warrior with severe punishment, as the young man reluctantly apologized.

✂ FOUR ✂

The Tribesman

"THIS IS the tepee of solitude."

Yozip was led by the chief's plump daughter to a thin, tall tepee. She was a woman of eighteen who wore a bone necklace and large circular metal earrings.

After her announcement she paid him scant attention. She was assured, calm, almost austere. He admired and feared her. An Old Country boy finds it hard to forget where he was born.

Their walk through the high grass, the sight of the long valley below sloping upward toward distant green hills, awoke in Yozip a hunger to be out of the forest and on his way. If only a man knew where to go. It shamed him still to think that one place was as good as another. What does one attach himself to?

Yozip had never been able to understand his inclination for a complex fate. Many men lived lives that flowed easily. Others tangled their fates with every word they spoke: Yozip was that type. Best say little.

He dutifully followed the Indian girl. She was good-looking though stout, her business if that was how she liked the shape of things. But he couldn't call her fat without thinking pretty. Yozip warned himself to keep his mind clear and his options open. He guessed he would need all his wits, whether he expressed himself in plain Yiddish or by Indian signs.

"Our people use this tepee to meditate," said the girl. "My father, our highest chief, wants you to be in touch with your self

16

so that you can feel the Great Spirit's presence in the light on earth."

"So why is it," Yozip asked, "that everybody here speaks such a good English?"

"Not all," said the chief's daughter. "My father was raised in a Christian school after the murder of his father and mother in a raid by white settlers. So was I, many years later, with my father's permission, after the death of my mother. And Indian Head, my true friend, attended a school in Pocatello. When the People broke into two tribes my father became chief of the lower tribe, and now we are one tribe in this long valley."

She said some of the braves spoke a few white words but not many. She said that once a few People had been enrolled in Christian schools in the past, but nobody was now.

"We detest all pale skins."

"If I had another skin," he told her, "I would take this off and put on the other.

"So who is Indian Head?" Yozip then asked. "What kind of a name is this for an Indian man?"

"He was so named in the Christian school. His name in our tongue means 'He who fights eagles.' His true name also means 'Man of strong feeling.' "

She pressed two fingers to her lips.

"Indian Head loves me."

Yozip offered sincere congratulations.

"So what is your name?" he asked.

"One Blossom. I was named after a small flower."

"About flowers I don't know much," he confessed. "Where I was born was no flowers. If somebody found one she cooked it."

One Blossom led Yozip into the tepee of solitude. She glanced in, listened to the heavy silence, and hastily left.

*   *   *

Yozip, sitting alone in the silent tepee with his thoughts in his fingers, tried to think out his situation. It looked as though the chief had plans to turn him into an Indian. On the other hand, he wanted to go back to his own life, not very rewarding but bound to improve. America was a fine country. Who had ever heard of such opportunities for an uneducated man? He had already given his word he would do his best for the tribe, whatever that meant. Yozip felt strongly sympathetic to the Indians and their furrow-faced old chief.

He considered speaking to him and perhaps probing the chief's plans for him, and with luck maybe even being delivered home to his boardinghouse if the plans came to nothing much and the red man agreed to let him go.

Yozip thought he ought to try to convince the chief that what the People needed was a better man to represent them—certainly not a greenhorn, at least somebody educated in the lore and history of the tribe; someone who would know how to speak for them against the self-serving whites. He had heard of their dirty tricks against the Indians. But Yozip had serious doubts he could do anything for them, or they for him.

An Indian brave entered the tepee of solitude.

"Our chief commands your initiation to being."

Yozip recognized the young warrior.

"Why did you spit me in my eye?" he cried. "This you learned in a Christian school?"

"It was meant to tell you to keep your nose out of Indian affairs."

"My nose was invited by the chief."

Indian Head glanced into the tepee, then turned to Yozip. "The chief of the People ordered me to make sure of your presence. The trials will begin now. This is your initiation."

"Why should I have a trial if I didn't do a crime?"

"These are trials, not a court trial. This is an initiation according to our customs."

Yozip allowed himself to think of breaking away from Indian Head, leaping onto the back of his mare, and galloping off as fast as he could in whichever direction.

Instead, he accompanied the warrior to the chief's tepee, where more than three dozen braves were crowded together, several of whom seemed to be in a mood of celebration. Some of the Indians stared at Yozip as if he were a small animal they preferred not to name.

Among them was an elderly medicine man with a missing front tooth, wearing a headdress of purple flowers. He shook his flowered head.

"How," he greeted Yozip.

The old chief frowned at the expression.

The medicine man frowned at Yozip.

The chief, standing near them, addressed the ex-peddler: "We will now begin the ceremony of your entrance into our tribe."

Maybe it's like a bar mitzvah, Yozip thought. If it is, why should I say no?

The chief addressed the sub-chiefs, warriors, medicine man, and braves in a dialect strange to Yozip's ears. He spoke solemnly in words that sounded like Chinese, though Yozip was sure he had never heard Chinese; yet he would not be surprised if the dialect he was listening to resembled it. A remarkable thing about a language was that it sometimes sounded like a different language. He remembered once hearing a Hungarian play in Warsaw that, for all he got from it, might have been Chinese. On the other hand, his Russian was fair and he was tempted to address the chief with a quotation from Pushkin, but didn't want to astound him. The chief addressed him with probing eyes as he said these words in the language of the People:

"I have chosen a man whose bravery I witnessed, and whose words I trust, to be among us as one of our brothers. I may ask him to speak in our names to some of the whites, and once more tell them who we are, and why our words and ways must be honored. He knows he must pass our tests of initiation, and if he does I shall order you, my people, to accept him as I already do deep in my bowels, and as I have been instructed by the Great Spirit, whose presence I feel on my back and shoulders and in the depths of my being."

"Ha yai," said the chief.

"Yai ha," said the medicine man in the purple-flowered hat, breaking into a long-legged dance. The chief clapped his hands, then spoke first in Indian words and then in English: "Braves, warriors, medicine man, and sub-chiefs: I will speak to you. Listen: I propose this Yozip, who seems to me to be a good man, to work and speak in the name of our tribe. You must honor his efforts."

Those who listened answered with silence.

The old chief clapped his hands and pointed in the direction of a flock of Indian ponies, among them Yozip's mare chewing grass in a nearby hollow.

"We begin our ceremonies and rites."

Then he said the same in their tongue, and the Indians broke their silence in muttered words.

At this moment One Blossom entered the chief's tepee in the company of three squaws. He, observing their entrance, spoke to them: "I will order my daughter, One Blossom, to accept her new brother under these conditions I have spoken, after they are justified by rites of initiation."

One Blossom turned pale and Indian Head swallowed his spittle as if he had been chewing a dead mouse.

The three squaws standing nearby whispered among themselves. Indian Head threw up his mouse head as the medicine man in purple chanted a blessing in reverse.

The first contest, Yozip learned, was to be a circular horse race to a rotting oak tree about three miles away, then around the split oak and back. First returned, first winner, and bets were permitted by the braves, though the chief himself thought it was a waste of good beads. Yozip had not participated in a horse race even when he was a marshal in charge of public safety, although he had once led a Fourth of July parade. But now he was personally instructed concerning the rules of the horse races, as some of the braves sniggered. He also listened attentively to the chief's instructions in his native tongue, trying to pick up a word here and there.

The ex-peddler, edgy on his mare, hoped to perform well, yet feared he would make a mess of the old chief's faith in him as a talisman meant to come up with some sort of unusual performance. It was not only a question of the importance of the race, but it would also give him a chance to explore the surroundings on Bessie's back, and maybe make practical plans to escape to his boardinghouse.

The five riders lined up by a stand of pines, four braves seated on slender, speedy ponies. Indian Head rode a small white horse,

Corn Talk sat on a prancing chestnut, and Foolish Eyes reined an Appaloosa. Seven Fists was mounted on a strong gray, and Yozip, the stranger, sat on Bessie's warm back.

The chief cleared his breath of a pocket of phlegm, then uttered a strange harsh cry that shook Bessie to her withers and threw her off stride for six steps. Indian Head and his friends had streaked past Yozip on his mare, but Bessie impelled herself forward in leaps and exalted bounds, and was soon pursuing the Indian racers and gaining quickly on their lithe ponies.

The course was a short one, about three miles through rough turf and then into what might be a section of smooth terrain.

At the first half circle Indian Head led on his white charger, pursued by Corn Talk wearing black braids, and followed by Yozip's Bessie, making nightmare noises as though in pursuit of a dream; she quickly overtook Corn Talk, then Indian Head, and completed the circle with her immigrant master triumphantly in the lead.

The chief grunted when Yozip stopped before him as if expecting his blessing; One Blossom stared at the white stranger in embarrassment; at the same time her poignant eye met Indian Head's in an expression of regret at his loss of the race. Since no one had cheered for him, Yozip let out a sob of self-approval and Bessie produced a gay fart.

*   *   *

When he had dismounted after the horse race, Yozip was surrounded by the braves he had competed with and had left in the dust. He extended both hands to forgive them, or to acknowledge congratulations, but got instead a sharp slap on the mouth by each Indian. One by one each plucked five red hairs from Yozip's inflamed chin.

And the chief slapped him on the face on three separate occasions.

In this way they will make me into a red man, Yozip thought. So who needs paint when a slap shows better?

The ex-peddler remembered Gussie, his mother, plucking feathers off a dead hen.

At the chief's whispered request Indian Head informed Yozip

that the forthcoming trial would measure his skill with a bow and arrow, and his courage under pressure. Yozip then explained he wasn't sure about his courage, and he barely knew a bow from an arrow. His landlady's son in the boardinghouse had once shown him a picture of an Indian gentleman in a fur cap shooting a tufted arrow with a long bow. The ex-peddler asked Indian Head if he would mind a fistfight instead. Yozip hated fighting in any form but occasionally he had such an experience.

"To tell you the truth, I don't like to hurt somebody who doesn't hurt me."

"I don't like fist games," said Indian Head.

"So let's play something else."

Indian Head said the chief wouldn't permit that. It would nullify the contest and Yozip wouldn't be allowed to enter the tribe.

The ex-peddler feigned disappointment. He sighed audibly. Indian Head then produced a long large sheep-horn bow and cutting arrow. To test them he aimed at a tiny cloud in the sky. A black hawk striving for altitude shrieked and fell to the ground. Neither Indian Head nor Yozip had seen the bird begin its fall and both were astonished.

Bessie bolted, attempting to run, but Yozip grabbed her by the tail and deftly held tight until the horse, kicking at imaginary enemies, gradually calmed down.

The Indian braves, standing in a circle around their venerable chief, now looked at the peddler as if he might be human. Though on the verge of crying gevalt after he had been slapped red and raw by them, and chastened by the objectivity of the chief, Yozip forcibly biting his lips managed to keep his mouth shut.

Bessie whinnied in sympathy and was severely whacked on the rump by Indian Head. She moaned, shivered, and took the blow without moving. Yozip felt embarrassed for his faithful black steed.

The chief then touched Yozip's left eye with his arthritic pinky. He blew on it. The eye was bone dry.

The medicine man in the purple headdress that resembled a dish of rags performed a frenetic short dance and uttered three bleating cries at the sky.

Then the old chief, walking backward in his soiled feathered bonnet, hoarsely announced the next contest.

*   *   *

Indian Head explained the rules of the bow-and-arrow game. Yozip would shoot first at the red apple Indian Head was about to place on his head. Should Yozip miss, Indian Head would then shoot at the red apple on Yozip's head. The purpose was to hit the apple, not the head. Indian Head smiled mysteriously, and Yozip then had serious doubts about his future. This bothered him, because essentially he was an ambitious man who wanted to live a long, accomplished life.

Yozip could barely manipulate the heavy sheep-horn bow Indian Head gave him to shoot with. To pull the sinewed gut string burdened his heart. He envisioned himself falling to the ground in weakness. Again he heard snorting and derision among the braves.

The chief lectured them on courtesy and then told Yozip what he had said.

Yozip lifted his heavy bow. His arrow, after a slow shot, rose ten feet and skidded along the ground before it came to a stop.

No one laughed.

The betting commenced again and Yozip thought the odds on him could not be very high.

In the next round Indian Head, pulling his bow so strongly that his fingers quivered, seemed to be carefully aiming at Yozip's skull. It occurred to the ex-peddler that he was on his way to being a dead man.

The arrow, shot high into the air, eventually descended before his face; he felt it cut the tip of his nostril as the apple fell off his head. Yozip was slightly wounded by the barbed edge of the expiring arrow, and thus a bit of flesh was snipped from the tip of his long nose.

Blood streamed from the wound.

A cry went up from the braves in the tribe.

The chief called the blood a magic sign.

"Your nose is pierced but you are not wounded."

"My nose bleeds," Yozip cried, touching the blood. He feared he would be disfigured for life.

The medicine man bent to inspect the fleshly bleeding, but he saw nothing to get excited about. He hawked up a glob of phlegm and caught it in his hand. Then he spoke aloud to the Great Spirit, but apparently the Great Spirit advised him to omit the spittle.

The chief told Yozip to rub earth on his bleeding nose. The earth would stop the blood.

Yozip followed his advice. He then picked up the heavy bow for his second shot. To everyone's surprise the arrow rose from fifty yards away quickly and strongly in a straight line toward Indian Head's cranium.

One Blossom shrieked, but Indian Head, after giving the matter a moment of serious consideration, was able to catch the expiring arrow with his left hand.

The braves mumbled and grunted.

The chief then sternly informed One Blossom that her cry had interfered with the sacred initiation and she would be suitably punished.

The girl gasped, for a war-painted brave was rising from the bushes and aiming his massive arrow squarely at Yozip's head.

From a tall tree nearby a shrieking eagle rose aloft and flew with talons and wings outstretched at the painted brave with the shaven skull who had aimed to shoot Yozip in the back of his head. The other braves grabbed for their bows and arrows and swiftly shot them into the sky. Shaved Head, cursed by the chief, dived into a nearby muddy pond. The Indians loosed a stream of arrows at the black eagle and bloodied its feathers as the bird rose with magnificent force until it vanished.

*   *   *

One night Yozip stayed awake until the moon drew in its horns. He intended to count a thousand stars in the diamond sky but did not stop until 1,033. Dawn came serenely as he promised to do something splendid for his tribe.

*   *   *

Fifty buffalo had been imported from Montana and caged in a corral. When they saw the Indians approaching they battered the logs with their heavy horns and, when the fence gave way, stampeded toward a ravine. Indian Head and thirty tribesmen carrying white-feathered lances were trapped amid the frightened animals and tossed like boats on a stormy sea. The buffalo scattered thunderously among the red men. They milled around frantically and the Indians, in self-protection, began to shoot their whirring arrows at the shaggy beasts. Yozip did not know what to do with himself or where to go. He had been given a tomahawk to bring down a buffalo, but he was a confirmed vegetarian and could not bring himself to crack open a buffalo's skull.

Indian Head shouted at him: "The trophy we must present to the chief is a buffalo's head."

"So let us look for another trophy."

Indian Head raised his tomahawk at Yozip. The sight of the uplifted weapon incensed a bull, who let out a roar of fright and charged Indian Head's pony. The bull struck the pony a blow on the hip. Indian Head's horse screamed, reared, and dumped its rider at its feet. He went head down as though off a chute.

Yozip jumped from Bessie's back to the ground. With all his strength he lifted Indian Head and, before the massive bull could move, settled the youthful brave on Bessie's back and clucked loudly. Holding the brave tightly with one arm he mounted his horse and pushed forward. The other braves surrounded them for protection, but the buffalo had disappeared down the side of the ravine.

Yozip reined in Bessie, lifted Indian Head down, and began to try to revive him as the braves on their ponies looked on.

Indian Head's eyes fluttered as he came slowly to life. His expression, as he stared at Yozip, was one of surprised affection.

A brave slapped the ex-peddler on the back.

"You Big Chief," he muttered.

"Denks," said Yozip.

*   *   *

After being accepted as winner of the contests he had entered, and theoretically as a brave who had proved his courage in the face of peril, Yozip, after receiving the old chief's congratulations and a reluctant peck on the cheek by his sister One Blossom, became depressed, feeling he had no fate other than to win and take his place among the Indians of the tribe.

FIVE

Washington, D.C.

THE CHIEF SAID he would send Yozip to Washington, D.C. "We have not been in touch with our American friends recently."

"Keep me here," Yozip cried. "What do I know from strange cities?"

"It is in some respects an evil city. My father cursed it when that actor Booth shot Mr. Abraham Lincoln."

"So if it is evil why will you send there a man who is not far from a greenhorn? What can I tell them which they don't know? Will they believe me if I tell them the truth?"

"I am sending you there to tell them the truth."

The chief nodded at Indian Head, who nodded to One Blossom. She dipped her head to Yozip, to his surprise.

"We wish you to represent our tribe," said the chief. "We wish you to speak in our name for our cause. You must tell the Americans that we will never leave our land."

"How can I tulk with my short tongue? Where will I find the words? When I open my mouth to tulk they will laugh at me."

"No one will laugh at you. No one will laugh at the sound of your voice which speaks for all of us—the People. We wish you to speak to the Commissioner of Indian Affairs. He has asked me to sign a new paper that I will not sign. I don't trust these papers which they send us. Others have signed and have been betrayed, but I will not sign though they threaten to move our tribe out of this valley."

"Where will we go?" asked Yozip.

"No doubt they have in mind an inferior reservation where the soil and fishing can hardly compare to ours. I have told them that death lives on that reservation, and we cannot live with death."

"Ai," said Indian Head.

"Ai," said One Blossom.

The chief said the Indian Commissioner's threat bled their morale.

"We have managed for years through great efforts to hold the bloodsucking whites at a distance. But the time may come when we shall have to defend ourselves with arms. This is a great disadvantage because they have superior arms and all we have is our will. Although our will is of iron it does not shoot bullets."

"I don't like bullets," Yozip said.

"We are sending you to Washington to speak with your eloquence on our behalf. We send you to speak for our tribe that has chosen you to be our brother. We must now do what we have never done before. You will go in our name and plead with the Commissioner to soften his heart to our request. He must be merciful to his brothers who walk in rain in their red skins."

But Yozip was still worried. "What can a greenhorn do for you in such a city as Washington? Suppose they say I am not yet a citizen and so they keep from me my citizen papers?"

"None of us have citizen papers," said Indian Head. "They call us native Indians and treat us as native strangers. When an American looks at an Indian he expects to see lice crawling on his head. One Blossom hides her head with her hat. The whites have no respect for us. They cheat us of our past."

"You must go," announced the chief. "You are capable. I am old and my children are not eloquent. If you don't go with your vibrant voice and presence to speak for our rights they will rob us of our last spot of green land."

"You must go," said One Blossom. Her eyes glistened.

Yozip was already on his feet.

"I will brush my Bessie."

"You will go on the iron train in Montana that eats up wood and spits out miles," said the chief.

One Blossom found a pair of beaded moccasins for Yozip. He wore buckskin pants, a deerskin shirt, and a thick headband over his reddish long hair. Since joining the tribe, Yozip's hair had turned a brownish red. Only his face was shaved clean. He shaved with a piece of plate glass the chief had presented to him. One Blossom wound a cord around a white feather in his thick hair. Yozip also wore three sets of heavy black beads around his neck. The chief had given him a pair of gold earrings, but the new Indian was too shy to wear them. And he carried a jacket a good-hearted squaw had given him, and was thinking of investing in a new pair of field boots.

Indian Head, three braves, and One Blossom accompanied him on their ponies to the iron horse that left from the station in Helena, Montana. Yozip sat in the rocking train astonished by the ride and the view. From one window he saw a herd of buffalo walking in single file in the snow. Farther up the line, two elephantine buffalo were fearfully facing the iron horse as it chugged along. Nearby a buffalo defecated in the snow.

I feel alone like him, Yozip thought, but I hope nobody will see me the way I see him.

On the train Yozip met a drummer who tried to engage him in a conversation.

"By God, an Indian. I didn't think they let you ride on trains. At least you don't look like a full-blooded Indian to me. Who the hell are you?"

"I go to Washington."

The drummer fell silent, then asked, "What's the difference between a horse's ass and a horse who is an ass?"

Yozip could not tell him.

"None."

"What did the hoor say to the Indian chief with the big prick?" the salesman asked with a chuckle.

"Excuse me, this I don't know."

"That will cost you double." The drummer laughed hoarsely.

In five days and nights Yozip arrived in Washington, D.C., excited to be in the capital of the United States of America.

He had been given the name of a boardinghouse on N Street, and though he was stared at by some people in the house who seemed to admire his white feather, Yozip was not embarrassed. Two middle-aged men were friendly to him, and so were a courteous government lawyer and his wife, who helped him locate the building in which the Commissioner of Indian Affairs had his office.

Yozip went to this building not far from the Washington Monument to look at it twice, and he twice returned to the boardinghouse ashamed of his English. He had talked to a stranger who had listened to him with a broad smile. Since his funds were low, one morning after a short inspirational look at the White House he walked forcefully to the Indian Commissioner's office and informed a young man with a part in his wavy hair why he had come.

"If you'll excuse me, they sent me from my tribe I should see the Commissioner of Indian Affairs."

The young man examined him closely. "Did you say you are a member of an Indian tribe?"

Yozip drew an unsteady breath. "I am a member of a tribe in Idaho, which they call themselves the People. The chief told me to talk to the Commissioner."

"The People sent you to talk to the United States Commissioner of Indian Affairs?" He looked doubtful. "Do you have any official papers with you?"

Yozip produced a sheaf of papers from his deerskin pouch pocket, which he asked the young man to return to him because they belonged to the tribe. He noticed a redheaded young woman sitting on a bench nearby, regarding him with interest.

He was tempted to talk to her but said nothing.

The young man left with the papers and soon returned.

"The Commissioner will see you late this afternoon if he can be certain you are not misrepresenting yourself and the tribe you call the People."

"This," said Yozip, "I wouldn't do. They told me to go to Washington, so I went."

"Should I call you chief?" asked the young man.

"If you will call me mister will be fine."

"This afternoon at 5 p.m., Mr. Indian."
"Denks," said Yozip.

*   *   *

At five o'clock, Yozip was led to the desk of the Commissioner of Indian Affairs and sat nervously still while the burly man looked him over, particularly at the white feather in his thick hair. He was a heavy man wearing pince-nez. He spat into a pocket handkerchief, brushed his lips, and then addressed Yozip.

"Where were you born if I might ask? Are you an American citizen? How did you become acquainted with the People tribe? The story you tell, as it has been conveyed to me, is not very convincing."

Yozip said his name was Yozip Bloom. He explained that he had been initiated into his tribe. They had permitted him to become a member after he had gone through the rites of initiation.

"And you deliberately altered your nose in order to accept initiation into this tribe?"

"Indian Head hit me on the nose with a loose arrow that he shot. When it stopped to bleed it did not anymore hurt me."

"I'm quite sure that your chief had more than one decently educated brave available who could have represented him adequately in this office. What is your explanation why you were chosen to do that?"

Yozip began a sentence and stopped. Then he said, "The chief told me I am capable. Long ago he signed once with the United States government a paper that it says the tribe could stay in Idaho in their valley where they live there many years. The old braves are buried there. The government now says to leave this valley but we do not wish to go.

"My chief told me also to tell you that one day he planted two poles in the valley where we live, which is fifty miles wide. He said the white men could take the land outside, but the land inside the poles is the land of our people. Inside this boundary the land goes around the graves of our fathers. We will never give up these graves. My chief says he will not sign any more papers because they all lie to him. He says they don't speak to him the truth."

The Indian Commissioner smiled thinly. "Why didn't he come here to this nation's capital and say it himself?"

"He is now an old man. It is not easy to walk if you got arthritis."

"But I understand he speaks English?"

Yozip's face turned red. "I told you his words."

"Be that as it may, eventually our entire Indian population will be placed on reservations. That will be just, as well as the best possible thing for them."

"If you will podden me," Yozip said, "the chief and also my brothers do not like to change our reservation. He likes, and also the tribe likes, our valley, which they wish to stay there. The chief told me to say that our people don't attack white people. He told me to say, with respect, if you will kindly let us live where our ancestors lived, and do not force us to go to another reservation, for this we will be thankful to you and also to the Great Spirit."

Yozip had memorized this speech.

"When you refer to 'ancestors,' " said the Commissioner, "do you refer to American Indians or to Hebrews?"

Yozip considered the question slowly. "I mean any kind ancestors that they lived before us and believed in the Great Spirit Chief in the sky."

"Considering all things," said the Commissioner, "I will tell you we would be happy to assist your tribe if we possibly can. However, you must understand that the United States of America is an expanding nation. We grow in great haste because our opportunities are manifold. We would like to set aside this valley you have so much affection for, but we must ask you to understand that our country's foremost need, far into the future, will be land. And more land. We are a great nation with an important future. Therefore, we have to ask you not to make requests we can't possibly fulfill, and which ultimately embarrass us."

"We do not wish to embarrass anybody," said Yozip. "We wish you to consider what is our need. We wish to live in peace with you."

"What did you say your name was?" the Commissioner asked, playing with an ivory letter opener on his desk.

"Yozip Bloom."

The Commissioner laughed as he removed and thoroughly cleaned his pince-nez. "That's what I thought. Still another Joseph to deal with. I'm sure you know your chief is called Joseph?"

Yozip blushed. "Now I know," he admitted. "He is also Tuk-Eka-Kas."

"In any case, I must advise you and your fellow 'tribesmen' not to interfere in the legitimate aims and aspirations of the United States government." The Commissioner stood up. "I regret I am pressed for time and therefore must conclude this interview."

Yozip rose, anguished. "Please, Mr. Indian Commissioner, don't say to the Indians no. The United States of America is a very big country that it takes a week to go anyplace. We are a small tribe. Please give me a letter to take back to my chief which will make him be happy. He is an old man. This is my request to you."

The Commissioner rang a melodious little silver bell on his desk.

"Mr. Cluett," he told the young man with wavy hair who entered, "will you kindly tell this half-ass Hebrew Indian that the quicker he leaves these premises, the better it will be for him and his fellow tribesmen."

The door opened and the young redheaded woman Yozip had seen in the hall stepped up to the desk and presented the recently initiated Indian with a shasta daisy.

"Foh," said the Commissioner to his daughter. "Lucinda, why the hell don't you stay out of government business?"

Yozip and his white daisy chugged back to the West on the iron horse.

He had meant to stop in Chicago to have a look at his citizenship papers at his cousin Plotnick's, but he forgot.

✖ SIX ✖

Chief of the Tribe

THE KEROSENE LAMP on the locomotive cab flickered on the rails. The train, clackity-clacking, rattled into the space across the wide prairies. Yozip, unable to sleep with eyes shut, slept with his eyes open. He slept staring at the tribe's documents he had left behind in the Commissioner's office. They were scattered everywhere. He ran after them in dreams to retrieve the papers, but they were forever flying out of sight. Yozip had lost the documents Chief Joseph had entrusted to him and asked him to return. The ex-peddler woke to punish himself whenever he momentarily slept.

"The first time they send me on a job I come back without papers and without any luck. Everybody in the tribe will be ashamed and disgusted."

At Helena, the train slowed and Yozip considered jumping off and disappearing into the night. But as the locomotive drew to a slow stop dawn was beginning and the new Indian, with a cry of surprise, recognized Bessie herself waiting for him untied at a hitching rail. He looked for Indian Head and some of the other braves and saw none. The horse alone had come for him. Bessie let out a motherly whinny. Either she had been sent to get him or had remembered where to find him, and had gone there by herself. Or perhaps she had waited for him, foraging what she could until his return. Dear Bessie.

Yozip kissed his horse on the head, mounted her with his meager bundle of clothes, and rode off in the direction of the valley. From time to time he pulled at the mare's halter, trying to turn her and go elsewhere, in another direction; but the animal insisted on carrying him toward the long valley. Yozip in anger slapped Bessie with his hand. The horse froze and refused to budge. Yozip gave up and let her bring him back to the tribal grounds. Neither apologized to the other.

He went, after a while, to the chief's tall blue tepee, stopping outside a minute to revive his wits. He whistled to himself and waited. Yozip then poked his head into the tepee and saw that One Blossom wasn't there. Entering, he found the old chief lying on his back on the frozen ground.

The new tribesman moaned. "So are you all right?" he asked the old chief.

The chief muttered that he was not far from death.

"So stay alive, Chief Joseph," Yozip said. "What will we do without you? If you go away where will we go? What will the tribe do?"

"Ah, you have called me by my father's name," said the old chief. "He was a wise man who taught me in few words the depth of his experience."

"In Washington," Yozip said, "I told them what you said I should tell them, but I didn't do a first-class job. Nobody wished to tulk to me there. Also I lost the papers of the tribe. I was stupid to let the assistant man take them away even for five minutes. I feel now to cry like a child because I did not protect the property of the People. I was not a first-class manager."

"Crying is for children," said Joseph hoarsely. "And it is not useful, because I had these papers copied by a scribe after I had signed the first treaty for this valley. I did not trust the whites."

"That made me a heartache because I thought I had lost them."

"We may know where evil begins, but not where it ends."

Yozip asked the old chief what he could do for him now. "Should I call maybe the medicine man with the purple feathers that he sometimes makes you laugh?"

"Keep him away from me. He smells of goat turd." The old man's laugh racked him. He coughed brutally. Yozip wished he knew how to help him. It struck him again how ignorant he was.

He sat on the ground warming Joseph's head with his hands.

The chief was dying, his voice was thickly hoarse.

"Where is One Blossom?" Yozip asked. "Where is also Indian Head?"

The chief smiled as though to himself. "They speak their words of love."

"Now? When you are so sick?"

"What better time to love? For myself I have no fear. The Great Spirit touches me with his finger. I am warm."

Yozip said he would look for them.

"There will be time for that. Now I want to talk to you. There is something to do for us. Yozip, the council of sub-chiefs agrees with me at least to ask you to become chief of our people. I know your qualities. You must help us to go on living our lives. You must protect us from the evil the white men lay on us. We cannot live without air. We love this valley. It is our place of freedom. You must help our people to live as the Great Spirit says we must."

He coughed gratingly, holding his fingers against his head.

Yozip gazed at the withered, whispering man.

"Who wants me here? I come also from Quodish, but what can I do for the People. What do I know?"

"I trust you to learn what you must know. I want you to become Chief Joseph. I have chosen you in my place. I believe you will make a fine leader."

"Why? How? What can I bring to the tribe?"

"You are a protector. Those who can must protect those who cannot protect themselves. These are the words of the Great Spirit in the open sky."

"But why me? Indian Head would be better."

"Indian Head speaks twelve words when there are six to say. You must teach him to protect himself. And you must help One Blossom, who does not always help herself. She is not as serene or wise as her gentle mother."

"Indian Head will take care of her. He is her lover. What can I tell her if her lover says no?"

"You must look after my child as well as her lover."

Yozip told the old man he would protect his children as best as he could. "I will try, but I don't think they will like it if a stranger says he will protect them."

"Keep them together," whispered the dying man. "Teach them to be disciplined. Tell them to respect our leader, and whom to respect. And they must honor their ancestors. My father lived his life in love of peace."

"I will mention to them your father, also I will mention my father that he died in Zbrish."

"Now I must begin my journey into the sky."

Two red tears rolled down his cheeks of parchment.

Chief Joseph coughed harshly once and breathed quietly. He then stopped breathing.

Yozip wept for the old chief.

Indian Head and One Blossom entered the tepee and she began wailing over the dead chief as she tenderly arranged his feathers.

"Now I know what solitude means," said Indian Head.

One Blossom, the youthful daughter of an aged father, kissed his eyes and wept in silence.

Now the warrior chiefs and the medicine man drifted into the tepee and stared at their dead chief.

The purple-flowered medicine man gave out a cry and, addressing the Great Spirit through the sunny opening at the top of the tepee, lamented the chief's death.

The braves looked on silently.

Indian Head spoke to them, saying that their chief was dead, their new chief was Jozip, who had been initiated into the tribe according to their ancient customs.

Some of the Indians in the tepee uttered a noise of protest, and Yozip shrank to the wall of buffalo hide; but Indian Head addressed them eloquently, and soon each of the braves and warriors approached the new chief and touched his head with warm and cold fingers. Yozip memorized the faces of those whose fingers were cold.

"Your name also Joseph," Broken Ear said, and again they welcomed him into the tribe.

"Jozip," said the new chief.

SEVEN

The Burial

JOZIP MOVED among the mourners of the old chief at his burial as though he were a close relative. Lately he had become more facile in the language of the People, saying his words without excessive grunting. It was an easier language to acquire, he thought, than Russian, a difficult language, yet he had spoken Russian well.

"One day you will be a smart chief," said Foolish Eyes.

"How can somebody who is not smart be smart?"

"You will find out."

"I have too much to find out," said Jozip.

For a time the body of old Chief Joseph, dressed in ancient garments and decorated with bone necklaces, lay under the open sky by the pine trees. The medicine man with the purple headdress had painted his face white with pink stripes, according to an ancient rule of the tribe. One Blossom, in torn garments, hacked off her braids with a knife and threw them into a fire that burned near where the old chief lay. When Indian Head saw her hair burning he bit his lips. Nor could Jozip bear to look at the burning braids of the beautiful young woman. She had changed; her figure was firmer, no longer plump. She lived in a world without a father. Indian Head told Jozip that she made his life joyous. Yet her eyes saddened as though she had looked at something she did not care to see.

After two days, Tuk-Eka-Kas, wrapped in deerskin by the women of the tribe, was lifted up by the braves and laid on six long poles.

His woven bier was raised on the shoulders of four warriors, Jozip permitted among them, and it was carried to the grave site that four braves and Indian Head had dug in the earth. A dozen women followed the bier, tearing their hair, mourning, sobbing. One Blossom was among them.

The warriors, with Jozip's assistance, holding hemp ropes, lowered the corpse into the newly dug grave, the chief's head turned to the east. Amen, thought Jozip; they walk to the west with their heads turned east.

The medicine man then spoke a mournful mouthful about the old chief who now lay in his new grave. The shaman called him a noble man. Once he had confronted a mother bear hunting for a lost cub. She approached Joseph, smoking his pipe in the woods, with a roar that fluttered his eardrums; but he had frightened the bear away by blowing a mouthful of the buffalo-dung smoke into her eyes. She had galloped away, stopping only to roar at the brave chief.

And once Chief Joseph, hunting bear in the forest, had come upon another hunter who had been struck by a fallen tree and was pinned under it. Straining to lift the huge tree and hold it off the warrior, the good chief gave the wounded man, whose head was bloody, a moment to crawl forth, and then carried him in his arms to be treated by the medicine man, who snapped his bones into place and massaged his wounded back. In a week the hunter had recovered. Thus had Joseph rescued his brother in the tribe.

When the shaman had completed his eulogy, One Blossom tossed six of her most treasured trinkets into her father's grave. Indian Head had contributed a long bow and six sharp arrows. He bowed to the east.

Then several braves filled the grave, scooping up handfuls of earth, and the squaws and unmarried women wailed for the dead chief.

Afterward an old brown dog of the tribe—he belonged to no one and used to go along with the other dogs to hunt buffalo—lay on the chief's grave as the dead man was growing used to death. The shaman screamed at the dog but Jozip asked him to stop lest he disturb the sleep of the old chief. "The Great Spirit has sent the animal here out of love for the good Chief Joseph. He will not take away his dog."

But to keep the ghost of the dead man from bringing madness to those who were still alive, the tepee of Joseph was moved fifty feet to the west. The medicine man then blew smoke from his pipe across every corner of it to remove the ghost-spirit before Jozip began to live alone in his new tepee.

A moon passed, then One Blossom and Indian Head held a feast in the old chief's honor, at which a pair of his worn buckskin trousers and other personal belongings were given away to five of the assembled guests.

One Blossom gave the new chief a leather shirt that she had once made for her father, and Indian Head gave him a swift silver arrow to hunt buffalo when meat was scarce.

After the burial ceremonies, at Indian Head's whispered suggestion, Yozip, who now openly called himself "Jozip," although he thought of himself still as Yozip, gathered the braves together for a long ride over the Montana mountains to hunt the fat buffalo and store smoked and jerked meat for the long winter.

So now I am a real Indian, Jozip sadly, yet not unhappily, thought. So what can I do for my people?

EIGHT

The New Jozip

JOZIP OFTEN THOUGHT of himself as Yozip and experienced days of wonderment and doubt. He questioned his abilities, yet felt he had taken up a cause he increasingly cared about, that of the People. Many of his Indian brothers were still unknown to him, but he thought of them as his Indians and had begun to feel responsible for their welfare, as though there was a gap in their experience he might fill. "Don't ask me why," he said to himself. "Ask the Great Spirit who looks at us from the sky." But the cause he had taken up helped him understand what he had lacked in his former, lonely life.

"If I am a man like me, what should I do next?" he asked Indian Head.

"First we must settle the land question with the whites, but before that we must prepare for the long winter. We will hunt buffalo in the mountains and in the snow. The animals will not know which way to run when we appear before them with drawn bows. They will stampede and thunder away as our braves shoot their bellies full of arrows."

"This I don't like to do," said Jozip.

"You will get used to it."

After ascending the western pass for two weeks of hunting on the cold plains in Montana, Jozip, when the meat was plentiful and the hides many, called a halt and the hunters descended toward their long valley accompanied by a dozen shaggy huge beasts, lassoed and led by squaws who had traveled with the hunters.

The buffalo, Jozip observed, was not a very intelligent animal, yet if treated humanely it would go where it was led. The hunt had gone well: they had not encountered any rival tribes and this was a year of plentiful beef. Jozip had been told that large numbers of buffalo were crossing the railroad tracks and interfering with the movement of trains. Conductors distributing rifles, and passengers potshooting from windows, were energetically slaughtering droves of animals before the trains could plow free of them and chug forward on the bloody tracks.

Jozip, from youth a vegetarian at heart, disliked this useless destruction of innocent animals, but now he was an Indian and lived as they lived. Yet he was also the grandson of a shochet, a religious slaughterer in the Old Country, who killed devoutly, gently, aware of the sin of taking a living life even though he blessed the beast as he slit its throat. Maybe it was in partial revulsion to his grandfather's holy profession that the grandson avoided eating animal flesh and had ultimately become a vegetarian. Night after night, as the braves gorged themselves on meat, the new chief devoured buckwheat groats and fresh vegetables when available. Though some braves snickered at Jozip's ways, still for a novice he was a decent chief—organized in his head, and sensibly aware of the needs of the braves and of the pride of warriors and sub-chiefs.

"Passable anyway," grunted the warrior known as Hard Head.

The Indian hunters climbed down the Idaho foothills and moved toward their green land, where they at once encountered bad news that caused them quickly to forget the pleasures of the hunt. When they returned to the tribal grounds they were at once surrounded by women, children, and older men, who informed them that there had been a visitation of settlers, and one of the young women describing the incident angrily cried out, "Rape!"

"So who made a rape?" Jozip asked indignantly. "Who did such a terrible thing?"

One cheery woman with wild hair spoke up: "I was raped by a disgusting fiend."

"Who is she?" Jozip cautiously asked Indian Head.

"She was raised in a missionary school and is interested in rape.

Her name is Penelope. Her father was one of our best hunters. Her mother is a loudmouth."

"Do you think someone raped her?"

"I am not a medicine man and you are the chief of our tribe."

Indian Head asked One Blossom, "Were you bothered by anyone? Touched?"

"One fool tried to touch me but I hit my knee between his legs. He slapped my mouth but the other whites called him off."

"If I had seen that I would have killed him," said Indian Head.

"Why did they come here, these men?" Jozip asked.

"Six of them appeared on their ponies," One Blossom said, "and they told us we would have to leave our valley in thirty days. They said the valley belonged to them, and the tribe must leave. I told them they were liars, and they listened as if their tongues had turned to stone. Some of the women began to shout and cry. The Americans said they would come back after our hunters returned. What can we do?"

"We have our papers that your father signed them," Jozip said. "If we stay here and don't make trouble for them, they should not make trouble for us."

"They are whites," she said. "They don't think as we do. And I don't want to go to another valley. I have lived all my life here."

"Maybe we should get a lawyer?" Jozip asked Indian Head.

"We have no rights in their thoughts," he said. "When they get ready to drive us out they will try it. They have their Winchester rifles, and we only have bows and arrows and small voices."

"I will tulk to them," Jozip said. "And I will say we will not move from here because this is our land. Maybe if we tulk to them soft, they will answer soft."

The Indians spoke among themselves and then disbanded.

Jozip sat with his head full of difficult thoughts.

The next day a crier called out the approach of twenty white men on horses.

Jozip appeared instantly from his tepee, where he had been drinking tea brewed from valley plants he had discovered. He put on his war bonnet and, going out to the white men, asked them to state their business.

"Who might you be?" asked a tall rider wearing a blue military cape. He had thin lips and a long jaw. His eyes were deep-socketed and he made no attempt to smile.

"I am Jozip, who is now the chief of this tribe. We are the People. I did not ask for this honor but they gave it to me anyway, so I tulk to you like the chief."

"I am Colonel Gunther of Fort Boise," said the visitor in a husky voice. He unbuttoned his cape and cleared his throat. "The Commissioner of Indian Affairs, Mr. Horace Sedgewick in Washington, D.C., has ordered me to inform the people of your tribe that the Great White Father in Washington has lost patience with you for not obeying his orders. Now I will tell you this: The U.S. government has once more decided to extend your time of departure for thirty days beginning today, with no further extensions. I am here to say that if you haven't left these surroundings within that stated thirty days, the cavalry at Fort Boise will round you up and deliver you to a reservation of our choice."

"So where is this reservation, tell us?" Jozip said. "We hear about such a reservation but nobody says to us where it is. Is it in the sky maybe? Who will move us there? Maybe twelve eagles that they come from the sky?"

"I can't provide you with any information any more specific than the message that I have just delivered," replied Colonel Jacob Gunther. "But if I were you I would certainly make ready to leave this area pronto."

"Please, Mr. Cohnel, I will speak to you with soft words. This is the valley of our tribe. The Great White Father gave to us this valley and also our Chief Joseph signed the papers. For fifteen years our people lived here and also they have fished here in our big river, and we love this earth and bury in it our dead."

Jozip said that from the time of Quodish the valley had belonged to the red man. "If the Great White Father wants now to have the valley back, he must give us another place where we can live, and which is as good as this valley. We must have someplace to go and live there, otherwise we will be like animals."

"We have our papers," said the colonel. "You are Indians and not citizens of our country. You are dealing with the President of the United States and you must yield to him. If you don't want to make serious trouble for your tribe, you had better behave without further complaint or resistance, verbal or otherwise. No doubt we will lead you to another reservation. I have no further details of that matter in this moment. In the meantime, you are impeding the manifest destiny of a young and proud nation. We will give you just thirty days in which to prepare for a move in accordance with our plans for you."

"Please, Mr. Cohnel, we ask for more time and also a little more consideration. We are men with the worries and troubles of men. We got to have justice. If somebody takes away from you your house and your garden but he doesn't pay you for it, is this justice?"

"Yah," said three of the Indians. The others stoically shook their heads.

The colonel yanked his horse's bridle as he signaled his men.

"There are ways to listen," he said to Jozip. "One is with deaf ears, which is what you do. The other is with intelligent awareness of the possibility of change for the better, which is what you are avoiding doing. We must therefore affirm our right to this land in the name of our nation, and our inalienable right to direct your next move within this country. If you disregard us we will exercise the right of eminent domain and do with our land what we have to do to fulfill our destiny."

"So what is eminent domain?" Jozip whispered to Indian Head.

"The strong man does what he wants. The weak man listens."

"Will they make a war against us?"

"We will fight back."

"I am a man of peace."

"You are chief of this tribe."

"If you will speak to us the truth, we are not afraid of your words," Jozip replied to the colonel.

"We don't need any lessons in ethics, my good man," said the colonel. "And preachment won't put any pork in your pot."

"From pork I am not interested," said Jozip, speaking for himself.

The colonel said "Giddap" to his horse and the soldiers began to ride off the reservation.

One of them, puzzled by Jozip's eloquence, said aloud, "Who

the hell is he? He don't sound like no Indian to me. Who the hell are you?" he said to Jozip.

"Let's get on along," said the colonel to the soldier.

"I am Jozip," said Jozip.

"That means Joseph," said Indian Head. "He is a man of peace. We do not want war with the white people."

Jozip nodded. He had not spoken as well as he would like, yet he heard dignity in the words he had said. "If you speak with your heart," he told himself, "the words fix themselves together in the right way. They will say what you want them to say."

"Sounds like Jew talk to me," said the colonel in the capacious cape. "Nobody can trust these goddamn Indians in any way at all."

"That's as true as anything," said the cavalry soldier.

❧ NINE ❧

The Settler

ONE NIGHT three young braves beheld a white settler wandering in their woods. He was carrying an empty kerosene lamp, and every forty feet or so he sat down in the snow and tried to light the lamp. The wind blew out his sulphur matchsticks. The settler shook out the dead matchsticks and one by one flipped them over his shoulder into the bushes.

"He is in our woods," whispered Small Horse. "He moves as if he is drunk."

"He must be looking for a place to piss," said Windy Voice.

"He's spying on us," Foxglove said. "We are fifty miles from the white fort. The big-ass colonel has sent him to spy on us to see if the tribe is getting ready to leave the valley."

The three braves gravely observed the white settler sitting in the snow watching the rising half-moon.

"Let us show ourselves," Small Horse whispered. "We will say we are ghosts. He will jump out of his shoes."

"If we had brought a feathered bonnet with us," Windy Voice said, "I would do a war dance around him."

"I say he's a spy," said Foxglove. "He has no business being on this land. Let's find his horse and take it with us. He'll freeze to death trying to find his way out of the woods."

The three Indians approached the white settler. He was a sturdy man of sixty, half asleep, still staring at the half-moon.

Then the settler rose and wheeled around. After an instant of fright he casually studied their Indian faces and laughed. They could smell his whiskey breath.

"Welcome, friends," said the white man. "I have strayed off the beaten path and have to ask you to point me in the right direction. I left my horse in the woods and can't find him. I tried to figger out where I was by studying the moon, but all I can figger is it's rising in the east. This is for your trouble." He handed Foxglove a half-empty whiskey bottle.

Foxglove then handed the settler an almost empty whiskey bottle. The settler shook that bottle to see if the stuff fizzed. It didn't, so he took a half pull and held up the bottle to see how much was left. It was empty so he tossed it into the snow.

Small Horse took a long pull of the new bottle and handed it back to the settler; he took another pull, wiped his wet chin with his coat sleeve, and passed the whiskey to Foxglove.

"I am feeling no pain," the elderly man said to the three Indians. "You gents are my friends—right?" He said he was on his way back to the fort and had got lost.

None of them spoke.

"No speak?" he said. "When we make powwow?"

The settler resumed sitting on the snowy ground. After a while each of the three Indians sat with him, first Small Horse, then Foxglove, then Windy Voice holding his ankles.

"What should we do with him?" Windy Voice asked in the tongue of the People.

"Are you talking about me?" asked the settler.

"No," said Windy Voice. "We talk about your firewater. Where you get it? It steals my breath away."

The settler said, "I hoped you wasn't talking about me."

The Indians said nothing. Their faces were motionless.

"He must be the one who tried to rape Penelope," said Foxglove. "He also touched One Blossom in the crotch. Indian Head said he would kill him on sight if he ever came across the white bastard who had done that."

Small Horse pulled out a short pipe and lit it with sparks from two pieces of flint. The settler also had a corncob, which he lit with a spark from Small Horse's pipe.

They smoked.

"What will we do with this white bastard?" Windy Voice asked in their tribal tongue.

"Where you want to go?" he asked the white man.

"Home," said the settler, "if I knew where it was. I thought I came from the east, but my head is spinnin' so it feels like east, west, and north. Still and all, what I want to do most is take a hot piss and go back to the fort. My horse is waitin' somewhere t'other side of them pines."

"We take you back," said Windy Voice, imitating a white man.

"Will you? Thanks, old chum. You boys are the nicest fucking Indians I do believe I have ever met."

Even Foxglove laughed at the man's expression.

*   *   *

A brave came galloping into camp one morning as Jozip was sensing spring on its way. The brave ran to Jozip's tepee, tossed open the tent flap, and proclaimed trouble. "Chief Jozip, we have found a dead settler in the woods. He is a bald-headed man who was scalped."

"What do you mean, scolped?" said Jozip. "This tribe does not do such terrible things. We don't teach our braves to scolp strangers. This we don't do. My God, where did they leave the body? First we must bury it. No. First call for me Indian Head. Tell him to come fast."

Indian Head came on the run. Jozip asked the brave to repeat his story. The brave said he had been in the woods and had found a dead white man lying in the bloody snow. He swore he had never seen him before.

Jozip told Indian Head the man had been scalped. "Is this possible?"

Indian Head said it was. "It is not possible until it happens."

"Who would do such a terrible thing?"

"Some stupid fool. Maybe somebody who wants to make trouble between us and the Indian agent at Fort Boise, or the fat-ass colonel. What will you do?" he asked Jozip.

"Maybe I will ride to the fort and talk to Cohnel Gunther. Also

I will tell him our braves did not kill this man. I say that this man who got killed was lost on our land. If he got lost this is no crime, but we did not kill him. We are a lawful people. I will say this to the cohnel."

"Maybe you ought to call a council meeting."

"I will call this meeting after I talk to the white man."

"Do you want me to ride with you to the fort?"

"No, I will go alone. One Indian makes them suspicious. If they see two it's already an attack. This way they will see that I come in peace."

Jozip rode off to the fort. Bessie had lost weight and traveled swiftly and lightly.

It took Jozip a while to get into the colonel's office; and once inside he wasn't sure he should have come. The aide-de-camp searched Jozip's pockets, ran his hands over his buckskin pants, then reluctantly admitted him into the office. Jozip did not like being searched.

The colonel appeared when he heard an Indian had come to see him.

They recognized each other.

"Good morning, Chief," said the colonel. "I have to request that you tell me quickly the reason for your visit to this office. I have a painful toothache. I hope you've come to tell me that your tribe is getting ready for its move."

"Excuse me that I come when you have such a bad toothache," said Jozip, "but since I bring now some bad news I will tulk fast."

"The faster the better."

"Cohnel, I am very sorry that we found on our reservation this morning a dead white gentleman that he was scolped and died there in the woods. I came to ask you what we should do with the body."

"A dead settler?" The colonel brooded. "Was his name Ezra Pence? His wife reported him missin' last night."

Jozip was sorry he did not know the man's name.

"But you found him scalped by your Indians? This happens to be a very drastic offense, Chief Josephs."

"Cohnel Gunther, I wish to mention to you that I came here on my free will to explain you what hoppened."

The colonel went to the door and called his aide.

"Mr. Carpenter," he said when the man entered, "this is Chief Josephs. At least that's what he calls himself. They have found a dead settler on the reservation ground that may be the man we are missin'. Lock him up in the hoosegow until I get a dentist to pull my goddamn tooth in the morning. After that we will assemble fifty men to accompany us to the reservation. I want to get to the bottom of this scalpin' incident. A mean thing like that could start off a war."

Jozip said in astonishment, "You wish to arrest me and put me in jail? Mr. Cohnel, I don't think my tribe will like this."

"Don't threaten me, Chief. I am locking you up because I think it might be the best thing under the circumstances. Now don't make any more trouble or you will get your ass broke."

Jozip, disliking the man, said nothing. He wondered what Indian Head would do if he did not return before nightfall. Then he decided to let the colonel get away with the arrest though it humiliated him. Tomorrow he would be free, and when he got back to the reservation he would call a meeting of the tribe's council. Too much was happening too fast. He needed the council's advice.

The aide led Jozip to a small cell in the interior of the fort. Jozip spent half an hour reading the filthy inscriptions on the wall and decided the white race did not know what to do with itself. He was glad he had become an Indian.

That night he dreamed a woman had got into the cell and was beating him with the handle of her umbrella. He woke in pain. A woman with an umbrella was beating him in the dark. He shouted at her, "Stop, stop, you bitch, go home!" He tried to grab the umbrella but she was strong and fought him for it. Jozip struggled for breath, vigor, enlightenment.

"You bastard murderer!" she screamed. "You have killed my husband!"

He caught the umbrella handle in the dark but she clawed his face. Jozip cried out.

Two men appeared then in the dimly lit cell. Jozip shouted for help but there was none. The men beat him brutally. One man held him down while the other hit him until his face was wet with blood. The second man kicked him in the head. He could not recall what had happened after that.

Jozip fainted and lay on the cold planks until the colonel's aide came for him in the morning. He was allowed to wash his swollen face before appearing in the colonel's office.

"Chief," said the colonel, looking at him with distaste, "I am sure distressed to hear about your unhappy adventure last night. I had a toothache and took a slug of gin before I went to sleep. I owe you an apology, but this revenge against you was done behind my back. You have to believe that one of your assailants was the wife of Ezra Pence, the settler who was killed by Indians of your tribe. The other was his brother, and with him came a dear friend of Ezra's. We had all we could do to prevent the brother and Ezra's friend from cuttin' your throat and scalpin' you. I always said that bad leads to worse. I assure you I was dismayed by this incident and am releasin' you at once. I would have done it sooner but I had my toothache to attend to."

The colonel permitted Jozip to wash his face in a bucket of water in the toilet. He looked at the mirror and shrank from the sight of his battered head.

"This serves me right," he said to himself, "because I went to the fort and first I did not tell the tribe. This was wrong, to go without a friend."

Indian Head was waiting for him on his pony. He let out a shout. "Great God, what has happened to your face? Who beat your head like that?"

"I made a mistake," said Jozip, "which I will not make the same mistake again."

One Blossom was disturbed by his face but said nothing.

"Now we must find those braves that they killed the settler," Jozip said.

"We know those who killed the settler in the woods," said Indian Head.

"Aha," said Jozip. "Did they confess to you?"

"Nobody confessed but we know who they are."

"I will tulk to them," said Jozip.

Windy Voice, Foxglove, and Small Horse assembled with Indian Head in Jozip's tepee. They stared in surprise at his black-eyed, beaten face but said nothing. Two were young men. Only Foxglove was as old as thirty.

Jozip shook his finger in their faces. "Why did you kill a white man for nothing, which we have never done such a bad thing before?"

Small Horse said they had drunk firewater before going into the woods. "The old man had another bottle with him and we drank it and gave him ours. It was a fair exchange."

"Except that he is now scolped and dead, and you are all alive. Who took his scolp off?"

The braves said nothing.

"Are you sorry you did this terrible crime? If you don't answer me, then I got to ask you to leave this tribe. Now is not a time for more trouble than we already got. Now is the time to stay together because they want to take away from us our land."

"I don't feel sorry for that drunk bastard," said Foxglove.

"I will apologize," Small Horse said, "because it was the wrong time."

"That goes for me too," said Windy Voice after a minute.

"I will not apologize," Foxglove said. "The whites are spying on our tribe. They are trying to force us off the land. I have no love to waste on them."

"This is not a question of love, this is a question of justice."

"How much justice have they given to the Indians?" Small Horse asked.

"I fuck them all," said Foxglove.

"Who took his scolp off?" Jozip said.

No one spoke.

Jozip studied them.

He told Small Horse he could stay. He told Windy Voice to watch himself or he would be in grave trouble. He told Foxglove he was expelled from the tribe.

Foxglove spat on the ground. "Does he know what he's doing?" he asked Indian Head.

"He knows."

"I am doing what Chief Joseph also would tell me to do."

"Don't look at me with those bad-luck eyes," said Foxglove. "I don't want your bad luck on my head."

"My luck is good," said Jozip. "I asked the Great Spirit what I must do and He told me to do what was right. The medicine man said it would be wrong to exile Foxglove alone, but when I look in your eyes I see who murdered the settler. And I have to send you out of the tribe."

"I will leave with hatred for you," Foxglove said to Jozip.

Jozip did not reply.

Foxglove went for his horse and left the tribe without clearing his lodge.

Within ten minutes Colonel Gunther came galloping up to Jozip's tepee accompanied by fifty armed cavalry men.

"Hear me," he commanded, as he tried to control his pawing horse. "I have come to tell you that the U.S. government has already informed you that your tribe must leave this land in three weeks of time. Those words are out of the mouth of the Great White Father, U. S. Grant, President of these United States of America."

Jozip, thinking what he must look like to this man, and ashamed of his broken-faced appearance before his tribe, said slowly, "Mr. Cohnel, you said last time that we had a month to leave this valley."

"That was before you began to murder our settlers," said the colonel.

"But where will we go, where?" Jozip said. "How can you take away overnight where we live and also our property? We are human beings, not animals."

"I intend to refer this matter for additional adjudication by the proper authorities in the War Department. They will inform you where your tribe will have to go. I will telegraph Washington and at the same time put this tribe on strict notice that it must prepare itself for a major move of departure out of this valley forever."

"This is a long time," Jozip sighed.

The colonel wheeled his horse and with his fifty troops galloped over a hill and disappeared beyond it.

TEN

When We Go Where Shall We Go?

MANY SCHEMES tempted Jozip but nothing could he seriously propose. Where could a whole tribe of Indians go? Flight, if it came to that, had to be prepared for. It was impossible without a strategy, a way of holding together, renewed commitment to their way of life.

It is my responsibility, Jozip thought, but without a careful plan, a hasty move—the wrong move—might mean the end of the People. This thought frightened the new chief.

Jozip then called a tribal council, reluctantly seeing himself addressing his tribe in a tongue he was still trying to master. Was there a word for chutzpah in their language?

Jozip, after whitening his black eyes with paint, opened the council of sub-chiefs in his tepee. The council of ten men sat in a circle on the ground with the medicine man, Last Days, and around them sat many other braves. Some smoked pipes whose odor all but nauseated their chief. If he remained with the tribe he must introduce the cultivation of a mild tobacco; buffalo manure was too much for his nerves.

At last he spoke some reluctant words, squirming at all he had to say in a new tongue, but going on with greater ease as the words came to him.

"My brothers," Jozip said, "you know the contempt the whites have for us, as if they were the firstborn of the Everlasting Power. Our reservation in this valley is one in which our tribe has lived for fifteen years, and it was promised to us to live in forever. Chief Joseph told me this before he left us to walk in the Everlasting Fields. He spoke these words in the presence of One Blossom, who still mourns for the father who is not now with us. Now the paleskins want us to give up our land and go somewhere to a place that they have not yet told us the name, and which we do not want to go to, though we are not cowards. Nobody asked us where we would like to go or whether we are willing to live somewhere else. Also, nobody gave us a date of departure, though they must know it in their own minds. We were told three weeks from now but first we were told four. They count in bad numbers. They warn us of our fate but they do not ask if we will accept it. They will let it fall on our heads like rotten fruit.

"Now is the time to speak from my heart," he said. "I will call on our sub-chiefs and ask Wilderness Man, Split Jug, Fast Turtle, One-Leg-Is-Bad, and Indian Head to speak good words to us which course of action we ought to take. What shall we do now? I am your chosen chief. Give me your best words so I can weigh them before we act."

Wilderness Man wore his hair long and tightly braided. His voice was deep and his speech unhurried. He spoke, saying that each treaty they had signed in the recent past until they gave up signing treaties had deceived them as to its true intent, until they realized that the intent always was to expel them from the valley they thought they had been given to live in forever. The word of the white man was never more than the yapping of dogs. "We should have nothing more to do with them. They are men of broken words. They break them with their teeth and spit them on the ground." Wilderness Man spat on the ground. The Indians of the inner circle grunted in approval.

Then Split Jug, a lanky man with a black feather in his headband, struck his chest and spoke. He was a congenial bent-nosed man, who liked to challenge Jozip in games of arm wrestling. Jozip had won a handful of wampum from him in two trials.

"My brothers," said Split Jug in a high voice, "let us fool our childish enemies who are born with ghostly faces and stupid thoughts. Seven days ago I saw a miner on our land fouling our fresh water as he stood in a stream tapping his hammer on a dirty rock he held in his hand; and when the rock crumbled and fell apart, the glow of the metal lit his face. If his companion had not grabbed him by the seat of his pants he would have drowned in a foot of water.

"I say let us get rid of enemies by seeking out an unknown private place in this great land, where we will be able to go without asking permission or pardon from the whiteskins. When in our long history have our people needed men of bleached skin to tell us where and how to live? In some corner of this vast territory there must be at least some hidden valley full of elk and buffalo, and where the salmon leap out of the streams to greet our fishermen. Let us now depart this valley they have spoiled for us by taking away our sacred rights, and seek new hunting grounds where the whites won't be able to find us." Split Jug grunted as he resumed smoking his pipe. His brothers also grunted.

Now Fast Turtle spoke swiftly and vehemently. "My brothers, we have bows and arrows and many lances. But we have not enough deadly weapons to destroy these men if the pony soldiers should attack us with all their forces. I want to fight and annihilate them, but I will not in my conscience try to persuade my brothers to begin a war against our enemies under such odds, although this thought pleases me. Since this is so I will forbear to give advice to our good Chief Joseph."

"Jozip," said Jozip.

"His name is Jozip," said Indian Head.

"Jozip," Fast Turtle agreed.

Then One-Leg-Is-Bad spoke angrily: "I would want to draw the whites into battle and destroy them as Custer of the Golden Curls was destroyed by Sitting Bull." He turned to Jozip for a nod of approval but the chief did not want the words to inflame the braves, so he looked away. One-Leg-Is-Bad shrugged and puffed on his smelly pipe.

Last Days, the medicine man, said he would talk.

The medicine man of the purple headdress said he would speak plainly. He said he would prepare a formula only he knew. He would make of certain weeds tobacco with an aroma the white settlers would be unable to resist. "We will give them bad medicine weeds to smoke, and afflict them with a spicy smell they will never in their lives escape from. When they smoke this magic tobacco weed, one after another they will forget they want to force us to leave our peaceful valley. Their minds will waver and go lame."

Indian Head then spoke: "How will you get the settlers to smoke your magic weed? Won't they distrust it if we give it to them and urge them to smoke the bad weed?"

"Wherever the aroma is they will forget their purpose."

"But won't we have to smoke it first to produce an aroma?"

"We will smoke for a minute and they will forget forever."

The medicine man laughed, but Indian Head said he didn't think it would work.

Last Days disagreed with him. "Still, if you don't trust my magic weed I can think up other things to try. It won't take me long to think of a better plan."

Indian Head, speaking from where he sat, said to Jozip, "Is there nothing we can do to persuade the whites to change their minds and let us go on living where we have lived so many moons?"

Jozip, still speaking slowly in the tribal tongue, said these words: "I often think of our old chief, One Blossom's father. He was an enlightened man who taught himself new things every day. One reason I don't want to leave this valley is that his grave lies here.

"Now, if you ask me what I think we ought to do I must say, in truth, that I do not believe in any act that will lead to war with the whites, no matter how they trouble the Indians and make our lives very difficult. If they offer us nothing we will take nothing, yet defeat them in quiet ways. I do not mean by fighting a war against them. What we must do is outwit them. Let me tell you how."

"Yah," said the Indians sitting in Jozip's lodge.

"We could surprise them by starting an action that will trick them and overturn them if the Great Spirit helps us. Do you want to know what this action might be?"

"Yah," said the Indians.

"We know that the white man has betrayed us many times and will betray us until the skies turn purple in order to take away our land. So I think we must leave this country as soon as we can and move into Canada, which is moons away, but is still a friendly country where we will not have to face the American pony soldiers anymore. I give you this thought for your consideration."

Indian Head then said, "Canada is our grandmother's country. Maybe it will welcome our people."

Split Jug spoke in his deep voice: "My brothers, I do not think that the Americans will let us just pack our goods, take our cattle and our horses, and walk out of this land. I don't think we will be allowed to leave without engaging in an act of war. I think they will try to keep us from entering Canada. And what good is this long trek northward if we have no promise from the Canadians that we could stay there? We have heard that Sitting Bull is in Canada now, but all he is allowed to do is sit."

"I will tell you what I have done," said Jozip. "I have sent messengers to Canada. The Canadians have already agreed to accept us because they know our reputation for peace through a long correspondence they had with our Great Chief Joseph. As for the American pony soldiers, they may try to make it hard for us to leave but that is a chance we will have to take. Otherwise there is no future for us here. They offer us nothing, not even charity if we ask for it. I did not know this until I thought it out, but now I am secure in my thoughts. If the Americans are as civilized as they say they are, they will step aside at our approach. We must depart from here, my brothers, before we find ourselves prisoners in some smelly reservation much unlike this that they are forcing us to leave. We can't trust them. Shouldn't we attempt to escape from those people who still think of us as animals? If we succeed in outwitting them the whole world will laugh."

"Yah, yah," the Indians laughed.

*   *   *

Two nights later six youths of the tribe shed their clothes to the breech clout and painted their bodies with red and yellow stripes.

On the warpath they killed two settlers, an old man and his wife of eighty, but refrained from scalping them.

Chief Jozip, formerly a pacifist, cursed his luck for having been made a fool of by Foxglove and a half dozen irresponsible youths.

"This shows me that a first-class chief I am not," Jozip muttered to himself in Yiddish. "Otherwise I would have warned these young Indians never to murder another human being. If you murder somebody, first of all you murder yourself."

✗ ELEVEN ✗

The Long North Trek

ONE MORNING the herald spoke these words in the People's tongue:

"This is the second day of our long trek to Canada, our grandmother's country. We hastened our packing, we worked ourselves sick, in order to make a departure sooner than the whites could guess. However, we moved slowly and thought broken thoughts. After weeks of much labor we left in the dark before the black moon ascended. We had stationed two braves close to the American fort; they told us they could see no military activity and they rejoined us. We were 212 men and 438 women and children, each, whenever possible, mounted on a horse. Chief Jozip ordered me to make this count. We drove before us a thousand horses with remounts of a thousand more. We chose our animals with care, abandoning those that were lame or too wild to run free. Those we left behind will crop the grass of the greening earth until the white men discover and perhaps destroy them. They hate anything of Indian origin.

"Chief Jozip has marked out our route to Canada over the Buffalo Mountains. We will then move west and northward on that trail along which we often hunted buffalo. Most of you know these mountains and will welcome the sight of them. Once we cross them, we shall be that much closer to our freedom. Also, we counted the children and apportioned them among our women. Each child will remain with his mother as long as there is no peril. If any mother of a child should leave us for whatever reason, her mother or sister will care for the child, and see to it, every night, that it has a place to sleep.

"I have more to say. We left late at night, moving in silence in the dark. At the river the water was in full flood. The crossings were difficult. We had made tight rafts from buffalo hides and the horsemen towed us across, ferrying helpless old people and their duffels. Men and women fended for themselves, yet no lives were lost. Then the range horses, hundreds of them, as they passed their old grounds, unexpectedly stampeded; we never recovered more than half of them. Yet we counted no lives lost and considered we had made a good beginning of our planned escape.

"After we cross the mountains that lie before us, we will hunt buffalo as we move east, before we turn north. At night ten braves will guard our camp. We will hide our fires until we are three to five days ahead of those who will come to seek us.

"The palefaces are an accomplished people who have invented wires that sing. One day they will sing out where we are, but Chief Jozip has told the sub-chiefs that he hopes he will trick and delay them by contriving false leads to keep them off our trail, and by traveling at night as often as we can while the pony soldiers are asleep in their blankets. Our chief says that he hopes our people will be out of the United States before another full moon appears, if we can keep our present pace. Tonight is the moon of late spring, our time for planting. But we can't plant while we run. Chief Jozip has asked me to report to you each day so that you will know our daily purpose. He said this to me before we had left our valley."

Jozip muttered to Indian Head, "He makes it sound like a story, but without the madness of a tribe that is being forced out of its homeland." He was mounted on Bessie, Indian Head on a gray Appaloosa. They rode together. Indian Head had collected horses and many wagons for the very small children.

"If we can stay three days ahead of the soldiers on horses, maybe we could hold the same speed the rest of the way," Jozip said. "Do you think this is possible?"

"You're the chief," said Indian Head.

"What else could we do?" Jozip asked uneasily. "Would you go to that reservation in the Western states which finally they say they will offer us, where nobody from our tribe has lived there before and the land bakes hot in the summertime? Is this where we should go, so far away from our home in the valley, to live like animals?"

"Why do you ask me? We are of one mind about the decision to leave," said Indian Head.

"Denks for your good words," Jozip said as their horses trotted on together.

Indian Head then asked Jozip if he was religiously inclined. "You speak easily of the sky and in my presence you have often named the Great Spirit, but we have not exchanged thoughts about our beliefs. How much do you believe? Do you think of yourself as a religious man?"

"I have not made up my mind on this subject," Jozip confessed. "But I feel comfortable to believe in the Great Spirit. Who, otherwise, can explain the heavens and the light of the stars?"

"You speak good words," said Indian Head. "Why is it I make up my mind yes on some days and no on others, when the weather of my mood is the same each day?"

"Now we tulk like friends," Jozip said. "We will be friends— no?"

Indian Head nodded, then fell back with his steed, and before long One Blossom rode forward on her bay.

"The women and children are very tired," she said. "How much longer do you expect us to go on today?"

Jozip removed a bulky cloth map from the leather pouch he kept in his saddlebag. He pointed a stubby finger at the mountain range they were approaching in the near distance, then pointed to the foothills that lay before them. "This is where we turn off into Montana. You must speak to the women and tell them we will stop before the sun goes down. Tell them that the men expect to eat hot food. There is plenty of jerked beef and pemmican."

One Blossom lowered her head a moment. But when she raised her eyes toward him, Jozip faced her sternly and she put on a stern face. "I am sad to be leaving the land of my father's grave," said One Blossom. "I don't know when I shall ever see it again." She went on, "The whites have stolen our land from us. They say they go by democracy, but to me it seems that none of them knows what it truly is. If they had respected our rights and property we would still be living in the valley of the snaking river we love, and there would be no thought of a new reservation, or of fleeing into Canada."

"A reservation will be a miserable place to live if it feels like a prison roof on our heads. This must not hoppen," Jozip said.

One Blossom spoke in a low tone: "Jozip, I trust your judgment."

"Denks," said Jozip. Then, as if he had just invented the thought, he told her that Indian Head was his first true friend.

He said this while her eyes refused to leave his.

One Blossom turned back to carry the chief's message to the women.

When she had gone Jozip reflected on himself as the leader of the tribe. He had many doubts about his performance. Yet the Indians chose me, he thought. Chief Joseph himself picked me to be chief in his place. Otherwise why did they kidnop me in the middle of the street?

Jozip turned on his horse and signaled his people. He waved them toward the wood he wanted them to enter.

*   *   *

The tribe ate in silence.

Indian Head was one of those on guard that night. He said to Jozip, "The braves have been drinking firewater. They speak of their disgust that we don't stand and fight."

"Who will they fight?" Jozip asked. "Maybe I should go with you when you speak to them? Maybe we should spill their firewater into the fire."

Indian Head said he thought he could handle it alone. He had told One Blossom that she had better get some rest. They had miles to go before dawn broke.

"I will rest," she said. "I wanted first to tell Jozip what my father said to me." She looked at Jozip.

"Tell me too," said Indian Head.

"I will tell you," she said. "Once my father said that if it ever became necessary for his children to leave our valley he would be present to guide us on our way."

"Do you believe that?" Indian Head asked her.

"I do," she said. "I believe his word."

"I would enjoy to have his good advice," Jozip said.

He thought he ought to get a few hours of sleep if he could.

Indian Head then asked One Blossom why she looked as if she had been crying.

"I haven't been," she said. She glanced at Jozip but he wouldn't look at her. One Blossom went off into the deep grass to the wagon where some of the young women slept.

Jozip, in his tent, pulled off his buckskin pants, untied his leggings, then found he was too wide awake to sleep.

The next morning, after the tribe was moving, One Blossom rode forward to talk to Jozip and confessed her fear of dying young.

*   *   *

In the morning the herald spoke to the People:

"The ascent of the mountains was tedious. It had begun to rain hard. The muddy, slippery trails were impossible to ride or walk along. They were crowded with huge rocks and fallen trees. We made our descent, slipping, crawling, scrambling over wet rocks and thick underbrush. At last we found an opening in the forest and stopped to feed and rest our animals. Last Days thanked the Great Spirit for stopping the cold rain.

"We had come ten miles since daybreak, and Chief Jozip told the People we would have to go faster. The trails we followed over the Buffalo Mountains were obstructed by fallen trees, uprooted by winds, and matted together in troublesome ways. We abandoned two of the wagons for children, and divided them among the women. Then we found animals with torn bodies stretched along the trail where others had been, who Indian Head said were buffalo hunters from another tribe.

"Our march this day was to be sixteen miles. We climbed ridge after ridge in the wilderness; sometimes the only possible passage was filled with fallen trees, crossed and uncrossed. We traveled more miles and camped on the slope of another mountain. Now the grazing was poor. We had lost one wagon full of hay, and all we had left for the poor horses was wild lupine and wire grass. We made camp in the late afternoon. Two of the children had fevers.

"We had come ten miles since daybreak, but Chief Jozip said we ought to do another three before the day ended. We went another four. In the morning a messenger caught up with us and gave us bad news. He said that the soldiers under Colonel Gunther had discovered our early departure from the Long Valley and had begun to pursue us. Some of the braves were eager to stand and fight, but no one urged our chief to change the course of our flight. Chief Jozip said he thought he could see Canada when he looked into the deepest distance. I looked too but I could not see it."

*   *   *

Long Wind, a brave with a sharp tongue, came to talk with Jozip as he sat alone at his campfire. Long Wind said he must talk to Chief Jozip and they sat together. They spoke to each other as best they could.

"What will you do when the soldiers catch up with us and begin to shoot their rifles?" the brave asked. "They are only two days behind us."

"If they shoot at us we will shoot back," Jozip said in the language of the People, "but I will not shoot at them if they ask for a powwow and say they have come in peace and wish to live in peace with us. If they say that, I will tell them once more that we will not go to a new reservation. The only reservation where we will live is our own in the Long Valley. If they say that it is not our reservation anymore, then I will ask them to let us go on without delaying us.

"I will say that we are on our way to Canada and bear them no ill will. I will say that Canada is our mother now. I can see her in my heart.

"Do you feel sad at leaving America? Our people have lived on this land since they arrived on earth."

"But suppose they don't let us go where we want to go and instead interfere with the People?" said Long Wind.

"Then I will break off the meeting with the colonel and announce that we must move on again."

"Suppose the whites shoot at us?"

"We will take care of that when it comes to that."

"Without arms?"

"We are not without arms," Chief Jozip said. "We don't want to use our arms if we don't have to."

"You will get nothing from the white faces but scorn and lies."

"We will see."

"By the time you begin to see," said the young Indian in a tight rage, "half our people will be dead."

"We will say we want peace, that peace leads to peace."

"They will say, 'Peace leads to war when two nations collide,' although you don't seem to understand that."

"Don't speak to me with murder in your heart, Long Wind."

"That is what I have in my heart," said Long Wind bitterly. He walked away, leaving Jozip sitting alone by his fire.

Now One Blossom came forth from the dark to speak to Jozip. Jozip did not tell her what Long Wind had said to him.

One Blossom spoke angrily: "Don't you take any pleasure in being with me?"

"Of cuss," the chief said, "but how much pleasure can I take if you belong to Indian Head?"

"Indian Head belongs to Indian Head," One Blossom said. "He is my friend, but I have never said I will be his squaw. I am Chief Joseph's daughter, and will tell my man when I have chosen him. My father never gave me to anyone. I will love who I please. That is my message to Jozip the chief."

Jozip told her he was in no mood to hear that message.

"Our tribe is now being followed by an American army," he said. "I have to think of the tribe first. I have also Indian Head to think about. He is my friend. And I have our long journey, and at last the escape to think of which the council has planned."

Jozip said, "My name is like your father's name. Think of that and what it means."

"Please don't tell me what I must think."

One Blossom fled into the dark wood.

Jozip called out an affectionate name, but she did not return.

He scattered the glowing embers of his fire.

✕ TWELVE ✕

Three Indians

ON THE MORNING of the twentieth day of the tribe's long trek to Canada, One Blossom rode with Jozip, who had been riding with Indian Head. For a while all rode together. No one said much to the others. Jozip, uncomfortable with himself, tried to think out a way to put them at ease with each other.

He spoke his mind openly. "My friend Indian Head and my friend One Blossom, let us tulk in such a way that it makes us comfortable to be together. Our big purpose must still be to protect the people from any kind harm, while we gradually leave our country. On this subject I am not always happy, but I have made up my mind what I must do and I will do it. What bothers me the most is that I feel we are angry and without trust for each other.

"Indian Head," Jozip asked, "are you angry and without trust on account of me, and if so, why? It feels to me like all of a sudden you are suspicious of me."

"I will tell you at once," Indian Head said curtly. "Are you trying to take One Blossom from me?"

"God forbid," said Jozip.

"I am not yours to be taken away from you," One Blossom said.

"Your father, the good Chief Joseph, wanted us to marry," Indian Head said. "He told me so."

"He never said that to me," One Blossom said.

Indian Head asked her whether she thought he was lying.

"No," she said. "You and I are good friends. I want us to stay friends, but I don't want you to try to push me to marry."

"Why didn't you tell me that before?" Indian Head said. "We have known each other since we were children."

"I was not clear in my own mind," One Blossom said. "I thought I was but I wasn't. I learn more slowly than I thought. I have told you that often. That's true, isn't it?"

"I am not pushing you to do anything, but I want you to be honest when we talk. Have you given me up for Chief Jozip? If this is true in your thoughts, don't hide them from me."

"No," said Chief Jozip. He said it twice.

Indian Head did not hear it twice. He said to One Blossom, "If you don't want me to feel my feeling for you, you must tell me why, and who you want instead of me."

One Blossom said, "I will ask the chief of our people to speak now. Jozip, do you feel in your heart any feeling for me? Speak truly and earnestly."

"Yes, I have my affection for Indian Head, I also have in my heart affection for One Blossom. But I have more feeling for the Indian people than I have for either of you. This is my honest answer."

One Blossom grasped her horse's mane and turned him quickly. "We are running from the blue coats," she said. "I can run from them but I won't run from Jozip, and I don't want Indian Head to run after me."

"Please," Chief Jozip said, "please don't tulk anymore on this subject. Let us say we all have affection and maybe love each for the other, but nobody should tulk now—when we are running away from an army of white soldiers—about questions of love and marriage. Not now, please. We got to keep our mind on what is the important thing. Now is the time to move first to Canada. Indian Head, is this right?"

"It is right," said Indian Head, "but you ought to stay away from One Blossom."

One Blossom did not hear him because she was galloping away on her white pony.

Then Long Wind, on a black steed, came thundering toward Chief Jozip and Indian Head. "There is bad news," he said in the People's tongue. "Our messengers have seen white soldiers riding toward us, only two days away."

"We got to hurry to make it four days," Chief Jozip said.

"Why don't we just stand and fight?" said the young brave. "Our hatred for the blond soldiers will make us fight like battle gods."

"Like the warriors we are," said Indian Head.

"First we will tulk, then if they don't listen maybe we will have to fight," Chief Jozip said.

"There are no maybes," Indian Head said.

"Not maybe," said Long Wind.

That he was a vegetarian suddenly preoccupied and worried Jozip. "So how can I fight a war without the experience of a war?" he asked himself.

His war experience, thus far, had been to practice using the implements of war, bows and arrows, lances and rifles. Of course he had also shot at buffalo, some the size of a small railroad locomotive. Jozip had blessed the beasts as they thundered to their doom, and he did not eat their flesh. He silently explained these thoughts to his grandfather the shochet, long since dead and buried, and thus to himself.

He might fight, he thought, because he was an Indian, and Indians, more than whites, had to fight for their lives.

Later Jozip threw up and searched his vomit for barley grains, of which there were more than a few.

THIRTEEN

What Does the Dead Pigeon Say?

ONE NIGHT One Blossom feared death and screamed aloud. Indian Head came running to her tent and said there was nothing to fear.

"I am a child in my sleep," One Blossom said.

An old squaw appeared in the tent and told One Blossom she would stop screaming once she was married. "It is the screaming alone in bed that is hard to do," said the old woman. "I stopped when I was married," she said to them, "but now that my brave is dead I scream again like One Blossom. Maybe it is your father the chief who whispers in your ear and makes you scream. What does he say to you?" she wanted to know.

"I don't know what he said in my ear," One Blossom replied. "He said something I thought I understood, but then I awoke."

"You ought to take a husband," said the old squaw as she left the tent.

"You heard what she said," said Indian Head. "Why don't you take me as your husband? We have been friends since we were children in the missionary school."

"I enjoy you as a friend, Indian Head, but I don't think of you as my husband."

"The no is yes and the yes is no," said Indian Head. He shouted at her for having talked so badly to him that day when the two of them were riding with Jozip. Indian Head said her medicine was bad medicine and bad medicine was who she was. He said she was shaming her father's memory, and that was what the old chief had shouted into her ear. As he said these words Indian Head's nostrils were drawn thin and tight with anger.

One Blossom spoke coldly to him. She said that Chief Jozip was kinder to her than the friend she had had all her life. "What is this special kindness you ask for?" he said. "And why should I be kind to someone who shuns my wish to marry her and stands with two feet planted in her bad medicine? That is no life for me, and if that's all you give as my portion of your friendship, I will have no use for you, either as a mate or as a friend, or for anything else in my life. Possibly I will leave this tribe."

Indian Head left One Blossom's tent, his nostrils pinched white. He said he might go back to the States and not return.

"Perhaps that's what my father's ghost whispered in my ear," One Blossom said to herself. "For my part I want you to stay," she said as if she were still talking to Indian Head. "You are Jozip's friend as well as mine."

When One Blossom told Jozip that she feared death at night when she lay alone on the sack of branches she used as a bed in her small tent, he said, "So do I once in the while, but now I am alive, so if you will podden me, I will not tulk from death. When I think about you I think of life."

"Then why don't you say it," she said to him through the sadness in her eyes. "When you first came to our tribal home in the valley of the winding river, you smiled often as we talked, but now your face is always grim and you look too stiff and important when you wear your white feathered headdress."

"I smiled on account of I thought that someday I might love you in my heart," Jozip said.

"Then why don't you say you love me when I can see that feeling clearly in your eyes?"

"Sometimes my eyes tulk better than I tulk with my tongue," Jozip admitted to her.

He said this with hope, yet spoke as though with regret. He felt he spoke mildly when she wanted him to speak wildly.

"But don't you feel a heart-feeling for me now as we talk? I have that feeling for you."

He said perhaps he did, but there were reasons she already knew why he could not say that now. He thought he might say it after the tribe had passed safely into Canada.

"Will you speak your heart then?"

"I will say what I have to say to you and I will also say it to Indian Head."

"In English or in the People's tongue?" She laughed.

"You will hear the words when I will say them to you."

"I can see those words in your eyes as you look at me. I can feel your hands touching my flesh."

Jozip closed his eyes. "Please don't tulk to me like this when I said already I don't want to tulk to you this way now."

"Yes, Jozip," One Blossom said joyously.

* * *

Last Days privately told Chief Jozip, in the People's tongue, that he did not like the omens he had read in the body of a pigeon he had killed that morning.

"So what did the pigeon say?"

"The pigeon said nothing, but the omens were bad. I think we ought to break camp and go once more on the move."

"In this case I will break it," said Jozip. "The messenger said we were two days ahead of the soldiers, and tonight we have made it three days."

"What does our Crow spy say?"

"He says we are three days ahead," said Jozip.

"Do you trust him?"

"I have to trust him. He was also Chief Joseph's messenger and his best spy."

"I will read my omens again in the morning," Last Days said.

"Maybe we ought to leave this camp tonight," Jozip said. "Tell the warriors not to sleep with their wives tonight."

"You can tell them that, Chief Jozip," said Last Days. "I will tell them what the pigeon said."

Then Lone Bird, a tall warrior with a cracked face he had broken years ago when he fell off a wild running horse and landed on his head, came to Jozip and said his face and head hurt, and he took that to be a sign of danger.

"What kind of danger?"

"We ought to be on our way now."

"I have given already this order," Jozip said.

"Give it again."

Jozip said once was enough.

"We ought to go as fast as we can. This morning my father said he had received a strong impression of coming danger. The old man said, 'The danger thunders like a horse with four legs.' He also said, 'My shaking heart tells me that death will overtake us if we don't go faster on our way to Canada. I cannot hide what is revealed to me.' I too say we must hurry on to the North. We are taking much too long."

"Genuk," said Chief Jozip. "You should stop tulking like this. It will frighten the women."

Lone Bird said, "It is not wise to stop talking. Some who do that never say another word."

"Get all our horses together," the chief said calmly. "We will move as fast as we can go. Today should be a day of rest. It is the Sabbath. But if you rest on Sabbath you can die on Sabbath, so I guess we will move along on our trek to Canada tonight."

"We will have no real days of rest as long as the white dogs are in a pack behind us," Lone Bird said.

The tribe was on the road within two hours. The hard night trek made it a fourth day they were ahead when they stopped and wearily celebrated by cooking buffalo meat. When the fires were damped, the braves sought their wives in the dark.

FOURTEEN

Morning Massacre

JOZIP WRESTLED himself in his sleep.

He dreamed he was wrestling death, but when his eyes sprang open he had no company other than himself.

He rose in the moonlight and poured a jug of water on his freezing head. He wiped his moonlit body with a ragged cloth and drew on his breechclout and a pair of buckskin leggings. He wandered among the tepees trying to think about the tribe's next move.

Jozip reminded himself he was white. "I am white but I think like I am red. The old chief told me this when I went in his tribe, that I was an Indian. I said if you think so; then he asked me who I was and I couldn't answer him with the right words. When I told him this he said to me, 'I will tell you that you are a red man. Feel your face,' and when I felt my face I felt it was a red face. But I said, 'I am an Indian who is a Jew.' 'And I understand that too,' he said. And I said to myself, 'Why should an Indian give me this particular lesson?' "

Jozip went among the sleeping People lying on the ground or in the field, some naked, some covered with buffalo robes. They slept as if exhausted as he wandered among them trying to foresee the future of the tribe. What kind of warrior chief was a Jew who lived among a tribe of Indians with peace raging in his heart?

His thought troubled him when he saw his braves outstretched on the field as though wounded in war while Jozip urged them to run faster, run harder. Maybe they would outdistance the white soldiers, outrun them even in sleep, so there would be no war;

and once they were securely in Canada, they would deal with the Canadians about where they could live in the future. Or perhaps the Americans would send messages on the singing wires, saying they were ready to discuss better terms than before. And maybe the People would be allowed to return to their own valley, their own place on the earth, and live at last in peace.

"Who needs now a war?" Jozip said.

Then he realized he had awakened in the middle of the night, asking himself impossible questions, and rousing men and women who still wanted to sleep in the cool air. He heard himself being mocked in the distance by the young men, being called names he did not like.

But Chief Jozip responded to their taunts with these words: "I don't think there will come a war. So we will go to Canada, and when we reach there, we will meet in a council with other tribes and plan out where we should go next. Maybe these Canadians will let us live on their land near to the Eskimos, or maybe we will go someplace else that we don't know yet what is this place, or even where it is?"

So Jozip walked on, carrying his thoughts in a circle as he pondered a way to be free of them.

In the morning an army of blue-coated soldiers appeared in a forest, at the foot of which the People had camped by a stream after a night of dancing and celebration that Chief Jozip had disapproved of in silence. It was true that the tribe had thus far outrun the enemy, their soldiers thought to be three full days behind them, although they were not. And now the soldiers were hidden in the woods spying on the People as they planned an attack they hoped would turn into a slaughter of Indians.

Colonel Gunther was among the officers present, and so was General Stong, who had fought in the Civil War. Neither of them liked the other, but a war was a war and not much else mattered. Gunther was the envious one who had been harassing Chief Jozip. General Stong, the other officer on the chase, was surer of himself than the gravel-voiced colonel. In any case, they and almost a thousand men were closing in on the People. Colonel Gunther wanted the credit for the approaching victory to go to his regiment.

General Stong didn't care who got the credit, so long as the soldiers defeated and destroyed the blasted Indians. The general had been shocked by Custer's disaster, and he bore an uneasy hatred for Indians.

It was 5 a.m. The soldiers had slept in their greatcoats, and now the colonel's orderly woke them up one by one. They arose in silence for a cup of cold coffee. No fires had been lit anywhere, not so much as a flicker of flame. An officer with binoculars watched the Indians from across a rushing stream at the edge of the woods. There were no Indians watching the soldiers sipping their cold coffee, shivering.

An Indian woman came out of her tepee to stir up the fire. She swallowed a mouthful of water and spat it out on the sizzling flames. Another squaw was drawn to the campfire, and they talked. After she returned to her hut, the second woman told her brave that she sensed something wrong outside.

"What is wrong?" the brave asked.

"I smelled something dead," she said. "At the same time the coyotes were howling."

"You smell too much," he said. "You smell everything. The more you smell, the more I smell. I don't like to live like that."

"How do you like to live?"

"Without so much smelling," said the brave. "You go to sleep."

"I can't," she said. "I feel nervous."

"You are a stupid woman," the brave told his wife.

*   *   *

When dawn opened the sky, a single shot sounded within the woods and the soldiers pressed forward silently toward a hill of tepees arranged in a V-shape up a slope. They sloshed across the waist-deep stream and then charged with a roar to the lodges, shooting low to kill the families sleeping on the ground. The braves, when they could, bolted out of the tepees. Some remained where they were, wrestling the soldiers until they were killed or were able to escape into the woods. The soldiers shot or clubbed every-one in sight. They shot an old man reaching for his breechclout, and they beat the screaming children who got in their way. The

People scattered in panic, whenever they could grabbing up a child and running with it into the woods at the edge of the stream. One woman whose child had been shot in the face ran screaming with him deeper into the water. She laughed as she drowned.

Other women fleeing the soldiers were shot in the back and fell as they fled. Soldiers' boots crushed the skulls of infants, and the force of their rifle butts broke open the heads of dazed old men no longer able to fight. After a warrior shot at a captain, and the captain killed the warrior, his wife snatched up his rifle, shot the soldier in the head, and kept on shooting until she fell riddled with bullets.

$$* \quad * \quad *$$

Chief Jozip, who had taken for himself the topmost tepee, awoke running.

"Get together," he cried to the warriors. "We got to get together for defense." In a few minutes he succeeded in organizing the braves on the upper slope into a defense force. "Get ready to attack," he cried.

Then he realized that he carried no rifle. Jozip turned himself around and ran back to his lodge.

"Why were we so stupid that we didn't post guards last night? What did we celebrate if we are still running from the soldiers?"

One Blossom, half dressed, was waiting in his tepee. She handed Jozip his rifle. "Shoot," she said. "They are murdering the children."

"I will shoot," he said. "If you see Indian Head, tell him to look for me."

"And you must look for me."

He swore he would.

Jozip left the lodge and ran toward a group of soldiers who had appeared on horseback. He urged the warriors to fight them as best they could with their arrows, old guns, and single-shot rifles. The People were the better marksmen and knocked several soldiers out of their saddles. The troops, equipped with the latest arms, sprayed bullets blindly.

At the other end of the camp two sub-chiefs rallied the People and began to mount a counterattack there against the soldiers still coming up the hill. "Now is the time to fight," the scattered warriors shouted to each other.

Jozip divided his time fighting on the slope and directing operations at the bottom of the camp by the stream. He felt an urge to do battle but controlled the feeling lest it shame him when he wasn't attentive to his thoughts. How, he thought, can a pacifist fight in a war?

Jozip posted sharpshooters to the rear of the soldiers attacking from the opposite direction. Caught in a deadly cross fire, the soldiers were surprised to be falling, hit by bullets in the back. Only a few shots were exchanged with the Indian marksmen kneeling on the ground.

One soldier shook his bloody arm at the Indians. "You'll get yours, you red bastards."

"Shoot him again," Last Days ordered a marksman. "If he isn't dead, he ought to die."

The marksman shot; the soldier died.

"The pony soldiers are good fighters but they don't know where to shoot," Jozip said as Indian Head appeared from another part of the battleground. Jozip told him to get the older people to strap the children onto ponies and start them moving.

"I hope you know what you're talking about," Indian Head said. "We are dying like flies."

"You must get the children out of here before the whites try to stop us."

Jozip went from one group to another, pointing out where the soldiers were most exposed. That whole morning he fought among them. The People's situation was bad, but not as desperate as before. The soldiers were taking a fearsome punishment, but many of the People were also scattered dead on the field.

When he saw himself fighting against white men, Jozip was astounded. He never knew whether he had killed any of them. He assumed he had and he tried not to think of it.

I am chief of this tribe, he thought. I got to protect the Indians.

*   *   *

"Them Indians fight too damn well," General Stong said to Colonel Gunther. "I think we'll need about a hundred more bodies on horses before we can turn them back."

"I telegraphed for a hundred men just after we left to surprise the Indians," the colonel answered. "I got a message from the wireless operator that my request had been approved. I hope that don't interfere with any of your plans, General."

"That didn't," said the general, "but if you ever want to know what my plans are, you better get them direct from the horse's mouth. I am that horse. I don't want any of my subordinates out there guessing what I might attempt next. I want you to ask me. My plans at this very minute, if you would like to know them, are to wipe out these bloody savages before they eat our hearts with ketchup."

"There I go along with you," said Colonel Gunther in his gravelly voice.

*　　*　　*

Three Indian boys appeared in the meadow below with a dozen ponies. They led the animals forward at a fast trot, and quickly some of the warriors mounted and armed themselves with strong bows and arrows. They shot at whatever moved or fell out of a tree. They were sharpshooters.

Then Jozip heard the sound of a cannon bombarding them and felt sick. His horsemen rode forward to attack the cannon, but it had already fallen off an army wagon and lay with its nose in the mud.

A woman appeared on the battleground near the rifle pits the People had dug to protect themselves as they fired. Jozip said to her, "I have told the women not to fight against the white men. These men don't fight by rules. The rules frighten them."

She said to him, "One of the women asked me to go to you and say your friend is dead."

"Which friend? Oh, my God. Do you mean Indian Head?"

"No, not him. I mean One Blossom. She was loading guns for the braves. A soldier shot her in the teat."

"Is she alive?" Jozip asked.

"No, she is dead."

A cry broke in his throat. "I told her I would look for her. Where is she now?"

"There at the opening of the wood."

Jozip plunged into the wood and saw two white soldiers before they saw him. He beheld One Blossom's body lying on the blood-stained ground. Jozip aimed his rifle but did not shoot. He stood deep in the arms of a pine tree, waiting for the two soldiers to leave.

"Christ," said the younger man, "I feel kinda sorry we shot her. Why did she have to get herself shot?"

"Leave her be," said the lieutenant with him. "She is good and dead."

The young soldier touched One Blossom's body.

"I'm not doing anything wrong," he told the lieutenant. "I just want to feel how warm her cunt is." He lifted her dress and looked under it.

The lieutenant pointed his pistol at the young soldier's head, and at the same moment Jozip fired. The lieutenant fell heavily, sucking his last breath.

The young soldier ran, expecting a bullet to break his neck.

Jozip looked at the lieutenant lying on his back. "I killed already more than one human being," he said.

He dragged the lieutenant away and then fell on his knees before One Blossom. For a moment he embraced her body, then he lifted the girl and carried her in his arms.

"Meine kleine fegele," Jozip said as he carried her away. "My dear girl. Why did you go away from me if I love you?" He wanted to carry her until she came back to life. "My dear dead girl, don't go away from me."

He carried her out of the woods. But even as Jozip held her body, he rallied the Indians. "We fight for our lives," he shouted.

Indian Head appeared. He had been shot in the left shoulder. "I lost the ponies," he said bitterly. "I lost some of the old people and some of the children. I barely got away from the whites alive. You were wrong to order me to take them away when I did."

Then Indian Head realized it was One Blossom Jozip was carrying, and he let out an anguished cry.

"What happened to One Blossom?"

"She was shot by the soldiers. Do you want to hold her?"

"No," said Indian Head. "She was no longer mine to hold. She was not my woman."

Jozip held One Blossom as the battle went on around them.

Maybe she isn't dead, he thought.

"You were a fool to think you are the equal of an Indian," Indian Head said. "This trek to Canada has destroyed many of the People."

"I had the approval of the council," said Jozip. "Isn't that true?" he asked three braves watching him.

None of them said it was true.

Then two women appeared and took One Blossom away from Jozip. He tried to hold on to her but the older woman said it was time to bury her or she would stink forever.

"No," Jozip said, "she will smell like a flower."

"Indian Head should be our true chief," argued one warrior. "Now our medicine is bad because our chief is a stranger to us."

"I'm not a stranger to anybody in this tribe," Jozip said. Again he called on all the Indians to fight the whites. They heard his voice and fought well. At the end of the day, some of the soldiers charged up the hill to relieve others who had been trapped for hours without water. Then several Indians drifted back to see what remained of their camp. The soldiers heard a wail of mingled grief and rage that rose up as the People recognized the bodies of their warriors, women, and children. And they saw that the whites had let Indian scouts from other tribes scalp and mutilate the dead. Now the Indian sharpshooters kept the soldiers pinned while the People buried their dead. A bugle sounded retreat and the soldiers, carrying their own dead, moved toward the twilit woods, stopping now and then to fire back at Indian snipers.

Soon scattered bands under Jozip's guidance, after collecting the arms of the dead soldiers, slipped out of the camp, moving slowly to lessen the pain of the wounded. At twilight the warriors, leaving three sharpshooters behind, stole away one by one, and in the dark joined others of the tribe on their long trek to Canada.

General Stong cursed the war. "Who could've thought those blasted Indians would recover after our surprise assault?"

Chief Jozip cursed himself for the failure of his pacifism.

FIFTEEN

The White Flag

AFTER BARELY MANAGING to escape the murderous massacre, the People put themselves together as best they could. They had lost fourteen warriors as compared to fifty or sixty dead soldiers scattered over the battleground. And the Indians had lost four hundred remounts, yet Jozip decided they must flee faster. At times he had random thoughts of deserting the tribe, but they flew out of his head as quickly as they had flown in. He feared leaving the Indians in the midst of their flight to Canada. If the old chief had known his present mood, he would have cursed him with his ragged tongue. But Jozip, no matter his momentary doubts, had no serious plan to desert the People, who had become his brothers. "Coward!" he shouted at himself when his face wasn't looking.

Now he must be practical. The People were not immediately short of food: they carried hundreds of pounds of pemmican and jerked buffalo meat, but would have to replenish their stores at least once more before leaving the country. Jozip saw to it that the old people, the wounded warriors, and the children got what they needed. A warrior would shed his wounds more quickly if he was attended to at once and afterward heard his brothers give him praise for his feats in battle.

Although the People expected continuing pursuit, Chief Jozip dallied behind a bluff east of the soldiers' camp and invisible to them. Before another two days had gone by he learned from Nokomis, their best spy, that the soldiers were barely beginning to move out of the neighborhood of their failed massacre. Soon he was told that the white officers had ordered by telegraph many wagonloads of military supplies, including two cannons and scores of new repeating Winchester rifles. At the same time the enemy was resting their men until the supplies were delivered by covered wagon. "Denk God that they stop to rest now before we must fight them again. Tonight, when they can't see us leave, we will be gone. We will go after them and we will go before them. Let them figure out where we have gone."

"They will catch up with us quickly," said Indian Head.

"So what should we do, then?" Jozip asked in a moment of hesitation.

"Fortunately I am not chief of this tribe," Indian Head said, proud of himself.

"So if you are not," snapped Chief Jozip, "does this mean you have stopped thinking?"

"Oh, I have my thoughts," Indian Head said.

Chief Jozip walked away from him. He called a meeting of the tribe council. Five of its members were dead. Small Water was dead. Mad Storm was dead and his dearest friend, Long Light.

Jozip appointed five new members of the council to take the place of those who had not returned.

He then sat with the council for a powwow. The Indians sat cross-legged or crouched on their haunches, smoking their heady clay pipes. Jozip pretended not to notice. He spoke thus: "Nokomis and our Blackfoot scout, who is pledged to our cause, tell us that the whites have begun to receive military goods for a new battle against us. Our supplies are meager. All we can do is scrape the ground for their abandoned rifles. We have rusty guns and our faithful bows and arrows. There are good weapons but they will not win us a war or carry us into Canada. Another of their dangerous machines, which we have never learned to use, is the telegraph. When they need arms to be delivered, they telegraph Fort Missoula, and in a small time of days, tons of material are shipped to them from their supply depots. When we cut down or burn their telegraph poles, even if they send flights of eagles to shit on us while we are destroying the poles, we have to fight shit with birdshot. Our people are sick of fighting against unequal odds. I have thought long thoughts on this unequal situation and I have plans to suggest to you. Come, set aside those pipes that make me dizzy and let us talk sensibly to each other."

"Why should we set aside our pipes if they help us think?" asked Last Days.

Jozip told him to have it his way.

Then he asked, "What are these new plans I suggest to you? In the first place, we must go at once to the buffalo range and sacrifice a day to hunt and cut meat. The whites are getting ready to pursue us, but we must have food to fight with or soon the palefaces will be fighting our skeleton bones. Another choice is not to surrender but to continue to fly from our enemies as fast as we can go. This may be our best option but it may not come to pass. As we stretch the miles, the miles stretch us and continue to wear us out. Here is another of my thoughts. Maybe it is wise not to think of surrender but simply call for an end to the war and ask for peace without punishment because we are peaceable. We will say to the whites that we are willing to stop our flight into Canada. We will say as red brother to white that we want peace and will stop running from them if they stop pursuing us. We will turn in a westerly direction if they let us go freely where we want to go. This country is full of rich land and many good places to live comfortably. Why can't our tribe make its place here in this part of the United States, perhaps toward the far north before the land of Canada begins? That state is called Washington and is much like our former valley with its winding river and lakes. When this new land is ours we will make no further claims on the valley of the winding river that we have lost and now flee from. But the whites will have to sign a serious paper saying that part of the northern lands just under Canada will be ours forever, and that none of the whites will make any claim on them forever. Do you agree with these plans, my brothers?"

"Chief Jozip," said Indian Head, whose wounded shoulder seemed to give him more anger than pain, "you are speaking cleanly washed words and enjoying peaceful imaginings. But your words are not healthy. In fact I will call them crazy words. The whites will wipe us out overnight if we give in to them as you urge."

"No," cried Chief Jozip. "My words are sane and speak the truth. We ought once more to see what we can still do with the whites before we engage them in another bloody battle. Yesterday is not today. We should at once—now—make contact with their war officers and tell them that if the government will grant us several thousand acres in far-off Washington, we will accept this offer and then the long chase we are engaged in will be over for all time, and we will shift our journey north into Washington." Then Chief Jozip went on: "Now that the whites have fought us in battle, perhaps it will be easier to persuade them to exchange what was ours for what may be as good as ours."

There were members of the council who murmured words of encouragement to their chief.

Jozip said, "We must meet with the whites. We will go forth with a white flag. With us we will take the young lieutenant we captured in our battle of the Buffalo Mountains. Some of you wanted to kill and scolp him, but I persuaded you not to for just such an occasion as this. We will take this officer along to protect ourselves when we make contact with the whites. Three of our braves will lead him to the woods below. He will be properly tied up but not tortured. We will leave him below, miles from their lines, and we will keep him hidden and a captive until we need him. Then we will approach them with a white flag."

"It ought to be a black one," Last Days said.

Indian Head let out a guffaw, but no one acknowledged his noise.

"Small Brain will carry the white flag and he will wave it on his white horse. He will hold it high as we go forward on our ponies. We will cry out in loud words that we are the People and have come to speak in the cause of peace.

"After they hear us out they will talk among themselves," Chief Jozip went on. "After such talk I will tell them that we have, as a prisoner, a young lieutenant who says he is from Baltimore, wherever that is. We will ask the officers to speak to the Great White Father on their talking machine and ask from him that piece of land in northern Washington where we can live and hunt and fish as we once did in our long valley. If he agrees, that will end the war and our peoples will never be enemies again. The next week we will go to the other Washington in the East to sign the papers with the Great White Father.

"Now," said Chief Jozip, "we will put the white officer on a pony but keep him out of sight of the whites as we are powwowing with them. Those who may come with us are Indian Head, Small Brain, and Lightning Flies, because each of you knows the English tongue as well as I do. I speak the tongue of the People better than I do the tongue of the whites. One Blossom taught me our Indian tongue, and I am grateful to her for giving me a gift of speech when I needed it. Will those I have named come with me to powwow with the whites?"

"I think you are proposing a stupid plan and they will have no use for it," said Indian Head angrily. "They will give us nothing and waste our time. We can use our time more wisely in hunting for a day and then go on with our trek north, moving as quickly as we can."

"No, that is not a good plan," Small Brain said. "I like Chief Jozip's better. Let us go with him and see if we can reach an agreement to lay down all arms now as we consider where and how we can end this evil war and take care of our people."

"Your plan won't work," said Indian Head in exasperation. "Your thoughts, like Chief Jozip's, are twisted. We know that the white officers we meet will do nothing for us, as they did nothing for us in the past. We will suffer for our stupidity. We ought to push ahead at once to Canada and not waste time."

"Let us agree to the powwow," said Last Days. He said to Chief Jozip, "Who do you want to go with you? The rest of us will wait for you to hear your words on your return."

"I will ask Indian Head to come with us. I will also ask Small Brain. I will ask him to carry the white flag as we approach the palefaces."

Indian Head, who had been listening to Jozip, said he had thought it over and had no wish to go with anyone to the American soldiers. Only disaster could come from such a meeting.

"But another possibility is success," said Jozip.

"You will have no success."

"We will see."

Indian Head turned from him in disgust.

I will have to watch him, Jozip thought.

Last Days read his thoughts. He could do that on certain days. He would know what a person was thinking who had not yet expressed himself.

"Do you foresee disaster if we go to the whites in the cause of peace, Last Days?" Jozip asked.

"I foresee disaster if a white crow plucks a feather from the body of a black crow."

The Indians were startled.

"Then stay here," Jozip ordered. "Small Brain, you may come with me. You are our flag bearer. We will go to the whites and tell them we will make an agreement to end the war if they will meet our terms. If the Great White Father agrees on the telegraph instrument to let our representatives go to the capital Washington in the East and sign papers for a new reservation, we will turn at once to Montana to trek to the new land."

"I agree to go with you," said Small Brain.

Jozip then singled out three youthful braves. Lank Feet wore a yellow maple leaf in his black hair. Good Weather wore no decorations or head covering. Hard Head wore a white man's tattoo that he had got as a child before he came to the reservation. These young braves, without protest, accompanied Jozip to a cave where a white officer, with his arms bound, was sitting on the ground looking at the sky.

"If you are lucky, we will bring you to your friends," said Jozip.

The imprisoned officer was a heavily built second lieutenant who seemed to be relaxed despite his bound arms. He wore a Civil War hat that one young Indian coveted, but no one had tried to take it off his head.

"We are carrying the white flag to the Americans," Jozip said. "If we speak well with them we will return you to them. If we don't we will hold you as a prisoner until we get into Canada, and you will be freed then."

"I'm obliged to you," said the soldier, "and I'm praying you will send for me soon."

"The Indians will not return you to your friends until all of us return safely."

"I'll be praying for you," said the American soldier.

"Have you changed any of your thoughts about Indians since we took you as a prisoner?" Jozip asked. "I asked the Indians not to kill you—in the name of our former Chief Joseph, who was the father of One Blossom. She is not here now, but she protected you too."

"I'm grateful to the lady. I've learned that the world is a lot stranger than I thought," said the young officer. "And so far I've been a pretty lucky guy."

Jozip said that he and Small Brain would take the trail leading to the campgrounds of the white soldiers. They were encamped ten miles below the place of the massacre in the woods.

I'm doing what I must do, Jozip thought. If no one tries to make peace it will never be made.

Jozip was riding Bessie, and Small Brain rode a black pinto downhill along a rough trail through the woods.

"When we get to the soldiers' campgrounds we will wave the white flag and say we are peaceful people who come in the cause of peace."

They came out of the woods and once more were on level ground about a mile from the soldiers' camp.

"Raise your white flag," Jozip said to Small Brain.

The Indian raised the white flag, waving it back and forth.

Then to Jozip's horror a shot rang out.

"Don't shoot!" he cried out. "We come to be peaceful!"

He shouted as Small Brain, with a choked grunt, fell off his horse and toppled to the ground. The white flag fell with him. His horse, whinnying, bolted away from the sound of rifle shot, but Bessie, shivering, remained firmly present.

"No, no," Jozip cried, waving both arms. "We come in peace."

He was at once surrounded by a group of soldiers with raised rifles, one of whom was Colonel Gunther.

"You fools," cried Jozip. "We came here in peace to tulk good words. Why do you shoot us if we carry a white flag? Don't you know what it means to carry a white flag? This is an international sign. Everybody must respect it if we say we live like civilized human beings."

"That is more than enough outta you," snapped Colonel Gunther. "Somebody go get the bamboo cage for this wise-ass."

"You go against the law," Jozip said. "We came to you to be peaceful and also we carry a white flag."

"You know what you can do with your flag."

General Stong appeared. "What the hell is coming off here?" Seeing Jozip, he laughed aloud. "My, our foreign friend is with us again." He then announced loudly, "You are a deserter of the United States of America. In the name of the U.S. government I arrest you."

"I have already made that arrest," said Colonel Gunther.

"I'm making it official," said the general. "Get the bamboo cage," he ordered two soldiers.

"Don't try to put me in a cage," cried Jozip. "This cage is against the law to put an Indian in such a thing!"

The colonel slapped his face.

"You can kill me first," Jozip said.

"It would be simpler to break your ass," said the colonel. "Now get down here and slide your body into that cage."

"Shoot me first," Jozip said.

The colonel struck Jozip's face with his fist. The chief's nose bled.

Another general appeared on his horse. He was a red-bearded man whom Jozip had never seen before. He looked the Indian over carefully.

"Why are you hitting this Indian?" he asked the colonel.

"That's no Indian," said the colonel. "He calls hisself Chief Joseph, but that is a big lie."

"Why did you slap him?" said the general. He was a burly man with a large mustache.

"He wasn't following my orders, sir."

"Why should he if you were slapping him around?"

"An order is an order, sir."

"Orders are like everything else. There are good ones and bad ones."

"I had General Stong's permission, sir."

"Did he?" asked the general.

"He might of wanted to but he didn't ask me directly," said General Stong.

"The Indian chief is free to go," said the general on the horse. "You are free to go," he said to Jozip, making a wide movement of freedom with both arms. The officers looked at him as if he had gone mad, but the general fastened his gaze on them and stared them down.

"You are free to go," he repeated to Jozip.

"Denks," Jozip said. He mounted Bessie and took off at a gallop, urging the mare on, even threatening her with a whipping if she slowed down, until he thought she might come to dead stop to protest his threats. But a whistling bullet he feared might break his back made no sound in his ears.

*   *   *

Later in the morning Jozip sent back the young officer who had been held in the woods. The lieutenant thanked him sincerely. Jozip grunted and gave him an Indian pony to take him back to the army camp.

That night the Indian chief returned to the vicinity of the soldiers' camp with two braves, and in the pitch dark they found and buried Small Brain's stiffened body.

The next morning, after they had broken camp and were once more on the way to Canada, Jozip sought out Indian Head and said to him, "You were right and I was wrong. The whites did not honor the flag we carried. They shot at it the minute they saw it. I barely escaped with my life and our friend Small Brain is dead. I should not have made contact with the white men. They can't be trusted."

"Why do you always talk with shit in your mouth," said Indian Head.

✕ SIXTEEN ✕

The Last Battle

ONE DAY IN September, the People, still moving northward, where the world was frozen white, beheld a body of galloping troops across a wide river. The Americans, a cavalcade of sixty horsemen, had discovered the Indians and were moving against them at a crossing point of the river. Jozip scanned the soldiers with a pair of binoculars that a cross-eyed brave had given him after the battle of Buffalo Hills.

"What do you see?" Last Days asked.

"I don't think we will have to fight them," Jozip said, pointing upstream. "They are trying to ford the river, but it is too high for an easy crossing. They will lose supplies and some of their horses. We will let them cross the river, but when they have come to this shore, we will be gone when they arrive. After that we will be invisible to them. They won't know where we have gone, and by the time they discover our tracks, we will once more be on our way. My thought is that Canada can't be more than twenty miles to the north. That is what the map says."

The braves who had surrounded their leaders to hear them talk about their next move heard little concerning future plans. Later, talking among themselves in the lodges and tepees, they praised their chief's astuteness and his strength as a warrior. Usually he read a situation clearly, as it was, and not as he thought it might be. One of their sub-chiefs had led them into nasty scrapes; but this one, whom the tribe had adopted and made their leader, Jozip himself, thought of and carried out moves that had almost magical

consequences, once, for instance, stealing two hundred government mules, all stupidly left untethered. That was a successful
foray, inconvenient for the white soldiers, who were then forced
to comb the fields for miles before rounding up a single mule
braying on a hilltop.

Who is doing this to me? Jozip thought, or am I doing it to
myself? When I take chances I feel a big—almost too big—excitement, as though I had poured a two-quart pitcher of beer into a
one-quart glass. I know the People are happy when we outwit the
whites, although I have no idea what they will do or say if the
white men should outwit me. The old chief who is dead reluctantly
instructed me in matters of warfare. Jozip remembered in his first
battle being aimed at by a soldier fifty feet away who was shot in
the face by an Indian brave riding his pony behind Jozip.

The braves asked Indian Head what he thought of Jozip as a
warrior, and at first he refused to reply. "Have we nothing more
to do than play games of fantasy? I will say that he seems to be a
good leader, but I am not sure of him and will watch him as the
skirmishes increase. So far I can say that he hasn't made any big
stupid mistakes that some other chiefs have foolishly made."

Then one brave spoke aloud to Indian Head: "Do you, by some
chance, expect to replace him as our leader whose eyes sweep the
ground in a glance as he leads us north?"

Indian Head did not directly reply to his question.

"Let us watch what he does as he goes through the forested
mountains on our road to Canada. If he can go through them able
to read the lines of his map, risking no foolishly extended battles,
and holding us together and properly fed, then when we come out
of the mountains and descend to the Canadian plains with our
women and children safe, I will have no bad names to call him.
Nor will I rail against his leadership, even though I know there
are some among us who could lead better than he, without his
nervousness and signs of frequent doubt."

Once Chief Jozip had responded to the appearance of a detach-
ment of soldiers across a wide field by signaling the People to enter
a wood. They quickly followed his orders, and soon a small band

of troops trotted by, not knowing how close they had come to being ambushed. "But why didn't we ambush them?" one Indian complained. "They hadn't seen us enter the woodland, and we could have trapped them and slit open their throats before they could think what we were doing. Why didn't we take advantage of the opportunity to wipe out of this world a few more of our enemies?"

"In sparing them," Jozip said, "we have earned some credit with the Great Spirit, who protects us in the same way we protected them, by letting their soldiers live as they went by these woods."

"Let us not fool around with words," said Indian Head.

Jozip replied that he had answered the brave as honestly as he could. He was then tempted to flee the Indians and their pursuers the first chance he got.

Then a long thought crossed his mind how that might happen. Suppose Jozip had gone hunting alone one day, refusing to look at the pinched faces of the starving children who had less to eat than ever before. Jozip had waited most of the day with his rifle on his knees, watching for a deer to appear out of the woods. He would fire with his rifle on one knee and would knock the animal off its feet and with his knife slit its throat, saying a blessing. Then he would carry the bloody carcass on his shoulder to the Indians, who would have wondered why he had left the tribe so early in the morning without a word of explanation. They had not known what he intended to do, though they had tracked him and guessed his intentions, but weren't sure until they saw his bloodstained hands and face. Jozip would then hand the heavy carcass to the braves who had wordlessly appeared. He would not tell them it had been his first desire to flee from his brothers, even though he could not bring himself to do so.

*   *   *

One day behind the Indians, an American general and his troops caught up with them unexpectedly. Knowing that he outnumbered the People three to one, he had arranged his men on a rise that looked into the valley below. The general had brought his artillery, a four-inch howitzer and two Gatling guns, and began to spray shot at the dumbfounded Indians. Jozip realized at once that he must keep the army from going around a nearby ravine that would give the soldiers easy access to the Indian camp.

As the braves pulled and pushed their women and children out of sight, a number of Indians fought their way up the side of the hill and toppled the cannon to the ground. Some of the braves spat at it, others dragged it with ropes along the ground until it sank in a mud hole; then with a cheer, they went on fighting as they had before. At the same moment Jozip and his band of Indians attacked. He did this with twenty-four men. Their sharpshooters were so effective that the whites at the side of the hill were compelled to go on the defensive. The People were able to hold their lines throughout the daylight hours. Now the white troops, needing water, were pinned down by the Indian sharpshooters, so the Indian camp in the valley was comparatively safe. The battle temporarily stopped and renewed itself in the morning.

But the People were tired of fighting in the dark and wanted to end the engagement. They were not conditioned mentally and physically for long battles, but were accustomed to fight or leave as they chose. Jozip slept hurriedly for twenty minutes and woke to wonder where he was. The whites had about two hundred men. The Indians had fewer than a hundred on their line. They stepped away from the firing line a few at a time, and withdrew through the woods to last night's camping ground without the soldiers knowing that the number of their foe was diminishing.

Then Jozip regretfully informed the council of twelve that he could no longer stand the losses in battle of some of their best warriors, and the continuing pain of the People, so he had come before the brothers of the council with a request that the People surrender.

"We have fought well," he said, "but the Great Spirit has turned away his head to our needs. We cry for peace but his ears are deafened by the noise of men. The sounds we make are strange to him. The People must prepare for surrender. I speak with sorrow in my heart, with lamentation for those who have fought so well and never won, though our spirits are still indomitable."

None of the sub-chiefs argued against these words, but Indian

Head showed contempt for them, and he mocked the warriors for keeping Jozip chief of the tribe.

Jozip, resisting tears, thought of surrender as his last act of pacifism. Where will I live? he thought. I have nowhere to live.

The next morning he rose and put on his best buckskin shirt and his buckskin trousers, and hung three strings of glass beads around his neck. He took his battle sword out of its case and went from one tepee to another asking the braves and their women to accompany him, so that all, in the future, would have proof of the words they spoke if ever the whites should question them. About fifty Indian men and women offered to walk with him to the campgrounds of the army.

Jozip then handed his sword to a general, who greeted him respectfully and asked him to carry the sword to the colonel.

"The colonel is no friend of our people," Jozip said. He carried the sword to the colonel. "This is yours," he said. "I have no need for it anymore."

The colonel took the sword and kissed it. "I had my mind set on having it," he said to the officers present, "and I thank the general for passing it along to me. Not everybody gets what he deserves and I sure am happy I got it."

He lifted the sword and kissed it again.

Jozip felt slightly sick to his stomach.

He told himself that he must in his sadness not cry. He turned to watch the windy snow rising from the ground and he thought of himself as homeless.

The next day the Indian warriors, the People, were rounded up and given places on freight cars going to a reservation in Missouri that they had all heard of as a miserable place, although the good general had told them he would help to get them settled in a Northwest reservation they had once thought of asking the Great White Father in Washington to give them. Last Days said that he thought he would not live to see it happen. "We are being sent to a place of death and my thought is that I will die there. This is my only thought."

The moaning of the Indians began as the freight cars were moving along the tracks.

Author's Notes

"THE LONG TRAIN" was the title Bernard Malamud jotted down for Chapter 17, for which he wrote several pages of text in longhand, showing Jozip being kept in solitary confinement in one of the cars. Jozip feels remorse at his failure: "I was not a first-class fighter . . . My heart is not in this war business." Indian Head turns up surreptitiously, expresses contempt for Chief Jozip, spits at him, and knocks him down. The final handwritten words: "General Miles, basically a reasonable man, seemed annoyed with any Indian he laid eyes on, and that included . . ." At this point the handwriting breaks off.

In the notes for Chapters 18 through 21, Jozip has left the reservation and turned up in Chicago, where he joins Buffalo Bill's Wild West Show (Jozip calls it a circus) as a White Indian. After leaving the show, he resumes work as a peddler, becomes a U.S. citizen, and enrolls in night school to study law in order to help the Indians fight persecution and injustice.

The final chapter, "A Homage to One Blossom," shows Jozip at night, dancing in the woods—"a Hasidic dance, of the recovered self . . . He dances for the happiness he felt in his heart on becoming a man."

There are several differing versions of the author's notes, but his intention about the conclusion of *The People* is confirmed again in these jottings:

Chapter 18. Back to the world. Jozip has shivering fits when he wakes up in the morning in Chicago. He is drawn to the Buffalo Bill poster for his wild west show. Jozip calls it circus.

Chapter 19. Jozip wants to become a lawyer for the Indians. He teaches his teacher's night class. More on the business of language and making himself understood. What shall I say to them? Tell them who you are and what you've done with your life. It took me thirty years to find out. Tell them what you found out. What you say may answer their own questions about their own lives.

Chapter 20. The scene with One Blossom sitting with him on the wagon [a dream?]. He tries to hold her but all he has in his arms is air. He looks up at the heavens for her. Who speaks to the People?

Chapter 21. Last scene: "Hasidic" dance of the recovered self. A rejoicing of life when the self seems annealed. Leave with an Indian talking.

STORIES

Armistice

WHEN HE WAS A BOY, Morris Lieberman saw a burly Russian peasant seize a wagon wheel that was lying against the side of a blacksmith's shop, swing it around, and hurl it at a fleeing Jewish sexton. The wheel caught the Jew in the back, crushing his spine. In speechless terror, he lay on the ground before his burning house, waiting to die.

Thirty years later Morris, a widower who owned a small grocery and delicatessen store in a Scandinavian neighborhood in Brooklyn, could recall the scene of the pogrom with the twisting fright that he had felt at fifteen. He often experienced the same fear since the Nazis had come to power.

The reports of their persecution of the Jews that he heard over the radio filled him with dread, but he never stopped listening to them. His fourteen-year-old son, Leonard, a thin, studious boy, saw how overwrought his father became and tried to shut off the radio, but the grocer would not allow him to. He listened, and at night did not sleep, because in listening he shared the woes inflicted upon his race.

When the war began, Morris placed his hope for the salvation of the Jews in his trust of the French army. He lived close to his radio, listening to the bulletins and praying for a French victory in the conflict which he called "this righteous war."

On the May day in 1940 when the Germans ripped open the French lines at Sedan, his long-growing anxiety became intolerable. Between waiting on customers, or when he was preparing salads in the kitchen at the rear of the store, he switched on the radio and heard, with increasing dismay, the flood of reports which never seemed to contain any good news. The Belgians surrendered. The British retreated at Dunkerque, and in mid-June, the Nazis, speeding toward Paris in their lorries, were passing large herds of conquered Frenchmen resting in the fields.

Day after day, as the battle progressed, Morris sat on the edge of the cot in the kitchen listening to the additions to his sorrow, nodding his head the way the Jews do in mourning, then rousing himself to hope for the miracle that would save the French as it had saved the Jews in the wilderness. At three o'clock, he shut off the radio, because Leonard came home from school about then. The boy, seeing the harmful effect of the war on his father's health, had begun to plead with him not to listen to so many news broadcasts, and Morris pacified him by pretending that he no longer thought of the war. Each afternoon Leonard remained behind the counter while his father slept on the cot. From the dream-filled, raw sleep of these afternoons, the grocer managed to derive enough strength to endure the long day and his own bitter thoughts.

The salesmen from the wholesale grocery houses and the drivers who served Morris were amazed at the way he suffered. They told him that the war had nothing to do with America and that he was taking it too seriously. Some of the others made him the object of their ridicule outside the store. One of them, Gus Wagner, who delivered the delicatessen meats and provisions, was not afraid to laugh at Morris to his face.

Gus was a heavy man, with a strong, full head and a fleshy face. Although born in America, and a member of the AEF in 1918, his imagination was fired by the Nazi conquests and he believed that they had the strength and power to conquer the world. He kept a scrapbook filled with clippings and pictures of the German army. He was deeply impressed by the Panzer divisions, and when he read accounts of battles in which they tore through the enemy's lines, his mind glowed with excitement. He did not reveal his feelings directly because he considered his business first. As it was, he poked fun at the grocer for wanting the French to win.

Each afternoon, with his basket of liverwursts and bolognas on his arm, Gus strode into the store and swung the basket onto the table in the kitchen. The grocer as usual was sitting on the cot, listening to the radio.

"Hello, Morris," Gus said, pretending surprise. "What does it say on the radio?" He sat down heavily and laughed.

When things were going especially well for the Germans, Gus dropped his attitude of pretense and said openly, "You better get used to it, Morris. The Germans will wipe out the Frenchmen."

Morris disliked these remarks, but he said nothing. He allowed Gus to talk as he did because he had known the meat man for nine years. Once they had nearly been friends. After the death of Morris's wife four years ago, Gus stayed longer than usual and joined Morris in a cup of coffee. Occasionally he repaired a hole in the screen door or fixed the plug for the electric slicing machine.

Leonard had driven them apart. The boy disliked the meat man and always tried to avoid him. He was nauseated by Gus's laughter, which he called a cackle, and he would not allow his father to do business with Gus in the kitchen when he was having his milk and crackers after school.

Gus knew how the boy felt about him and he was deeply annoyed. He was angered too when the boy added up the figures on the meat bills and found errors. Gus was careless in arithmetic, which often caused trouble. Once Morris mentioned a five-dollar prize that Leonard had won in mathematics and Gus said, "You better watch out, Morris. He's a skinny kid. If he studies too much, he'll get consumption."

Morris was frightened. He felt that Gus was wishing harm upon Leonard. Their relations became cooler, and after that Gus spoke more freely about politics and the war, often expressing his contempt for the French.

The Germans took Paris and pushed on toward the west and south. Morris, drained of his energy, prayed that the ordeal would soon be over. Then the Reynaud cabinet fell. Marshal Pétain addressed a request to the Germans for "peace with honor." In the dark Compiègne forest, Hitler sat in Marshal Foch's railroad car, listening to his terms being read to the French delegation.

That night, after closing his store, Morris disconnected the radio and carried it upstairs. In his bedroom, the door shut tightly so Leonard would not be awakened, he tuned in softly to the midnight broadcast and learned that the French had accepted Hitler's terms and would sign the armistice tomorrow. Morris shut off the radio. An age-old weariness filled him. He wanted to sleep but he knew that he could not.

Morris turned out the lights, removed his shirt and shoes in the dark, and sat smoking in the large bedroom that had once belonged to him and his wife.

The door opened softly, and Leonard looked into the room. By the light of the street lamp which shone through the window, the boy could see his father in the chair. It made him think of the time when his mother was in the hospital and his father sat in the chair all night.

Leonard entered the bedroom in his bare feet. "Pa," he said, putting his arm around his father's shoulders, "go to sleep."

"I can't sleep, Leonard."

"Pa, you got to. You work sixteen hours."

"Oh, my son," cried Morris, with sudden emotion, putting his arms around Leonard, "what will become of us?"

The boy became afraid.

"Pa," he said, "go to sleep. Please, you got to."

"All right, I'll go," said Morris. He crushed his cigarette in the ashtray and got into bed. The boy watched him until he turned over on his right side, which was the side he slept on; then he returned to his room.

Later Morris rose and sat by the window, looking into the street. The night was cool. The breeze swayed the street lamp, which creaked and moved the circle of light that fell upon the street.

"What will become of us?" he muttered to himself. His mind went back to the days when he was a boy studying Jewish history. The Jews lived in an interminable exodus. Long lines trudged forever with their bundles on their shoulders.

He dozed and dreamed that he had fled from Germany into France. The Nazis had found out where he lived in Paris. He sat in a chair in a dark room waiting for them to come. His hair had grown grayer. The moonlight fell on his sloping shoulders, then moved into the darkness. He rose and climbed out onto a ledge overlooking the lighted city of Paris. He fell. Something clumped to the sidewalk. Morris groaned and awoke. He heard the purring of a truck's motor and he knew that the driver was dropping the bundles of morning newspapers in front of the stationery store on the corner.

The dark was soft with gray. Morris crawled into bed and began to dream again. It was Sunday at suppertime. The store was crowded with customers. Suddenly Gus was there. He waved a copy of *Social Justice* and cried out, "The Protocols of Zion! The Protocols of Zion!" The customers began to leave. "Gus," Morris pleaded, "the customers, the customers—"

He awoke shivering and lay awake until the alarm rang.

After he had dragged in the bread and milk boxes and had waited on the deaf man who always came early, Morris went to the corner for a paper. The armistice was signed. Morris looked around to see if the street had changed, but everything was the same, though he could hardly understand why. Leonard came down for his coffee and roll. He took fifty cents from the till and left for school.

The day was warm and Morris was tired. He grew uneasy when he thought of Gus. He knew that today he would have difficulty controlling himself if Gus made some of his remarks.

At three o'clock, when Morris was slicing small potatoes for potato salad, Gus strode into the store and swung his basket onto the table.

"Well, Morris"—he laughed—"why don't you turn the radio on? Let's hear the news."

Morris tried to control himself, but his bitterness overcame him. "I see you're happy today, Gus. What great cause has died?"

The meat man laughed, but he did not like that remark.

"Come on, Morris," he said, "let's do business before your skinny kid comes home and wants the bill signed by a certified public accountant."

"He looks out for my interests," answered Morris. "He's a good mathematics student," he added.

"That's the sixth time I heard that," said Gus.

"You'll never hear it about your children."

Gus lost his temper. "What the hell's the matter with you Jews?" he asked. "Do you think you own all the brains in the world?"

"Gus," Morris cried, "you talk like a Nazi."

"I'm a hundred percent American. I fought in the war," answered Gus.

Leonard came into the store and heard the loud voices. He ran into the kitchen and saw the two men arguing. A feeling of shame and nausea overcame him.

"Pa," he begged, "don't fight."

Morris was still angry. "If you're not a Nazi," he said to Gus, "why are you so glad the French lost?"

"Who's glad?" asked Gus. Suddenly he felt proud and he said, "They deserved to lose, the way they starved the German people. Why the hell do you want them to win?"

"Pa," said Leonard again.

"I want them to win because they are fighting for democracy."

"Like hell," said Gus. "You want them to win because they're protecting the Jews—like that lousy Léon Blum."

"You Nazi, you," Morris shouted angrily, coming from behind the table. "You Nazi! You don't deserve to live in America!"

"Papa," cried Leonard, holding him, "don't fight, please, please."

"Mind your own business, you little bastard," said Gus, pushing Leonard away.

A sob broke from Leonard's throat. He began to cry.

Gus paused, seeing that he had gone too far.

Morris Lieberman's face was white. He put his arm around the boy and kissed him again and again.

"No, no. No more, Leonard. Don't cry. I'm sorry. I give you my word. No more."

Gus looked on without speaking. His face was still red with anger, but he was afraid that he would lose Morris's business. He pulled two liverwursts and a bologna from his basket.

"The meat's on the table," he said. "Pay me tomorrow."

Gus glanced contemptuously at the grocer comforting his son, who was quiet now, and he walked out of the store. He threw the basket into his truck, got in, and drove off.

As he rode amid the cars on the avenue, he thought of the boy crying and his father holding him. It was always like that with the Jews. Tears and people holding each other. Why feel sorry for them?

Gus sat up straight at the wheel, his face grim. He thought of the armistice and imagined that he was in Paris. His truck was a massive tank rumbling with the others through the wide boulevards. The French, on the sidewalks, were overpowered with fear.

He drove tensely, his eyes unsmiling. He knew that if he relaxed the picture would fade.

1940

Spring Rain

GEORGE FISHER was still lying awake, thinking of the accident which he had seen on 121st Street. A young man had been struck by an automobile, and they had carried him to the drugstore on Broadway. The druggist couldn't do anything for him, so they waited for an ambulance. The man lay on the druggist's table in the back of the store looking at the ceiling. He knew he was going to die.

George felt deeply sorry for the man, who seemed to be in his late twenties. The stoical way in which he took the accident convinced George that he was a person of fine character. He knew that the man was not afraid of death, and he wanted to speak to him and tell him that he too was not afraid to die; but the words never formed themselves on his thin lips. George went home, choked with unspoken words.

Lying in bed in his dark room, George heard his daughter, Florence, put the key in the lock. He heard her whisper to Paul, "Do you want to come in for a minute?"

"No," said Paul after a while, "I've got a nine o'clock class tomorrow."

"Then good night," said Florence and she closed the door hard.

George thought, This is the first decent boy Florence has gone out with, and she can't get anywhere with him. She's like her mother. She doesn't know how to handle decent people. He raised his head and looked at Beatie, half expecting her to wake up because his thoughts sounded so loud to him, but she didn't move.

This was one of George's sleepless nights. They came just after he had finished reading an interesting novel, and he lay awake imagining that all those things were happening to him. In his sleepless nights George thought of the things that had happened to him during the day, and he said those words that people saw on his lips, but which they never heard him speak. He said to the dying young man, "I'm not afraid to die either." He said to the heroine in the novel, "You understand my loneliness. I can tell you these things." He told his wife and daughter what he thought of them.

"Beatie," he said, "you made me talk once, but it wasn't you. It was the sea and the darkness and the sound of the water sucking the beams of the pier. Those poetical things I said about how lonely men are—I said them because you were pretty, with dark red hair, and I was afraid because I was a small man with thin lips, and I was afraid that I could not have you. You didn't love me, but you said yes for Riverside Drive and your apartment and your two fur coats and the people who come here to play bridge and mah-jongg."

He said to Florence, "What a disappointment you are. I loved you when you were a child, but now you're selfish and small. I lost my last bit of feeling for you when you didn't want to go to college. The best thing you ever did was to bring an educated boy like Paul into the house, but you'll never keep him."

George spoke these thoughts to himself until the first gray of the April dawn drifted into the bedroom and made the silhouette of Beatie in the other bed clearer. Then George turned over and slept for a while.

In the morning, at breakfast, George said to Florence, "Did you have a good time?"

"Oh, leave me alone," answered Florence.

"Leave her alone," said Beatie. "You know she's cranky in the morning."

"I'm not cranky," said Florence, almost crying. "It's Paul. He never takes me anyplace."

"What did you do last night?" asked Beatie.

"What we always do," answered Florence. "We went for a walk. I can't even get him into a movie."

"Does he have money?" asked Beatie. "Maybe he's working his way through college."

"No," said Florence, "he's got money. His father is a big buyer. Oh, what's the use? I'll never get him to take me out."

"Be patient," Beatie told her. "Next time, either I or your father will suggest it to him."

"I won't," said George.

"No, you won't," answered Beatie, "but I will."

George drank his coffee and left.

When he came home for dinner, there was a note for George saying that Beatie and Florence had eaten early because Beatie was going to Forest Hills to play bridge and Florence had a date to go to the movies with her girl friend. The maid served George, and later he went into the living room to read the papers and listen to the war news.

The bell rang. George rose, calling out to the maid, who was coming from her room, that he would answer the bell. It was Paul, wearing an old hat and a raincoat, wet on the shoulders.

George was glad that Florence and Beatie were not there.

"Come in, Paul. Is it raining?"

"It's drizzling."

Paul entered without taking off his raincoat. "Where's Florence?" he asked.

"She went to the pictures with a friend of hers. Her mother is playing bridge or mah-jongg somewhere. Did Florence know you were coming?"

"No, she didn't know."

Paul looked disappointed. He walked to the door.

"Well, I'm sorry," said George, hoping that the boy would stay.

Paul turned at the door. "Mr. Fisher."

"Yes?" said George.

"Are you busy now?"

"No, I'm not."

"How about going for a walk with me?"

"Didn't you say it was raining?"

"It's only spring rain," said Paul. "Put on your raincoat and an old hat."

"Yes," said George, "a walk will do me good." He went into his room for a pair of rubbers. As he was putting them on, he could feel a sensation of excitement, but he didn't think of it. He put on his black raincoat and last year's hat.

As soon as they came into the street and the cold mist fell on his face, George could feel the excitement flow through his body. They crossed the street, passed Grant's Tomb, and walked toward the George Washington Bridge.

The sky was filled with a floating white mist which clung to the street lamps. A wet wind blew across the dark Hudson from New Jersey and carried within it the smell of spring. Sometimes the wind blew the cold mist into George's eyes, and it shocked him as if it were electricity. He took long steps to keep up with Paul, and he secretly rejoiced in what they were doing. He felt a little like crying, but he did not let Paul guess.

Paul was talking. He told stories about his professors in Columbia at which George laughed. Then Paul surprised George by telling him that he was studying architecture. He pointed out the various details of the houses they were passing and told him what they were derived from. George was very much interested. He always liked to know where things came from.

They slowed down, waited for traffic to stop, crossed Riverside Drive again, and walked over to Broadway to a tavern. Paul ordered a sandwich and a bottle of beer, and George did the same. They talked about the war; then George ordered two more bottles of beer for Paul and him, and they began to talk about people. George told the boy the story of the young man who had died in the drugstore. He felt a strange happiness to see how the story affected Paul.

Somebody put a nickel into the electric phonograph, and it played a tango. The tango added to George's pleasure, and he sat there thinking how fluently he had talked.

Paul had grown quiet. He drank some beer, then he began to speak about Florence. George was uneasy and a little bit frightened. He was afraid that the boy was going to tell him something that he did not want to know and that his good time would be over.

"Florence is beautiful with that red hair," said Paul, as if he were talking to himself.

George said nothing.

"Mr. Fisher," said Paul, lowering his glass and looking up, "there's something I want you to know."

"Me?"

"Mr. Fisher," Paul told him earnestly, "Florence is in love with me. She told me that. I want to love her because I'm lonely, but I don't know—I can't love her. I can't reach her. She's not like you. We go for a walk along the Drive, and I can't reach her. Then she says I'm moody, and she wants to go to the movies."

George could feel his heart beating strongly. He felt that he was listening to secrets, yet they were not secrets because he had known them all his life. He wanted to talk—to tell Paul that he was like him. He wanted to tell him how lonely he had been all his life and how he lay awake at night, dreaming and thinking until the gray morning drifted into the room. But he didn't.

"I know what you mean, Paul," he said.

They walked home in the rain, which was coming down hard now.

*　　*　　*

When he got in, George saw that both Beatie and Florence had gone to bed. He removed his rubbers and hung his wet hat and raincoat in the bathroom. He stepped into his slippers, but he decided not to undress because he did not feel like sleeping. He was aware of a fullness of emotion within him.

George went over to the radio and turned on some jazz softly. He lit a cigar and put out the lamps. For a while he stood in the dark, listening to the soft music. Then he went to the window and drew aside the curtain.

The spring rain was falling everywhere. On the dark mass of the Jersey shore. On the flowing river. Across the street the rain was droning on the leaves of the tall maples, wet in the lamplight, and swaying in the wind. The wind blew the rain hard and sharp across the window, and George felt tears on his cheeks.

A great hunger for words rose in him. He wanted to talk. He wanted to say things that he had never said before. He wanted to tell them that he had discovered himself and that never again would he be lost and silent. Once more he possessed the world and loved it. He loved Paul, and he loved Florence, and he loved the young man who had died.

I must tell her, he thought. He opened the door of Florence's room. She was sleeping. He could hear her quiet breathing.

"Florence," he called softly, "Florence."

She was instantly awake. "What's the matter?" she whispered.

The words rushed to his lips. "Paul, Paul was here."

She rose on her elbow, her long hair falling over her shoulder. "Paul? What did he say?"

George tried to speak, but the words were suddenly immovable. He could never tell her what Paul had said. A feeling of sorrow for Florence stabbed him.

"He didn't say anything," he stammered. "We walked—went for a walk."

Florence sighed and lay down again. The wind blew the spring rain against the windows and they listened to the sound it made falling in the street.

1942

The Literary Life of Laban Goldman

COMING UPSTAIRS, Laban Goldman was rehearsing arguments against taking his wife to the movies so that he could attend his regular classes in night school, when he met Mrs. Campbell, his neighbor, who lived in the apartment next door.

"Look, Mrs. Campbell," said Laban, holding up a newspaper. "Again! This time in *The Brooklyn Eagle*."

"Another letter?" Mrs. Campbell said. "How do you do it?"

"They like the way I express myself on the subject of divorce." He pointed to his letter in the newspaper.

"I'll read it over later," Mrs. Campbell said. "Joe brings home the *Eagle*. He cuts out your letters. You know, he showed everyone the one about tolerance. Everyone thought the sentiments were very excellent."

"You mean my *New York Times* letter?" Laban beamed.

"Yes, it had excellent sentiments," said Mrs. Campbell, continuing downstairs. "Maybe someday you ought to write a book."

A tremor of bittersweet joy shook Laban Goldman. "With all my heart, I concur with your hope," he called down after her.

"Nobody can tell," Mrs. Campbell said.

Laban opened the door of his apartment and stepped into the hallway. The meeting with Mrs. Campbell had given him confidence. He felt that his arguments would take on added eloquence. As he was hanging up his hat and coat on the clothes tree in the hall, he heard his wife talking on the telephone.

"Laban?" she called.

"Yes." He tried to make it sound cold.

Emma came into the hallway. She was a small woman, heavily built.

"Sylvia is calling," she said.

He held up the paper. "The editor printed a letter," he said quickly. "It means I will have to go to school tonight."

Emma clutched her hands and pressed them to her bosom. "Laban," she cried, "you promised me."

"Tomorrow night."

"No, tonight!"

"Tomorrow night."

"Laban!" she screamed.

He held his ground. "Don't make an issue," he said. "Tomorrow is the same picture."

Emma bounded over to the telephone. "Sylvia," she cried, "you see, now he doesn't go."

Laban tried to duck into his room, but she was too quick for him.

"Telephone," she announced coldly. Wearily he walked over to the phone.

"Poppa," said Sylvia, "why have you broken your promise that you gave to Momma?"

"Listen, Sylvia, for a minute, without talking. I didn't break my promise. All I want to do is to delay or postpone it till tomorrow, and she jumps to conclusions."

"You promised me today," cried Emma, who was standing there, listening.

"Please," he said, "have the common decency to refrain from talking when I'm talking to someone else."

"You are talking to my daughter," she declared with dignity.

"I am well aware and conscious that your daughter is your daughter."

"All the time big words," she taunted.

"Poppa, don't fight," said Sylvia over the telephone. "You promised you would take Momma to the movies tonight."

"It just so happens that my presence is required in school tonight. *The Brooklyn Eagle* printed a vital letter I wrote, and Mr. Taub, my English teacher, likes to discuss them in class."

"Can't it wait till tomorrow?"

"The issue is alive and pertinent today. Tomorrow, today's paper will be yesterday's."

"What is the letter about?"

"It's a sociological subject of import. You will read it."

"Poppa, this can't go on," said Sylvia sharply. "I have two young children to take care of. I can't keep tearing myself away from my family every other night to take Momma to the movies. It's your duty to take her out."

"I have no alternative."

"What do you mean, Poppa?"

"My education comes first."

"You can get just as much education four nights a week as you can five."

"That will not hold water mathematically," he said.

"Poppa, you're a pretty smart man. Couldn't you stay home just one night a week, say on Wednesdays, and take Momma out?"

"To me, the movies are not worth it."

"You mean your wife is not worth it," broke in Emma again.

"I wasn't talking to you," said Laban.

"Don't fight, *please*," said Sylvia. "Poppa, try to be considerate."

"I'm *too* considerate," Laban said. "That's why I didn't advance in my whole life up to now. It's about time I showed some consideration for myself."

"I'm not going to argue with you about that anymore, but I warn you, Poppa, you will have to take more responsibility about Momma. It isn't fair to let her stay home all alone at night."

"That's her problem."

"It's yours," broke in Emma.

Laban lost his temper. "It's yours," he shouted.

"Goodbye, Poppa," said Sylvia hastily. "Tell Momma I'll come over at eight o'clock."

Laban hung up the receiver. His wife's face was red. Her whole body was heaving with indignation.

"To who you married," she asked bitterly, "to the night school?"

"Twenty-seven years I have been married to you in a life which I got nothing from it," he said.

"You got to eat," she said, "you got to sleep, and you got a nice house. From your wife who brought up your child, I will say nothing."

"This is ancient history," sneered Laban. "Tell me, please, have I got understanding? Did I get encouragement to study to take civil-service examinations so I am now a government clerk who is making twenty-six hundred dollars a year and always well provided for his family? Did I get encouragement to study subjects in high school? Did I get praise when I wrote letters to the editor which the best papers in New York saw fit to print them? Answer me this."

"Hear thou me, Laban—" began Emma in Yiddish.

"Talk English, please," Laban shouted. "When in Rome, do what the Romans do."

"I don't express myself so good in English."

"So go to school and learn."

Emma completely lost her temper. "Big words I need to clean the house? School I need to cook for you?" she shouted.

"You don't have to cook for me!"

"I don't have to cook?" she asked sarcastically. "So good!" Emma drew herself up. "So tonight, cook your own supper!" She stomped angrily into the hall and turned at the door of her room. "And when you'll get an ulcer from your cooking," she said, "so write a letter to the editor." She banged the door of her room shut.

* * *

Laban went into his room and stuffed his books and newspaper into his briefcase. "She makes my whole life disagreeable," he muttered. He put on his hat and coat and went downstairs. His first impulse had been to go to the restaurant, but his appetite was gone, so he went to the cafeteria on the corner of the avenue near the school. The quarrel had depressed him because he had counted on avoiding it. He ate half a sandwich, drank his coffee, and hurried off to school.

He went through his biology and geometry classes without paying much attention to the discussions, but his interest picked up in his Spanish class when Miss Moscowitz, who was also in his English class, came into the room. Laban nodded to her. She was a tall, thin young woman in her early thirties. Except for her glasses and a few pockmarks on her cheek, almost entirely hidden by the careful use of rouge, she wasn't bad-looking. She and Laban were the shining lights of their English class, and it thrilled him to think how he would impress her with his letter. He debated with himself on the procedure of introducing the letter into the discussion. Should he ask Mr. Taub for permission to read the letter to the class, or should he wait for a favorable moment and surprise the class by reading the letter then? He decided to wait. When he thought how dramatic the scene would be, Laban's excitement grew. The bell rang. He gathered up his books and, without waiting for Miss Moscowitz, walked toward his English room.

Mr. Taub began the lesson with a discussion on the element of fate in *Romeo and Juliet*, the play the class had just read. The class, adults and young people, both American and foreign-born, gave their opinions on the subject as Laban nervously sought for an opening. He was usually very active in this type of discussion, but he decided not to participate too much tonight in order to give his full attention to discovering a subject relevant to the letter. Miss Moscowitz was particularly effective in her answers. She analyzed the various elements of the plot with such impressive clarity that the class held its breath as she talked. Laban squirmed uncomfortably in his seat as the period grew shorter. He knew that he would feel miserable if he had not read his letter, especially since he had not even participated in the discussion. Mr. Taub brought up another question: "How did the lovers themselves contribute to their tragedy?"

Again Miss Moscowitz's hand shot up. The teacher looked around, but no hands were raised so he nodded to her.

"Their passion was the cause of the tragedy," said Miss Moscowitz, rising from her seat; but before she could go on, Laban Goldman's hand was waving in the air.

"Ah, Mr. Goldman," said the teacher, "we haven't heard from you tonight. Suppose we let him go on, Miss Moscowitz?"

"Gladly," she said, resuming her seat.

Laban rose and nodded to Miss Moscowitz. He tried to appear at ease, but his whole body was throbbing with excitement. He stepped into the aisle, thrust his right hand into his trouser pocket, and cleared his throat.

"A young woman like Miss Moscowitz should be complimented on her very clear and visionary answers. There was once a poet who quoted 'Passions spin the plot,' and Miss Moscowitz saw that this quotation is also true in this play. The youthful lovers, Romeo and Juliet, both of them were so overwhelmed and disturbed by their youthful ardor for each other that they could not discern or see clearly what their problems would be. This is not true only of these Shakespeare lovers, but also of all people in particular. When a man is young, he is carried away by his ardor and passion for a woman with the obvious and apparent result that he don't take into consideration his wife's real characteristics—whether she is suited to be his mate in mind as well as in the body. The result of this incongruence is very frequently tragedy or, nowadays, divorce. On this subject I would like to quote you some words of mine which were printed in a newspaper, *The Brooklyn Eagle*, today."

He paused and looked at the teacher.

"Please do," said Mr. Taub. The class buzzed with interest.

Laban's hands trembled as he took the paper from his briefcase. He cleared his throat again.

To the Editor of *The Brooklyn Eagle:*

I would like to point out to your attention that there are many important problems that we are forgetting on account of the war. It is not my purpose or intention to disavow the war, but it is my purpose to say a few words on the subject of divorce.

New York State is back in the dark ages where this problem is concerned. Many a man of unstained reputation has his life filled with the darkness of tragedy because he will not allow his reputation to be defiled or soiled. I refer to adultery, which, outside of desertion, which takes too long, is the only practicable means of securing a divorce in this state. When will we become enlightened enough to learn that incompatibility "breeds contempt," and that such a condition festers in the mind the way adultery festers in the body?

In view of this fact, there is only one conclusion—that we ought to have a law here to provide us with divorce on the grounds of incompatibility. I consider this to be *Quod Erat Demonstrandum.*

Laban Goldman
Brooklyn, January 28, 1942

Laban lowered his paper, and in the pause that ensued he said, "I don't have to explain to the people in this class who are taking Geometry 1 or 2 what this Latin quotation means."

The class was deeply impressed. They applauded as Laban sat down. His legs trembled, but he was filled with the great happiness of triumph.

"Thank you, Mr. Goldman," said Mr. Taub. "It pleases me to see that you are continuing your literary pursuits, and I should like the class to note that there was a definite Introduction, Body, and Conclusion in Mr. Goldman's composition—that is to say—his letter. Without having seen the paper, I feel sure that there are three paragraphs in the letter he read to us. Isn't that so, Mr. Goldman?"

"Absolutely!" said Laban. "I invite all to inspect the evidence."

Miss Moscowitz's hand shot up. The teacher nodded.

"I don't know how the class feels, but I for one am honored to be in a class with a man of Mr. Goldman's obvious experience and literary talent. I thought that the gist of the letter was definitely very excellent."

The class applauded as she sat down. The bell rang, and school was over for the night.

*   *   *

Laban caught up with Miss Moscowitz in the hall and walked downstairs with her. "The bell rang too soon before I could reciprocate the way you felt about me," he said.

"Oh, thank you," said Miss Moscowitz, her face lighting with happiness. "That makes it mutual."

"Without doubt," said Laban, as they were continuing downstairs. He felt very good.

The students poured out into the street and began to disperse in many directions, but Laban did not feel like going home. The glow of triumph was warm within him, and he felt that he wanted to talk. He tipped his hat and said, "Miss Moscowitz, I realize I am a middle-aged man and you are a young woman, but I am young in my mind so I would like to continue our conversation. Would you care to accompany me to the cafeteria, we should have some coffee?"

"Gladly," said Miss Moscowitz, "and I am not such a young woman. Besides, I get along better with a more mature man."

Very much pleased, he took her arm and led her up the block to the cafeteria on the corner. Miss Moscowitz arranged the silverware and the paper napkins on the table while he went for the coffee and cake.

As they sipped their coffee, Laban felt twenty years younger, and a sense of gladness filled his heart. It seemed to him that his past was like a soiled garment which he had cast off. Now his vision was sharp and he saw things clearly. When he looked at Miss Moscowitz, he was surprised and pleased to see how pretty she was. Within him, a great torrent of words was fighting for release.

"You know, Miss Moscowitz—" he began.

"Please call me Ruth," she said.

"Ah, Ruth, ever faithful in the Bible," Laban mused. "My name is Laban."

"Laban, that's a distinguished name."

"It's also a biblical name. What I started out to say," he went on, "was to tell you the background of my letter which they printed today."

"Oh, please do, I am definitely interested."

"Well, that letter is true and autobiographical," he said impressively.

"Without meaning to be personal, how?" she asked.

"Well, I'll tell you in a nutshell," Laban said. "You are a woman of intelligence and you will understand. What I meant," he went on, acknowledging her smile with a nod, "what I meant was that I was the main character in the letter." He sought carefully for his words. "Like Romeo and Juliet, I was influenced by passion when I was a young man, and the result was I married a woman who was incompatible with my mind."

"I'm very sorry," said Miss Moscowitz.

Laban grew moody. "She has no interest in the subjects I'm interested in. She don't read much and she don't know the elementary facts about psychology and the world."

Miss Moscowitz was silent.

"If I had married someone with my own interests when I was young," he mused, "—someone like you, why I can assure you that this day I would be a writer. I had great dreams for writing, and with my experience and understanding of life, I can assure you that I would write some very fine books."

"I believe you," she said. "I really do."

He sighed and looked out of the window.

Miss Moscowitz glanced over his shoulder and saw a short, stout woman with a red, angry face bearing down upon them. She held a cup of coffee in her hand and was trying to keep it from spilling as she pushed her way toward Laban's table. A young woman was trying to restrain her. Miss Moscowitz sized up the situation at once.

"Mr. Goldman," she said in a tight voice, "your wife is coming."

He was startled and half rose, but Emma was already upon them.

"So this is night school!" she cried angrily, banging the half-spilled cup of coffee on the table. "This is education every night?"

"Momma, please," begged Sylvia, "everyone is looking."

"He is a married man, you housebreaker!" Emma shouted at Miss Moscowitz.

Miss Moscowitz rose. Her face had grown pale, and the pockmarks were quite visible.

"I can assure you that the only relationship that I have had with Mr. Goldman is purely platonic. He is a member of my English class," she said with dignity.

"Big words," sneered Emma.

"Be still," Laban cried. He turned to Miss Moscowitz. "I apologize to you, Miss Moscowitz. This is my cross I bear," he said bitterly.

"Poppa, please," begged Sylvia.

Miss Moscowitz picked up her books.

"Wait," called Laban, "I will pay your check."

"Over my dead body," cried Emma.

"That will not be necessary," said Miss Moscowitz. "Good night." She paid her check and went out through the revolving door.

"You ignoramus, you," shouted Laban, "look what you did!"

"Oh, he's cursing me," Emma wailed, bursting into tears.

"Oh, Poppa, this is so mortifying," said Sylvia. "Everyone is staring at us."

"Let them look," he said. "Let them see what a man of sensitivity and understanding has to suffer because of incompatible ignorance." He snatched up his briefcase, thrust his hat on his head, and strode over to the door. He tossed a coin on the counter and pushed through the revolving door into the street. Emma was still sobbing at the table, and Sylvia was trying to comfort her.

Laban turned at the corner and walked down the avenue in the direction away from his home. The good feeling was gone and a mood of depression settled upon him as he thought about the scene in the cafeteria. To his surprise he saw things clearly, more clearly than he ever had before. He thought about his life with quiet objectivity and he enjoyed the calmness that came to him as he did so. The events of the day flowed into his thoughts, and Laban remembered his triumph in the classroom. The feeling of depression lifted.

"Ah," he sighed, as he walked along, "with my experience, what a book I could really write!"

1943

The Grocery Store

THEY SAT in the kitchen in the rear of the grocery store, and Rosen, the salesman from G. and S., chewing a cigar stump in the corner of his mouth, quickly and monotonously read off the items from a mimeographed list that was clipped to the inside cover of his large pink-sheeted order book. Ida Kaplan, her small, fleshy chin raised, was listening attentively as Rosen read this week's specials and their prices. She looked up, annoyed at her husband, whose eyes showed that he wasn't listening.

"Sam," she called sharply, "listen please to Rosen."

"I'm listening," said Sam absently. He was a heavy man with thick, sloping shoulders and graying hair which looked grayer still in the glare of the large, unshaded electric bulb. The sharp light bothered his eyes, and water constantly trickled over his reddened eyelids. He was tired and he yawned ceaselessly.

Rosen stopped for a minute and smiled cynically at the grocer. The salesman shifted his large body into a more comfortable position on the backless chair and automatically continued to drone forth the list of grocery items: "G. and S. grape jam, $1.80 a dozen; G. and S. grape jelly, $1.60 a dozen; Gulden's mustard, $2.76 a carton; G. and S. canned grapefruit juice Number 2, $1.00 a dozen; Heckers flour, 3½ lbs., $2.52 a half barrel—"

Rosen stopped abruptly, removed his cigar, and said, "Well, whaddayasay, Sam, you gonna order one item at least?"

"Read," said Sam, stirring a bit, "I'm listening."

"You listening, yes," said Ida, "but you not thinking."

Rosen gripped the wet cigar butt between his teeth and went on reading: "Kippered herrings, $2.40 a dozen; Jell-O, 65¢ a dozen; junket, $1.00 a dozen."

Sam forced himself to listen for a moment, then his mind wandered. What was the use? True, the shelves were threadbare and the store needed goods, but how could he afford to place an order? Ever since the A&P supermarket had moved into the neighborhood, he had done less than half his original business. The store was down to $160 a week, just barely enough to pay for rent, gas, electricity, and a few other expenses. A dull feeling of misery gnawed at his heart. Eighteen hours a day, from 6:00 a.m. to midnight, sitting in the back of a grocery store waiting for a customer to come in for a bottle of milk and a loaf of bread and maybe— *maybe* a can of sardines. Nineteen impoverished years in the grocery business to this end. Nineteen years of standing on his feet for endless hours until the blue veins bulged out of his legs and grew hard and stiff so that every step he took was a step of pain. For what? For what, dear God? The feeling of misery crept to his stomach. Sam shivered. He felt sick.

"Sam," cried Ida, "listen, for godsake."

"I'm listening," Sam said, in a loud, annoyed tone.

Rosen looked up in surprise. "I read the whole list," he declared.

"I heard," Sam said.

"So what did you decide to order?" asked Ida.

"Nothing."

"Nothing!" she cried shrilly.

In disgust, Rosen snapped his order book shut. He put on his woolen muffler and began to button his overcoat.

"Jack Rosen takes the trouble to come out on a windy, snowy February night and he don't even get an order for a lousy box of matches. That's a nice how-d'ye-do," he said sarcastically.

"Sam, we need goods," said Ida.

"So how'll we pay for the goods—with toothpicks?"

Ida grew angry. "Please," she said haughtily, "please, to me you will speak with respect. I wasn't brought up in my father's house a grocer should—you'll excuse me—a grocer should spit on me every time he talks."

"She's right," said Rosen.

"Who asked you?" Sam said, looking up at the salesman.

"I'm talking for your own good," said Rosen.

"Please," said Sam, "you'll be quiet. You are a salesman of groceries, not a counselor of human relations."

"It happens that I am also a human being."

"This is not the point," Sam declared. "I'm doing business with Rosen, the salesman, not the human being, if any."

Rosen quickly snatched his hat off the table. "What business?" he cried. "Who's doing business? On a freezing February night in winter I leave my wife and child and my warm house and drive twelve miles through the snow and the ice to give you a chance to fill up your fly-specked shelves with some goods, and you act like you're doing me a favor to say no. To hell with such business. It's not for Jack Rosen."

"Rosen," said Sam, looking at him calmly, "in my eyes you are common."

"Common?" spluttered the salesman. "I'm common?" he asked in astonishment. His manner changed. He slipped his book into the briefcase, snapped it shut, and gripped the handle with his gloved hand. "What's the use," he said philosophically. "Why should Jack Rosen waste his time talking to a two-bit grocer who don't think enough of his place of business to wash the windows or to sweep the snow off the sidewalk so that a customer can come in? Such a person is a peasant in his heart. He belongs in czarist Russia. The advantages of the new world he don't understand or appreciate."

"A philosopher," sneered Sam, "a G. and S. wholesale groceries' philosopher."

The salesman snatched up his bag and strode out of the store. He slammed the front door hard. Several cans in the window toppled and fell.

Ida looked at her husband with loathing. Her small, stout body trembled with indignation.

"His every word was like it come from God," she said vehemently. "Who ever saw a man should sit in the back of the store all day long and never go inside, maybe to wipe off the shelves or clean out under the counter the boxes, or to think how to improve his store a customer should come in?"

Sam said nothing.

"Who ever heard there should be a grocer," continued Ida, shaking her head scornfully, "who don't think enough about his place of business and his wife, he should go outside and sweep off the snow from the sidewalk a customer should be able to come to the door. It's a shame and a disgrace that a man with a place of business is so lazy he won't get up from a chair. A shame and a disgrace."

"Enough," said Sam quietly.

"I deserve better," she said, raising her voice.

"Enough," he said again.

"Get up," she cried. "Get up and clean the sidewalk."

He turned to her angrily. "Please," he cried, "don't give me orders."

Ida rose and stood near his chair. "Sam, clean off the sidewalk," she shouted in her shrill voice.

"Shut up!" he shouted.

"Clean off the sidewalk!" Her voice was thick with rage.

"Shut up," he roared, rising angrily. "Shut up, you bastard, you."

Ida looked at him uncomprehendingly; then her lips twisted grotesquely, her cheeks bunched up like a gargoyle's, and her body shook with sobs as the hot tears flowed. She sank down into her chair, lowered her head on her arms, and cried with a bitter squealing sound.

Sam groaned inwardly. The words had leaped from his tongue, and now she was crying again. The miserable feeling ground itself into his bones. He cursed the store and his profitless life.

"Where's the shovel?" he asked, defeated.

She did not look up.

He searched for it in the store and found it in the hallway near the cellar door. Sam bounced the shovel against the floor to shake off the cobwebs and then went outside.

The icy February wind wrapped him in a tight, cold jacket, and the frozen snow on the ground gripped his feet like a steel vise. His apron flapped, and the wind blew his thin hair into his eyes.

A wave of desperation rolled over him, but he fought against it. Sam bent over, scooped up a pile of snow, and heaved it into the gutter, where it fell and broke. His face was whipped into an icy ruddiness, and cold water ran from his eyes.

Mr. Fine, a retired policeman, one of Sam's customers, trudged by, heavily bundled up.

"For godsake, Sam," he boomed in his loud voice, "put on something warm."

The tenants on the top floor, a young Italian couple, came out of the house on their way to the movies. "You'll catch pneumonia, Mr. Kaplan," said Mrs. Costa.

"That's what I told him," Mr. Fine called back.

"At least put a coat on, Sam," advised Patsy Costa.

"I'm almost through," Sam grunted.

"It's your health," said Patsy. He and his wife pushed their way through the wind and the snow, going to the movies. Sam continued to shovel up the snow and heave it into the gutter.

When he finished cleaning the sidewalk, Sam was half frozen. His nose was running and his eyes were bleary. He went inside quickly. The warmth of the store struck him so hard that the back of his head began to ache, and he knew at once that he had made a mistake in not putting on an overcoat and gloves. He reeled and suddenly felt weak, as if his bones had dissolved and were no longer holding up his body. Sam leaned against the counter to keep himself from falling. When the dizziness went away, he dragged the wet shovel across the floor and put it back in the hall.

Ida was no longer crying. Her eyes were red and she looked away from him as he came into the kitchen. Sam still felt cold. He moved his chair close to the stove and picked up the Jewish paper, but his eyes were so tired that he could not make out the words. He closed them and let the paper slip to the floor. The overpowering warmth of the stove thawed out his chilled body, and he grew sleepy. As he was dozing off, he heard the front door open. With a start, Sam opened his eyes to see if Ida had gone inside. No, she sat at the table in frigid silence. His eyelids shut and opened again. Sam rose with an effort and shuffled into the store.

The customer wanted a loaf of bread and ten cents' worth of store cheese. Sam waited on her and returned to his place by the stove. He closed his eyes again and sneezed violently. His nose was running. As he was searching for his handkerchief, the store door opened again.

"Go inside," he said to Ida, "I must take a aspirin."

She did not move.

"I have a cold," he said.

She gave no sign that she had heard.

With a look of disgust, he walked into the store and waited on the customer. In the kitchen, he began to sneeze again. Sam shook two aspirins out of the bottle and lifted them to his mouth with his palm, then he drank some water. As he sat down by the stove, he felt the cold grip him inside and he shivered.

"I'm sick," he said to his wife, but Ida paid no attention to him.

"I'm sick," he repeated miserably. "I'm going upstairs to sleep. Maybe tomorrow I'll feel a little better."

"If you go upstairs now," Ida said, with her back turned toward him, "I will not go in the store."

"So don't go," he said angrily.

"I will not come downstairs tomorrow," she threatened coldly.

"So don't come down," he said brokenly. "The way I feel, I hope the store drops dead. Nineteen years is enough. I can't stand any more. My heart feels dried up. I suffered too much in my life."

He went into the hall. She could hear his slow, heavy footsteps on the stairs and the door closing upstairs.

Ida looked at the clock. It was ten-thirty. For a moment she was tempted to close the store, but she decided not to. The A & P was closed. It was the only time they could hope to make a few cents. She thought about her life and grew despondent. After twenty-two years of married life, a cold flat and an impoverished grocery store. She looked out at the store, hating every inch of it, the dirty window, the empty shelves, showing old brown wallpaper where there were no cans, the old-fashioned wooden icebox, the soiled marble counters, the hard floor, the meagerness, the poverty, and the hard years of toil—for what?—to be insulted by a man without understanding or appreciation of her sacrifices, and to be left alone while he went upstairs to sleep. She could hear the wind blowing outside and she felt cold. The stove needed to be shaken and filled with coal, but she was too tired. Ida decided to close the store. It wasn't worth keeping open. Better for her to go to sleep and come down as late as she chose tomorrow. Let him have to prepare his own breakfast and dinner. Let him wash the kitchen floor and scrub out the icebox. Let him do all the things she did, then he would learn how to speak to her. She locked the front door, put out the window lights, and pulled the cord of each ceiling lamp, extinguishing the light, as she made her way toward the hall door.

Suddenly she heard a sharp tapping against the store window. Ida looked out and saw the dark form of a man who was rapping a coin against the glass.

A bottle of milk, thought Ida.

"Tomorrow," she called out. "The store is now closed."

The man stopped for a second, and she thought with relief that he was going away, but once again he began to rap the coin sharply and insistently. He waved his hands and shouted at her. A woman joined him.

"Mrs. Kaplan!" she called, "Mrs. Kaplan!"

Ida recognized Mrs. Costa. A great fright tore at her heart, and she rushed over to the door.

"What's the matter?" she cried when she opened it.

"Gas," said Patsy. "Gas in the hall. Where's Sam?"

"Oh, my God," cried Ida, pressing her hands against her bosom. "Oh, my God," she cried, "Sam is upstairs."

"Gimme the key, quick," said Patsy.

"Give him the key, Mrs. Kaplan," said Mrs. Costa excitedly.

Ida grew faint. "Oh, my God," she cried.

"Gimme the key," Patsy repeated urgently.

Ida found it in the pocket of her sweater and handed it to Patsy. He ran upstairs, two steps at a time, his wife running after him. Ida closed the store and followed them upstairs. The odor of gas was heavy.

"Oh, my God," she cried over and over again.

Patsy was opening all the windows, and his wife was shaking

Sam in his bed. The sharp heavy stink of the gas tore at Ida's nostils as she came into the room.

"Sam!" she shrieked, "Sam!"

He woke from his sleep with a shock. "What's the matter?" he cried, his voice filled with fear.

"Oh, why did you do it?" cried Mrs. Costa in the dark. "Why did you do it?"

"I thank God he's alive," said Patsy.

Ida moaned and squeezed her hands against her bosom.

"What's the matter?" cried Sam. Then he smelled the gas, and for a moment he was paralyzed with fright.

Patsy put on the light. Sam's face was a dark red. He was per-spiring from every pore. He pulled up the quilt to cover his shoulders.

"Why did you do it for, Sam?" asked Patsy.

"What? What?" Sam said excitedly, "what did I do?"

"The gas. You turned on the gas radiator without making the light."

"It wasn't lit?" cried Sam in astonishment.

"No," said Mrs. Costa.

Sam grew quieter. He lay back. "I made a mistake," he said. "This is the first time I made such a mistake."

"Didn't you do it on purpose?" asked Mrs. Costa.

"What on purpose? Why on purpose?" Sam asked.

"We thought—"

"No," said Sam, "no, I made a mistake. Maybe the match was no good."

"Then you shoulda smelled the gas," said Patsy.

"No, I got a cold."

"The only thing that saved you was you got a lot of air. You're lucky this flat ain't windproof."

"Yes, I'm lucky," Sam agreed.

"I told you to put on a coat," said Mrs. Costa. "He was standing out in the snow without a coat," she said to Ida.

Ida was pale and silent.

"Well, come on," said Patsy, taking his wife by the arm, "every-body wants to go to sleep."

"Good night," said Mrs. Costa.

"Leave the windows open for a coupla minutes more, and don't light no matches," advised Patsy.

"I'm much obliged to you for your trouble you took," said Sam.

"Don't mention it at all," said Patsy, "but next time take more care."

"It was a mistake," said Sam. "Nothing more, I assure you."

The Costas left. Ida saw them to the door and turned the lock. Sam covered himself more securely with the quilt. The house was freezing with the windows open. He was afraid he would begin to sneeze again. Ida said nothing. Sam fell asleep very soon.

Ida waited until the house was free of the smell of gas. Then she closed the windows. Before undressing, she looked at the radiator and saw that the stopcock was closed. She got into bed, utterly fatigued, and fell asleep immediately.

It seemed to Ida that she had slept only a short time when she awoke suddenly. Frightened, she looked at Sam, but he was bulked up beside her with the covers over his head. She listened to his deep, heavy breathing, and the momentary fear left her. Ida was fully awake now, and the events of the day tumbled quickly through her brain. She thought of the episode of the gas, and a sharp streak of pain ripped through every nerve in her body. Had Sam really tried to take his life? Had he? She wanted to wake him and ask him, but she was afraid. She turned over and tried to sleep again, but she couldn't.

Ida reached over to the night table and looked at the luminous face of the clock. It was four-twenty-five. The alarm would ring at six. Sam would get up and she would ask him, then maybe she could sleep. She closed her eyes, but still no sleep came. She opened them and kept them open.

A faint tinkling on the window caused her to look out. By the light of the street lamp she could see that it was snowing again. The flakes drifted down slowly and silently. They seemed to hang in the air, then the wind rose and blew them against the windows. The windows rattled softly; then everything became quiet again, except for the ticking of the clock.

Ida reached over for the clock and shut off the alarm. It was nearly five. At six o'clock she would get up, dress, and go downstairs. She would pull in the milk box and the bread. Then she would sweep the store, and then the snow from the sidewalk. Let Sam sleep. Later, if he felt better, he could come downstairs. Ida looked at the clock again. Five past five. The sleep would do him good.

1943

Benefit Performance

MAURICE ROSENFELD was conscious of himself as he took the key from his pocket and inserted it into the door of his small apartment. The Jewish actor saw his graying hair, the thick black eyebrows, the hunch of disappointment in his shoulders, and the sardonic grimness of his face accentuated by the twisted line of the lips. Rosenfeld turned the key in the lock, aware that he was playing his role well. Tragedy in the twisting of a key, he thought.

"Who's there?" said a voice from inside the apartment.

Surprised, Rosenfeld pushed open the door and saw that it was his daughter who had called out. Sophie was lying in her bed, which became the couch when it was folded together, and her bedroom became the living room. There was one other room, a small one, where Rosenfeld and his wife slept, and an alcove for the kitchen. When her father was working and came home late after the performance, Sophie would set up three screens around her bed so that she would not be awakened by the light which he put on while heating up some milk for himself before going to bed. The screens served another purpose. Whenever Sophie and her father quarreled, she set them up and let him rant outside. Deprived of her presence, he became silent and sulked. She sat on her sofa, reading a magazine by the light of her own lamp and blessing the screens for giving her privacy and preserving her dignity.

The screens were stacked up in the corner, and Rosenfeld was surprised to see his daughter in bed.

"What's the matter?" he said.

"I'm not well," she answered.

"Where's Momma?"

"She went to work."

"Today she's working?"

"She had half a day off. She's working from five to ten."

Rosenfeld looked around. The table in the alcove was not set and it was nearly suppertime.

"She left me to eat, something?"

"No, she thought you were going to eat with Markowitz. Is there anything doing?"

"No," he said bitterly, "nothing is doing. The Jewish theayter is deep in hell. Since the war, the Jews stay home. Everybody else goes out for a good time to forget their troubles, but Jews stay home and worry. Second Avenue is like a tomb."

"What did Markowitz want to see you for?" Sophie asked.

"A benefit, something. I should act in a benefit for Isaac Levin."

"Don't worry," she said, "you had a good season last year."

"I'm too young to live on memories," he said.

Sophie had no answer to that.

"If you want me to make you something, I'll get up," she said.

He walked into the kitchen and looked into the pots on the gas range.

"No, I'll make for myself. Here is some potatoes and carrots left over. I'll warm them up."

"Warm up the hamburger in the oven. Momma made one for me, but I couldn't eat it."

Rosenfeld pulled down the door of the broiler and glanced distastefully at the hamburger on the wire grill. "No, it burns me my stomach when I eat chopmeat," he said, closing the broiler door.

"How is your stomach?" she asked.

He placed his hand underneath his heart. "Today I got gas." He was moved by her solicitousness.

"How are you feeling?" he asked her.

"Like always. The first day is bad."

"It will go away."

"Yes, I know," she said.

* * *

He lit the flame under the vegetables and began to stir the mashed potatoes. They were lumpy. The remnants of his appetite disappeared. Sophie saw the look on his face and said, "Put some butter in the potatoes." For a moment Rosenfeld did not move, but when Sophie repeated her suggestion, he opened the icebox.

"What butter?" he said, looking among the bottles and the fruit. "Here is no butter."

Sophie reached for her housecoat, drew it on over her head, and pulled up the zipper. Then she stepped into her slippers.

"I'll put some milk in," she said.

Without wanting to, he was beginning to grow angry.

"Who wants you to? Stay in bed. I'll take care myself of the—the supper," he ended sarcastically.

"Poppa," she said, "don't be stubborn. I've got to get up anyway."

"For me you don't have to get up."

"I said I have to get up anyway."

"What's the matter?"

"Someone is coming."

He turned toward her. "Who's coming?"

"Pa, let's not start that."

"Who's coming?"

"I don't want to fight. I'm sick today."

"Who's coming, answer me."

"Ephraim."

"The plum-ber?" He was sarcastic.

"Please, Pa, don't fight."

"*I* should fight with a plum-ber?"

"You always insult him."

"*I* insult a plum-ber? He insults *me* to come here."

"He's not coming to see you. He's coming to see me."

"He insults *you* to come here. What does a plum-ber, who didn't even finish high school, want with you? You don't need a plumber."

"I don't care what I need, Poppa, I'm twenty-eight years old," she said.

"But a plum-ber!"

"He's a good boy. I've known him for twelve years, since we were in high school. He's honest and he makes a nice steady living."

"All right," Rosenfeld said angrily. "So *I* don't make a steady living. So go on, spill some more salt on my bleeding wounds."

"Poppa, don't act, please. I only said *he* made a steady living. I didn't say anything about you."

"Who's acting?" he shouted, banging the icebox door shut and turning quickly. "Even if I didn't support you and your mother steady, at least I showed you the world and brought you in company with the greatest Jewish actors of our times. Adler, Schwartz, Ben-Ami, Goldenburg, all of them have been in my house. You heard the best conversation about life, about books and music and all kinds art. You toured with me everywhere. You were in South America. You were in England. You were in Chicago, Boston, Detroit. You got a father whose Shylock in Yiddish even the American critics came to see and raved about it. *This* is living. *This* is life. Not with a plum-ber. So who is he going to bring into your house, some more plum-bers, they should sit in the kitchen and talk about pipes and how to fix a leak in the toilet? This is living? This is conversation? When he comes here, does he open his mouth? The only thing he says is yes and no, yes and no—like a machine. This is not for you."

Sophie had listened to her father in silence.

"Poppa, that's not fair," she said quietly, "you make him afraid to talk to you."

The answer seemed to satisfy him.

"Don't be so much in the hurry," he said more calmly. "You can get better."

"Please drop the subject."

*   *   *

The bell rang. Sophie pressed the buzzer.

"Poppa, for godsake, please be nice to him."

He said nothing but turned to his cooking, and she went into the bathroom.

Ephraim knocked on the door.

"Come in!"

The door opened and he walked in. He was tall, very well built and neatly dressed. His hair was carefully slicked back, but his hands were beefy and red from constant washing in hot water, which did not remove the calluses on his palms or the grease pockets underneath his nails. He was embarrassed to find only Sophie's father in.

"Is Sophie here?" he asked.

"Good evening," said Rosenfeld sarcastically.

Ephraim blushed.

"Good evening," he said, "Is Sophie here?"

"She will be here in a minute."

"Thank you very much." He remained standing.

Rosenfeld poured some milk into the potatoes and stirred them with a fork. "So you working now in the project houses?" he asked.

Ephraim was surprised to be addressed so politely. "No," he said. "We're working in the Brooklyn Navy Yard on the new ships."

"Hmm, must be a lot of toilets on the battleships?" Rosenfeld asked.

Ephraim did not answer him. Sophie came out of the bathroom with her hair neatly combed and a small blue ribbon in it to match the blue in her housecoat.

"Hello, Eph," she said.

He nodded.

"Sit down," she said, placing a chair near her bed. "I'll get back into bed." She lifted her feet out of the slippers, fixed the pillow so she could sit up, and covered herself with her blanket. Ephraim was facing her. Over his shoulder she could see her father scooping out the vegetables onto a plate. Then he sat down at the table and began to mash them.

"What's new, Eph?" she asked.

He sat with his elbows resting on his knees, the fingers of both hands interlocked.

"Nothing new," he said.

"Did you work today?"

"Only half a day. I got three weeks overtime."

"What else is new?"

He shrugged his shoulders.

"Did you hear about Edith and Mortie?" she asked.

"No," he said. Rosenfeld lowered his fork.

"They got married Sunday."

"That's good," he said.

"Oh, another thing, I bought tickets for the Russian War Relief at Madison Square Garden. Can you go Friday night?"

"Yes," he said. Rosenfeld banged his fork down on his plate. Ephraim did not turn and Sophie did not look up. They were silent for a moment, and then Sophie began again.

"Oh, I forgot," she said, "I wrote to Washington for those civil-service requirements for you. Did your mother tell you?"

"Yes," he said.

Rosenfeld banged his fist on the table. "Yes and no, yes and no," he shouted. "Don't you know no other words?"

Ephraim did not turn around.

"Poppa, *please*," begged Sophie.

"Yes and no," shouted her father, "yes and no. Is this the way to talk to an educated girl?"

Ephraim turned around and said with dignity, "I'm not talking to you. I'm talking to your daughter."

"You not *talking* to her. You *insulting* her with yes and no. This is not talk."

"I'm not an actor," said Ephraim. "I work with my hands."

"Don't open your mouth to insult me."

Ephraim's jaw was trembling. "You insulted me first."

"Please, please," cried Sophie. "Poppa, if you don't stop, I'm going to put up the screens."

"So put up the screens to hide the plum-ber," her father taunted.

"At least a plumber can support a wife and don't have to send her out to work for him," cried Ephraim, his voice full of emotion.

"Oh, Ephraim, don't," moaned Sophie.

For a moment Rosenfeld was stunned. Then his face reddened

and he began to stutter, "You nothing, you. You nothing," he cried. His lips moved noiselessly as he tried to find words to say. Suddenly he caught himself and paused. He rose slowly. Rosenfeld crossed his arms over his breast, then raised them ceilingward and began to speak deliberately in fluent Yiddish.

"Hear me earnestly, great and good God. Hear the story of the afflictions of a second Job. Hear how the years have poured misery upon me, so that in my age, when most men are gathering their harvest of sweet flowers, I cull nothing but weeds.

"I have a daughter, O God, upon whom I have lavished my deepest affection, whom I have given every opportunity for growth and education, who has become so mad in her desire for carnal satisfaction that she is ready to bestow herself upon a man unworthy to touch the hem of her garment, to a common, ordinary, wordless, plum-ber, who has neither ideals nor—"

"Poppa," screamed Sophie, "Poppa, stop it!"

Rosenfeld stopped and a look of unutterable woe appeared on his face. He lowered his arms and turned his head toward Ephraim, his nostrils raised in scorn.

"Plum-ber," he said bitterly.

Ephraim looked at him with hatred. He tried to move, but couldn't.

"You cheap actor," he cried suddenly, with venomous fury. "You can go straight to hell!" He strode over to the door, tore it open, and banged it so furiously that the room seemed to shake.

By degrees Rosenfeld lowered his head. His shoulders hunched in disappointment, and he saw himself, with his graying hair, a tragic figure. Again he raised his head slowly and looked in Sophie's direction. She was already setting up the screens. Rosenfeld moved toward the table in the alcove and glanced down at the vegetables on the plate. They bored him. He went over to the gas range, carefully lit the flame under the broiler, and pulled down the door to see whether the hamburger was cooking. It was. He closed the door, lowered the flame a bit, and said quietly:

"Tonight I will eat chopmeat."

1943

The Place
Is Different Now

LATE ONE WARM NIGHT in July, a week after they had let Wally Mullane out of the hospital on Welfare Island, he was back in his old neighborhood, searching for a place to sleep. He tried the stores on the avenue first, but they were closed, even the candy store on the corner. The hall doors were all shut, and the cellars padlocked. He peered into the barbershop window and cursed his luck for getting there so late, because Mr. Davido would have let him sleep on one of the barber chairs.

He walked for a block along the avenue, past the stores, and turned in on Third Street, where the rows of frame houses began. In the middle of the block, he crossed the street and slipped into an alley between two old-fashioned frame houses. He tried the garage doors, but they were locked too. As he came out of the alley, he spotted a white-topped prowl car with shaded lights moving slowly down the street, close to the curb, under the trees. Ducking back into the alley, he hid behind a tree in the back yard and waited there nervously for the police car to go by. If the car stopped, he would run. He would climb the fences and come out in his mother's yard on Fourth Street, but he didn't like the idea. The lights moved by. In five minutes Wally sneaked out of the alley and walked quickly up the street. He wanted to try the cellars of the private houses but was afraid to because someone might wake and take him for a burglar. They would call the police, and it would be just his luck if his brother Jimmy was driving one of the radio cars.

All night long Wally hunted through the neighborhood, up Fourth, then Fifth Street, then along the parkway, all the way from the cemetery to the railroad cut, which was a block from the avenue and ran parallel to it. He thought of sleeping in the BMT elevated station but didn't have a nickel, so that was out. The coal yard near the railroad cut was out too, because they kept a watchman there. At five o'clock, tired from wandering, he turned into Fourth Street again and stood under a tree, across the street from his mother's house. He wanted to go into the cellar and sleep there, but he thought of Jimmy and his sister Agnes and said to hell with that.

Wally walked slowly down the avenue to the El station and stood on the corner watching it grow light. Gray light seeped into the morning sky, and the quiet streets were full of thinning warm darkness. It made Wally feel sad. The neighborhood looked the same but wasn't. He thought of the fellows who were gone now and he thought of his friend Vincent Davido, the barber's son, who had been gone since before the war. He thought of himself not having set foot in his own house for years, and it made him feel like crying.

There was an empty milk box in front of the delicatessen. Wally dragged it across the sidewalk and placed it against the El pillar to have a backrest. He was tired but didn't want to fall asleep, because soon the people would be going up the station and he wanted to see if there was anyone he knew. He thought if he saw two or three people he knew, maybe they would give him about fifty cents and he would have enough for a beer and some ham and eggs.

Just before the sun came up, Wally fell asleep. The people buying their papers at the newsstand looked at him before they went upstairs to the station. Not many of them knew him. A fat man in a gray suit who recognized him stood on the corner with a disgusted look on his face, watching Wally sleep. Wally sat heavy-bellied on the milk box, with his head leaning back against the pillar and his mouth open. His straw-colored hair was slicked back. His face, red and smudged, was unshaven and thick with loose flesh. He had on a brown suit, oily with filth, black shoes, and a soiled shirt, with a rag of a brown tie knotted at the collar.

"The bastard's always drunk," said the fat man to the man from the candy store who had come out to collect the pennies on the newsstand. The storekeeper nodded.

At eight o'clock, a water truck turned the corner of Second Street and rumbled along the avenue toward the El, shooting two fanlike sprays of water out of its iron belly. The water foamed white where it hit the sizzling asphalt and shot up a powdery mist into the air. As the truck turned under the El, the floating cool mist settled upon Wally's sweating face and he woke up. He looked around wildly, but it wasn't Jimmy and the feeling of fright went away.

The day was heavy with wet, blistering heat, and Wally had a headache. His stomach rumbled and his tongue was sour. He wanted to eat but he didn't have a cent.

Several people walked past him on their way to work, and Wally looked at their faces but saw no one he knew. He didn't like to ask strangers for money. It was different if you knew them. Looking into the candy-store window to see the time, he was annoyed that it was eight-twenty-five. From long experience Wally knew that he had missed his best chances. The factory workers and those who worked in the stores had passed by very early in the morning, and the white-collar employees who followed them about an hour or so later were also gone. Only the stragglers and the women shoppers were left. You couldn't get much out of them. Wally thought he would wait awhile, and if no one came along soon, he'd go over to the fruit store and ask them if they had any spoiled fruit.

At half past eight, Mr. Davido, who lived on the top floor above the delicatessen, came out of the house to open his barbershop across the street. He was shocked when he saw Wally standing on the corner. How strange it is, he thought, when you see something that looks as if it was always there and everything seems the same once more.

The barber was a small, dark-skinned man nearing sixty. His fuzzy hair was gray, and he wore old-fashioned pince-nez with a black ribbon attached to them. His arms were short and heavy, and his fingers were stubby, but he maneuvered them well when he was shaving someone or cutting his hair. The customers knew how quickly and surely those short fingers moved when a man was in a hurry to get out of the shop. When there was no hurry, Mr. Davido worked slowly. Sometimes, as he was cutting a man's hair, the man would happen to look into the mirror and see the barber staring absently out the window, his lips pursed and his eyes filled with quiet sadness. Then, in a minute, he would raise his brows and begin cutting again, his short, stubby fingers snipping quickly to make up for time he had lost.

"Hey, Wally," he said, "where you keep yourself? You don't come aroun for a long time."

"I was sick," Wally said. "I was in a hospital."

"Whatsamatter, Wally, you still drinkin poison whiskey?"

"Nah, I ain't allowed to drink anymore. I got diabetes. They took a blood test an it showed diabetes."

Mr. Davido frowned and shook his head. "Take care of yourself," he said.

"I had a bad time. I almost got gangrene. When you get that, they amputate your legs off."

"How you get that, Wally?"

"From my brother Jimmy when he beat me up. My whole legs was swollen. The doctor said it was a miracle I didn't get gangrene."

Wally looked up the avenue as he talked. The barber followed his glance.

"You better keep away from your brother."

"I'm watchin out."

"You better leave this neighborhood, Wally. Your brother told you he don't like you in this neighborhood. There's a lot of jobs nowadays, Wally. Why don't you get some kind of a job and get a furnish room to live?"

"Yeah, I'm thinkin of gettin a job."

"Look every day," said the barber.

"I'll look," said Wally.

"You better look now. Go to the employment agency."

"I'll go," said Wally. "First I'm lookin for somebody. There's a lot of strange faces here. The neighborhood is changed."

"That's right," said the barber, "a lot of the young single fellows is gone. I can tell in the shop. The married men don't come in for shaves like the single fellows, only haircuts. They buy electric razors. The single fellows was sports."

"I guess everyone is gone or they got married," said Wally.

"They went to the war but some never came back, and a lot of them moved away to other places."

"Did you ever hear from Vincent?" Wally asked.

"No."

"I just thought I'd ask you."

"No," said the barber. There was silence for a minute; then he said, "Come over later, Wally. I shave you."

"When?"

"Later."

Wally watched Mr. Davido cross the avenue and go past the drugstore and laundry to his barbershop. Before he went in, he took a key from his vest pocket and wound up the barber pole. The red spiral, followed by the white and blue spirals, went round and round.

A man and a woman walked by, and Wally thought he recognized the man, but whoever he was lowered his eyes and passed by. Wally looked after him contemptuously.

He became tired of watching the stragglers and drifted over to the newsstand to read the headlines. Mr. Margolies, the owner of the candy store, came out again and picked up the pennies on the stand.

Wally was sore. "What's the matter, you think I'm gonna steal your lousy pennies?"

"Please," said Mr. Margolies, "to you I don't have to explain my business."

"I'm sorry I ever spent a cent in your joint."

Mr. Margolies's face grew red. "Go way, you troublemaker, you. Go way from here," he cried, flipping his hand.

"Aw, screwball."

A strong hand grasped Wally's shoulder and swung him around. For an instant he went blind with fear and his body sagged, but when he saw it was his oldest sister, Agnes, standing there with his mother, he straightened, pretending he hadn't been afraid.

"What'd you do now, you drunken slob?" said Agnes in her thick voice.

"I didn't do anything."

Mr. Margolies had seen the look on Wally's face. "He didn't do anything," he said. "He was only blocking the stand so the customers couldn't get near the papers."

Then he retreated into the store.

"You were told to stay out of this neighborhood," rasped Agnes. She was a tall, redheaded woman, very strongly built. Her shoulders were broad, and her thick breasts hung heavily against her yellow dress.

"I was just standin here."

"Who is that, Agnes?" asked his mother, peering through thick glasses.

"It's Wallace," Agnes said disgustedly.

"Hello, Ma," Wally said in a soft voice.

"Wallace, where have you been?" Mrs. Mullane was a stout woman, big-bellied and stoop-shouldered. Her pink scalp shone through her thin white hair, which she kept up with two amber-colored combs. Her eyes blinked under her thick glasses and she clung tightly to her daughter's arm for fear she would walk into something she couldn't see.

"I was in the hospital, Ma. Jimmy beat me up."

"And rightly so, you drunken bum," said Agnes. "You had your chances. Jimmy used to give you money to go to the agencies for a job, and the minute he had his back turned, you hit the bottle."

"It was the Depression. I couldn't get a job."

"You mean nobody would take you after the BMT canned you for spendin the nickel collections on the racehorses."

"Aw, shut up."

"You're a disgrace to your mother and your family. The least you could do is to get out of here and stay out. We suffered enough on account of you."

Wally changed his tone. "I'm sick. The doctor said I got diabetes."

Agnes said nothing.

"Wallace," his mother asked, "did you take a shower?"

"No, Ma."

"You ought to take one."

"I have no place."

Agnes grasped her mother's arm. "I'm takin your mother to the eye hospital."

"Wait awhile, Agnes," said Mrs. Mullane pettishly. "Wallace, are you wearing a clean shirt?"

"No, I ain't, Ma."

"Well, you come home for one."

"Jimmy'd break his back."

"He needs a clean shirt," insisted Mrs. Mullane.

"I got one in the laundry," said Wally.

"Well, then take it out, Wallace."

"I ain't got the money."

"Ma, don't give any money to him. He'll only throw it away on drink."

"He ought to have a clean shirt."

She opened her pocketbook and fumbled in her change purse.

"A shirt is twenty cents," said Agnes.

Mrs. Mullane peered at the coin she held in her hand. "Is this a dime, Agnes?"

"No, it's a penny. Let me get it for you." Agnes took two dimes from the change purse and dropped them into Wally's outstretched palm.

"Here, bum."

He let it go by. "Do you think I could have a little something to eat with, Ma?"

"No," said Agnes. She gripped her mother's elbow and walked forward.

"Change your shirt, Wallace," Mrs. Mullane called to him from the El steps. Wally watched them go upstairs and disappear into the station.

He felt weak, his legs unsteady. Thinking it was because his stomach was empty, he decided to get some pretzels and beer with the dimes. Later, he could get some spoiled fruit from the fruit store and would ask Mr. Davido for some bread. Wally walked along under the El to McCafferty's tavern, near the railroad cut.

Opening the screen door, he glanced along the bar and was almost paralyzed with fright. His brother Jimmy, in uniform, was standing at the rear of the bar drinking a beer. Wally's heart banged hard as he stepped back and closed the screen door. It slipped from his hand and slammed shut. The men at the bar looked up, and Jimmy saw Wally through the door.

"Jesus Christ!"

Wally was already running. He heard the door slam and knew Jimmy was coming after him. Though he strained every muscle in his heavy, jouncing body, he could hear Jimmy's footsteps coming nearer. Wally sped down the block, across the tracks of the railroad siding, and into the coal yard. He ran past some men loading a coal truck and crossed the cobblestoned yard, with his brother coming after him. Wally's lungs hurt. He wanted to run inside the coal loft and hide, but he knew he would be cornered there. He looked around wildly, then made for the hill of coal near the fence. He scrambled up. Jimmy came up after him, but Wally kicked down the coal and it hit Jimmy on the face and chest. He slipped and cursed, but gripped his club and came up again. At the top of the coal pile, Wally boosted himself up on the fence and dropped heavily to the other side. As he hit the earth his legs shook, but fear would not let him stop. He ran across a back yard and thumped up the inclined wooden cellar door, jumping clumsily over a picket fence. Out of the corner of his eye he saw Jimmy hoisting himself over the coal-yard fence. Wally wanted to get into the delicatessen man's back yard so he could go down to the cellar and come out on the avenue. Mr. Davido would let him hide in the toilet of the barbershop.

Wally ran across the flower bed in the next back yard and lifted himself over the picket fence. His sweaty palms slipped and he pitched forward, his pants cuff caught on one of the pointed boards. His hands were in the soft earth of an iris bed, and he dangled from the picket fence by one leg. He wriggled his leg and pulled frantically. The cuff tore away and he fell into the flower bed. He pushed himself up, but before he could move, Jimmy had hurdled the fence and tackled him. Wally fell on the ground, the breath knocked out of him. He lay there whimpering.

"You dirty bastard," Jimmy said. "I'll break your goddamn back."

He swung his club down on Wally's legs. Wally shrieked and tried to pull in his legs, but Jimmy held him down and whacked him across the thighs and buttocks. Wally tried to shield his legs with his arms, but Jimmy beat him harder.

"Oh, please, please, please," cried Wally, wriggling under his brother's blows, "please, Jimmy, my legs, my legs. Don't hit my legs!"

"You scum."

"My legs," screamed Wally, "my legs, I'll get gangrene, my legs, my legs!"

The pain burned through his body. He felt nauseated. "My legs," he moaned.

Jimmy let up. He wiped his wet face and said, "I told you to stay the hell outta this neighborhood. If I see you here again, I'll murder you."

Looking up, Wally saw two frightened women gazing at them out of their windows. Jimmy brushed off his uniform and went over to the cellar door. He pulled it open and walked downstairs.

Wally lay still among the trampled flowers.

"Why didn't the policeman arrest him?" asked Mrs. Werner, the delicatessen man's wife.

"It's the policeman's brother," explained Mrs. Margolies.

He lay on his stomach, arms outstretched, and his cheek pressed against the ground. His nose was bleeding, but he was too exhausted to move. The sweat ran down his arms and the back of his coat was stained dark with it. For a long while he had no thoughts; then the nausea subsided a little, and bits of things floated through his mind. He recalled how he used to play in the coal yard with Jimmy when they were kids. He thought of the Fourth Street boys coasting down the snow-covered sides of the railroad cut in the winter. Then he thought of standing in front of the candy store on quiet summer evenings, with his shirtsleeves rolled up, smoking and fooling around with Vincent and the guys, talking about

women, good times, and ball players, while they all waited for the
late papers to come in. He thought about Vincent, and he remembered the day Vincent went away. It was during the Depression,
and the unemployed guys stood on the corner, smoking and chewing gum and making remarks to the girls who passed by. Like
Wally, Vincent had quit going to the agencies, and he stayed on
the corner with the rest of them, smoking and spitting around. A
girl passed by and Vincent said something to her which made the
guys laugh. Mr. Davido was looking out the window of the barbershop across the street. He slammed down the scissors and left
the customer sitting in the chair. His face was red as he crossed
the street. He grabbed Vincent by the arm and struck him hard
across the face, shouting, "You bum, why don't you go look for a
job?" Vincent's face turned gray. He didn't say anything, but
walked away, and they never saw him again. That's how it was.

Mrs. Margolies said, "He's laying there for a long time. Do you
think he's dead?"

"No," said Mrs. Werner, "I just saw him move."

Wally pushed himself up and stumbled down the stone steps of
the cellar. Groping his way along the wall, he came up the stairs
in front of the delicatessen. He searched through his pockets for
the twenty cents his mother had given him but couldn't find them.
The nausea came back and he wanted a place to sit down and rest.
He crossed the street, walking unsteadily toward the barbershop.

Mr. Davido was standing near the window, sharpening a straight
razor on a piece of sandstone. The sight of Wally that morning had
brought up old memories, and he was thinking about Vincent. As
he rubbed the razor round and round on the lathered sandstone,
he glanced up and saw Wally staggering across the street. His pants
were torn and covered with dirt, and his face was bloody. Wally
opened the screen door, but Mr. Davido said sharply, "Stay outta
here now, you're drunk."

"Honest I ain't," said Wally. "I didn't have a drop."

"Why you look like that?"

"Jimmy caught me and almost killed me. My legs must be black
and blue." Wally lowered himself into a chair.

"I'm sorry, Wally." Mr. Davido got him some water, and Wally swallowed a little.

"Come on, Wally, on the chair," the barber said heartily. "I shave you an you rest an feel cooler."

He helped Wally onto the barber's chair; then he lowered the back and raised the front so that Wally lay stretched out as if he were on a bed. The barber swung a towel around his neck and began to rub a blob of hot lather into his beard. It was a tough beard and hadn't been shaved for a week. Mr. Davido rubbed the lather in deeply with his gentle, stubby fingers.

As he was rubbing Wally's beard, the barber looked at him in the mirror and thought how he had changed. The barber's eyes grew sad as he recalled how things used to be, and he turned away to look out the window. He thought about his son Vincent. How wonderful it would be if Vincent came home someday, he would put his arms around his boy and kiss him on the cheek . . .

Wally was also thinking how it used to be. He remembered how it was when he looked in the mirror before going out on Saturday night. He had a yellow mustache and wore a green hat. He remembered his expensive suits and the white carnation in his buttonhole and a good cigar to smoke.

He opened his eyes.

"You know," he said, "the place is different now."

"Yes," said the barber, looking out the window.

Wally closed his eyes.

Mr. Davido looked down at him. Wally was breathing quietly. His lips were pulled together tightly, and the tears were rolling down his cheeks. The barber slowly raised the lather until it mixed with the tears.

1943

An Apology

EARLY ONE MORNING, during a wearying hot spell in the city, a police car that happened to be cruising along Canal Street drew over to the curb and one of the two policemen in the car leaned out of the window and fingered a come-here to an old man wearing a black derby hat, who carried a large carton on his back, held by clothesline rope to his shoulder, and dragged a smaller carton with his other hand.

"Hey, Mac."

But the peddler, either not hearing or paying no attention, went on. At that, the policeman, the younger of the two, pushed open the door and sprang out. He strode over to the peddler and, shoving the large carton on his back, swung him around as if he were straw. The peddler stared at him in frightened astonishment. He was a gaunt, shriveled man with very large eyes which at the moment gave the effect of turning lights, so that the policeman was a little surprised, though not for long.

"Are you deaf?" he said.

The peddler's lips moved in a way that suggested he might be, but at last he cried out, "Why do you push me?" and again surprised the policeman with the amount of wail that rang in his voice.

"Why didn't you stop when I called you?"

"So who knows you called me? Did you say my name?"

"What is your name?"

The peddler clamped his sparse yellow teeth rigidly together.

"And where's your license?"

"What license?—who license?"

"None of your wisecracks—your license to peddle. We saw you peddle."

The peddler did not deny it.

"What's in the big box?"

"Hundred watt."

"Hundred what?"

"Lights."

"What's in the other?"

"Sixty watt."

"Don't you know it's against the law to peddle without a license?"

Without answering, the peddler looked around, but there was no one in sight except the other policeman in the car and his eyes were shut as if he was catching a little lost sleep.

The policeman on the sidewalk opened his black summons book.

"Spill it, Pop, where do you live?"

The peddler stared down at the cracked sidewalk.

"Hurry up, Lou," called the policeman from the car. He was an older man, though not so old as the peddler.

"Just a second, Walter, this old guy here is balky."

With his pencil he prodded the peddler, who was still staring at the sidewalk but who then spoke, saying he had no money to buy a license.

"But you have the money to buy bulbs. Don't you know you're cheating the city when you don't pay the legitimate fees?"

" . . . "

"Talk, will you?"

"Come on, Lou."

"Come on yourself, this nanny goat won't talk."

The other policeman slowly got out of the car, a heavy man with gray hair and a red face shiny with perspiration.

"You better give him the information he wants, mister."

The peddler, holding himself stiff, stared between them. By this time some people had gathered and were looking on, but Lou scattered them with a wave of his arm.

"All right, Walter, give me a hand. This bird goes to the station house."

Walter looked at him with some doubt, but Lou said, "Resisting an officer in the performance of his duty."

He took the peddler's arm and urged him forward. The carton of bulbs slipped off his shoulder, pulling him to his knees.

"Veh is mir,"

Walter helped him up and they lifted him into the car. The young cop hauled the large carton to the rear of the car, opened the trunk, and shoved it in sideways. As they drove off, a man in front of one of the stores held up a box and shouted, "Hey, you forgot this one," but neither of them turned to look back, and the peddler didn't seem to be listening.

*　　*　　*

On their way to the station house they passed the Brooklyn Bridge.

"Just a second, Lou," said Walter. "Could you drive across the bridge now and stop at my house? My feet are perspiring and I'd like to change my shirt."

"After we get this character booked."

But Walter querulously insisted it would take too long, and though Lou didn't want to drive him home he finally gave in. Neither of them spoke on the way to Walter's house, which was not far from the bridge, on a nice quiet street of three-story brownstone houses with young trees in front of them, newly planted not far from the curb.

When Walter got out, he said to the peddler, "If you were in Germany they would have killed you. All we were trying to do was give you a summons that would maybe cost you a buck fine." Then he went up the stone steps.

After a while Lou became impatient waiting for him and honked the horn. A window shade on the second floor slid up and Walter in his underwear called down, "Just five minutes, Lou—I'm just drying my feet."

He came down all spry and they drove back several blocks and onto the bridge. Midway across, they had to slow down in a long traffic line, and to their astonishment the peddler pushed open the door and reeled out upon the bridge, miraculously ducking out of the way of the trailers and trucks coming from the other direction. He scooted across the pedestrians' walk and clambered with ferocious strength up on the railing of the bridge.

But Lou, who was very quick, immediately pursued him and managed to get his hand on the peddler's coattails as he stood poised on the railing for the jump.

With a yank Lou pulled him to the ground. The back of his head struck against the sidewalk and his derby hat bounced up, twirled, and landed at his feet. However, he did not lose consciousness. He lay on the ground moaning and tearing with clawlike fingers at his chest and arms.

Both the policemen stood there looking down at him, not sure what to do since there was absolutely no bleeding. As they were talking it over, a fat woman with moist eyes who, despite the heat, was wearing a white shawl over her head and carrying, with the handle over her pudgy arm, a large basket of salted five-cent pretzels passed by and stopped out of curiosity to see what had happened.

Seeing the man on the ground she called out, "Bloostein!" but he did not look at her and continued tearing at his arms.

"Do you know him?" Lou asked her.

"It's Bloostein. I know him from the neighborhood."

"Where does he live?"

She thought for a minute but didn't know. "My father said he used to own a store on Second Avenue but he lost it. Then his missus died and also his daughter was killed in a fire. Now he's got the seven years' itch and they can't cure it in the clinic. They say he peddles with light bulbs."

"Don't you know his address?"

"Not me. What did he do?"

"It doesn't matter what he tried to do," said Walter.

"Goodbye, Bloostein, I have to go to the schoolyard," the fat lady apologized. She picked up the basket and went with her pretzels down the bridge.

By now Bloostein had stopped his frantic scratching and lay quietly on the sidewalk. The sun shone straight into his eyes but he did nothing to shield them.

Lou, who was quite pale, looked at Walter and Walter said, "Let him go."

They got him up on his feet, dusted his coat, and placed his dented hat on his head. Lou said he would get the bulbs out of the car, but Walter said, "Not here, down at the foot of the bridge."

They helped Bloostein back to the car and in a few minutes let him go with his carton of bulbs at the foot of the bridge, not far from the place where they had first chanced to see him.

*   *   *

But that night, after their tour of duty, when Lou drove him home, Walter got out of the car and saw, after a moment of disbelief, that Bloostein himself was waiting for him in front of his house.

"Hey, Lou," he called, but Lou had already driven off so he had to face the peddler alone. Bloostein looked, with his carton of bulbs, much as he had that morning, except for the smudge where the dent on his derby hat had been, and his eyes were fleshy with fatigue.

"What do you want here?" Walter said to him.

The peddler parted his lips, then pointed to his carton. "My little box lights."

"What about it?"

"What did you do with them?"

Walter thought a few seconds and remembered the other box of bulbs.

"You sure you haven't gone back and hid them somewhere?" he asked sternly.

Bloostein wouldn't look at him.

The policeman felt very hot. "All right, we'll try and locate them, but first I have to have my supper. I'm hungry."

He went up the steps and turned to say something more, but a woman came out of the house and he raised his hat to her and went in.

After supper he would have liked very much to relax in front of the radio, but instead he changed out of his uniform, said he was going to the corner, and walked, conscious of his heavy disappointment, down the stairs.

Bloostein was planted where he had left him.

"My car's in the garage." Walter went slowly up the street, Bloostein following with his carton of bulbs on his back.

At the garage Walter motioned him into the car. Bloostein lifted the carton into the back seat and got in with it. Walter drove out and over the bridge to Canal Street, to the place where they had taken the peddler into the car.

He parked and went into three of the stores there, flashing his badge and asking if anyone knew who had got the bulbs they had forgotten. No one knew for sure, but the clerk in the third store thought it might be someone next door whose name and address he gave to Walter.

Before returning to the car Walter went into a tavern and had a few beers. Over the fourth he had a hunch and called the police property clerk, who said he had taken in no electric bulbs that day. Walter walked out and asked Bloostein how many bulbs he had had in the carton.

"Five dozen."

"At how much—wholesale?"

"Eight cents."

"That's four-eighty," he figured. Taking a five-dollar bill from his wallet, he handed it to Bloostein, who wouldn't accept it.

"What do you want, the purple heart?"

"My little box lights."

Walter then kidded, "Now you're gonna take a little ride."

They then rode to the address he had been given but no one knew where the one who had the bulbs was. Finally a bald-headed, stocky man in an undershirt came down from the top floor and said he was the man's uncle and what did Walter want.

Walter convinced him it wasn't serious. "It's just that he happens to know where these bulbs are that we left behind by mistake after an arrest."

The uncle said if it wasn't really serious he would give him the address of the social club where he could find his nephew. The address was a lot farther uptown and on the East Side.

"This is foolish," Walter said to himself as he came out of the house. He thought maybe he could take his time and Bloostein might go away, so he stopped at another beer parlor and had several more as he watched a ten-round fight on television.

He came out sweaty from the beers.

But Bloostein was there.

Walter scratched under his arm. "What's good for an itch?" he said. When he got into the car he thought he was a little bit drunk but it didn't bother him and he drove to the social club on the East Side where a dance was going on. He asked the ticket taker in a tuxedo if this nephew was around.

The ticket taker, whose right eye was very crossed, assured him that nobody by the name mentioned was there.

"It's really not very important," Walter said. "Just about a small carton of bulbs he happens to be holding for this old geezer outside."

"I wouldn't know anything about it."

"It's nothing to worry about."

Walter stood by the door a few minutes and watched the dancers, but there was no one whose face he could recognize.

"He's really not there."

"I don't doubt your word."

Afterward he said it was a nice dance but he had to leave.

"Stay awhile," said the ticket taker.

"I have to go," said Walter. "I have a date with a backseat driver." The ticket taker winked with his good eye, which had a comical effect, but Walter didn't smile and soon he left.

"Still here, kid?" he asked Bloostein.

*　　　*　　　*

He started the car and drove back to Sixth Avenue, where he stopped at a liquor store and bought himself a fifth of whiskey. In the car he tore the wrapper off the bottle and took a long pull.

"Drink?" He offered the bottle to Bloostein.

Bloostein was perched like a skinny owl on the back seat gazing at him.

Walter capped the bottle but did not start the car. He sat for a long time at the wheel, moodily meditating. At the point where he was beginning to feel down in the dumps, he got a sudden idea.

The idea was so simple and good he quickly started the motor and drove downtown straight to Canal, where there was a hardware store that stayed open to midnight. He almost ran into the place and in ten minutes came out with a wrapped carton containing five dozen 60-watt bulbs.

"The joyride's finished, my friend."

The peddler got out and Walter unloaded the large carton and left it standing on the sidewalk near the smaller one.

He drove off quickly.

*   *   *

Going over the bridge he felt relieved, yet at the same time a little anxious to get to sleep because he had to be up at six. He garaged the car and then walked home and upstairs, taking care to move about softly in the bathroom so as not to waken his son, a light sleeper, or his wife, who slept heavily but couldn't get back to sleep once she had been waked up. Undressing, he got into bed with her, but though the night was hot he felt like a cake of ice covered with a sheet. After a while he got up, raised the shade, and stood by the window.

The quiet street was drenched in moonlight, and warm dark shadows fell from the tender trees. But in the tree shadow in front of the house were two strange oblongs and a gnarled, grotesque-hatted silhouette that stretched a tormented distance down the block. Walter's heart pounded heavily, for he knew it was Bloostein.

He put on his robe and straw slippers and ran down the stairs.

"What's wrong?"

Bloostein stared at the moonlit sidewalk.

"What do you want?"

" . . . "

"You better go, Bloostein. This is too late for monkey business. You got your bulbs. Now you better just go home and leave me alone. I hate to have to call the police. Just go home."

Then he lumbered up the stone steps and the flight of carpeted stairs. Inside the bedroom he could hear his son moan in his sleep. Walter lay down and slept, but was awakened by the sound of soft rain. Getting up, he stared out. There was the peddler in the rain, with his white upraised face looking at the window, so near he might be standing on stilts.

Hastening into the hall, Walter rummaged in a closet for an umbrella but couldn't find one. Then his wife woke and called in a loud whisper, "Who's there?" He stood motionless and she listened a minute and evidently went back to sleep. Then because he couldn't find the umbrella he got out a light summer blanket, brought it into the little storage room next to the bedroom, and, taking the screen out of the window, threw the blanket out to Bloostein so he wouldn't get too wet. The white blanket seemed to float down.

* * *

He returned to bed, by an effort of the will keeping himself there for hours. Then he noticed that the rain had stopped and he got up to make sure. The blanket lay heaped where it had fallen on the sidewalk. Bloostein was standing away from it, under the tree.

Walter's straw slippers squeaked as he walked down the stairs. The heat had broken and now a breeze came through the street, shivering the leaves in summer cold.

In the doorway he thought, What's my hurry? I can wait him out till six, then just let the mummy try to follow me into the station house.

"Bloostein," he said, going down the steps, but as the old man looked up, he felt a sickening emptiness.

Staring down at the sidewalk he thought about everything. At last he raised his head and slowly said, "Bloostein, I owe you an apology. I'm really sorry the whole thing happened. I haven't been able to sleep. From my heart I'm truly sorry."

Bloostein gazed at him with enormous eyes reflecting the moon. He answered nothing, but it seemed he had shrunk and so had his shadow.

Walter said good night. He went up and lay down under the sheet.

"What's the matter?" said his wife.

"Nothing."

She turned over on her side. "Don't wake Sonny."

"No."

He rose and went to the window. Raising the shade, he stared out. Yes, gone. He, his boxes of lights and soft summer blanket. He looked again, but the long, moon-whitened street had never been so empty.

1957

Riding Pants

AFTER A SUPPER of fried kidneys and brains—he was thoroughly sick of every kind of meat—Herm quickly cleared the table and piled the dirty dishes in with the oily pans in the metal sink. He planned to leave like the wind, but in the thinking of it hesitated just long enough for his father to get his tongue free.

"Herm," said the butcher in a tired but angry voice as he stroked the fat-to-bursting beef-livered cat that looked like him, "you better think of getting them fancy pants off and giving me a hand. I never heard of a boy of sixteen years wearing riding pants for all day when he should be thinking to start some steady work."

He was sitting, with the cat on his knees, in a rocker in the harshly lit kitchen behind the butcher shop where they always ate since the death of the butcher's wife. He had on—it never seemed otherwise—his white store jacket with the bloody sleeves, an apron, also blood-smeared and tight around his bulging belly, and the stupid yellow pancake of a straw hat that he wore in storm, sleet, or dead of winter. His mustache was gray, his lips thin, and his eyes, once blue as ice, were dark with fatigue.

"Not in a butcher store, Pa," Herm answered.

"What's the matter with one?" said the butcher, sitting up and looking around with exaggerated movements of the head.

Herm turned away. "Blood," he said sideways, "and chicken feathers."

The butcher slumped back in the chair.

"The Lord made certain creatures designed for man to satisfy

164

his craving for food. Meat and fowl are full of proteins and vitamins. Somebody has to carve the animal and trim the meat clear of bone and gristle. There's no shame attached to such work. I did it my whole life long and never stole a cent from no one."

Herm considered whether there was a concealed stab in his words but he could find none. He had not stolen anything since he was thirteen and the butcher was never one to carry a long grudge.

"Meat might be good, but I don't have to like it."

"What *do* you like, Herm?"

Herm thought of his riding pants and the leather boots he was saving for. He knew, though, what his father meant—that he never stuck to a job. After he quit school he had a paper route, but the pay was chicken feed, so he left that and did lawn-mowing and cellar-cleaning, but that was not steady enough, so he quit that too, but not before he had enough to buy a pair of riding pants.

Since he could think of nothing to say, he tried to walk out, but his father called him back.

"Herm, I'm a mighty tired man since your momma died. I don't get near enough rest and I need it. I can't afford to pay a butcher's clerk because my take is not good. As a matter of fact it's bad. I'm every day losing customers for the reason that I can't give them the service they're entitled to. I know you're favorable to delivering orders but I need more of your help. You didn't like high school and asked me to sign you out. I did that, but you haven't been doing anything worthwhile for the past two months, so I decided I could use you in here. What do you say?"

"What am I supposed to say?"

"Yes or no, damn it."

"Then no, damn it," Herm said, his face flaring. "I hate butcher stores. I hate guts and chicken feathers, and I want to live my own kind of life and not yours."

And though the butcher called and called, he ran out of the store.

That night, while Herm was asleep, the butcher took his riding pants and locked them in the closet of his bedroom, but Herm guessed where they were and the next day went to the hardware store down the block, bought a skeleton key for a dime, and sneaked his riding pants out of his father's closet.

* * *

When Herm had just learned to ride he liked to go often, though he didn't always enjoy it. In the beginning he was too conscious of the horse's body, the massive frame he had to straddle, each independent rippling muscle, and the danger that he might have his head kicked in if he fell under the thundering hooves. And the worst of it was that sometimes while riding he was conscious of the interior layout of the horse, where the different cuts of round, rump, and flank were, as if the horse were stripped and labeled on a chart, posted, as a steer was, on the wall in the back of the store. He kept thinking of this the night he was out on Girlie, the roan they told him he wasn't ready for, and she had got the reins from him and turned and ran the way she wanted, shaking him away when he tried to hold her back, till she came to the stable with him on her like a sack of beans and everybody laughing. After that he had made up his mind to quit horses, and did, but one spring night he went back and took out Girlie, who, though lively, was docile to his touch and went with him everywhere and did everything he wanted; and the next morning he took his last twenty-five dollars out of the savings account and bought the riding pants, and that same night dreamed he was on a horse that dissolved under him as he rode but there he was with his riding pants on galloping away on thin air.

* * *

Herm woke to hear the sound of a cleaver on the wooden block down in the store. As it was still night he jumped out of bed frightened and searched for his riding pants. They were not in the bottom drawer where he had hidden them under a pile of his mother's clothes, so he ran to his father's closet and saw it was open and the butcher not in bed. In his pajamas Herm raced downstairs and tried to get into the butcher shop, but he was locked out and stood by the door crying as his father chopped the tightly rolled pants as if they were a bologna, with the slices falling off at each sock of the cleaver onto the floor, where the cat sniffed the uncurled remains.

*   *   *

He woke with the moon on his bed, rose and went on bare toes into his father's room, which looked so different now that it was no longer his mother's, and tried to find the butcher's trousers. They were hanging on a chair but without the store keys in the pockets, or the billfold, he realized blushing. Some loose change clinked and the butcher stirred in the creaking bed. Herm stood desperately still but, when his father had quieted, hung the pants and tiptoed back to his room. He pushed up the window softly, deciding he would slide down the telephone wires to the back yard and get in that way. Once within the store he would find a knife, catch the cat, and dismember it, leaving the pieces for his father to find in the morning; but not his son.

Testing the waterspout, he found it too shaky, but the wires held his weight, so he slid slowly down to the ground. Then he climbed up the sill and tried to push on the window. The butcher had latched it, not knowing Herm had loosened the screws of the latch; it gave and he was able to climb in. As his foot touched the floor, he thought he heard something scamper away but wasn't sure. Afraid to pull the light on because the Holmes police usually passed along the block this time of night, he said softly in the dark, "Here, kitty, here, kitty kitty," and felt around on the pile of burlap bags, but the cat was not where she usually slept.

He felt his way into the store and looked in the windows and they too were empty except for the pulpy blood droppings from the chickens that had hung on the hooks. He tried the paper-bag slots behind the counter and the cat was not there either, so he called again, "Here, kitty kitty kitty," but could not find it. Then he noticed the icebox door had been left ajar, which surprised him, because the butcher always yelled whenever anyone kept it open too long. He went in thinking of course the damn cat was there, poking its greedy head into the bowl of slightly sour chicken livers the butcher conveniently kept on the bottom shelf.

"Here, kitty," he whispered as he stepped into the box, and was completely unprepared when the door slammed shut behind him. He thought at first, so what, it could be opened from the inside, but then it flashed on him that the butcher had vaguely mentioned he was having trouble with the door handle and the locksmith was taking it away till tomorrow. He thought then, Oh, my God, I'm trapped here and will freeze to death, and his skull all but cracked with terror. Fumbling his way to the door, he worked frantically on the lock with his numbed fingers, wishing he had at least switched on the light from outside where the switch was, and he could feel the hole where the handle had been but was unable to get his comb or house key in to turn it. He thought if he had a screwdriver that might do it, or he could unscrew the metal plate and pick the lock apart, and for a second his heart leaped in expectation that he had taken a knife with him, but he hadn't.

Holding his head back to escape the impaling hooks, he reached his hand along the shelves on the side of the icebox and then the top shelf, cautiously feeling if the butcher had maybe left some tool around. His hand moved forward and stopped; it took him a minute to comprehend it was not going farther, because his fingers had entered a moist bony cavern; he felt suddenly shocked, as if he were touching the inside of an electric socket, but the hole was in a pig's head where an eye had been. Stepping back, he tripped over something he thought was the cat, but when he touched it, it was a bag of damp squirmy guts. As he flung it away he lost his balance and his face brushed against the clammy open side of a bleeding lamb. He sat down in the sawdust on the floor and bit his knuckles.

After a time, his fright prevented any further disgust. He tried to reason out what to do, but there was nothing he could think of, so he tried to think what time it was and could he live till his father came down to open the store. He had heard of people staying alive by beating their arms together and walking back and forth till help came, but when he tried that it tired him more, so that he began to feel very sleepy, and though he knew he oughtn't, he sat down again. He might have cried, but the tears were frozen in, and he began to wonder from afar if there was some quicker way to die. By now the icebox had filled with white mist, and from the distance, through the haze, a winged black horse moved toward him. This is it, he thought, and got up to mount it, but his foot slipped from the stirrup and he fell forward, his head bonging against the door, which opened, and he fell out on the floor.

*   *   *

He woke in the morning with a cutting headache and would have stayed in bed but was too hungry, so he dressed and went downstairs. He had six dollars in his pocket, all he owned in the world; he intended to have breakfast and after that pretend to go for a newspaper and never come back again.

The butcher was sitting in the rocker, sleepily stroking the cat. Neither he nor Herm spoke. There were some slices of uncooked bacon on a plate on the table and two eggs in a cardboard carton, but he could not look at them. He poured himself a cup of black coffee and drank it with an unbuttered roll.

A customer came into the store and the butcher rose with a sigh to serve her. The cat jumped off his lap and followed him. They looked like brothers. Herm turned away. This was the last he would see of either of them.

He heard a woman's resounding voice ordering some porterhouse steak and a chunk of calves' liver, nice and juicy for the dogs, and recognized her as Mrs. Gibbs, the doctor's wife, whom all the storekeepers treated like the Empress of Japan, all but kissing her rear end, especially his father, and this was what he wanted his own son to do. Then he heard the butcher go into the icebox and he shivered. The butcher came out and hacked at something with the cleaver and Herm shivered again. Finally the lady, who had talked loud and steadily, the butcher always assenting, was served. The door closed behind her corpulent bulk and the store was quiet. The butcher returned and sat in his chair, fanning his red face with his straw hat, his bald head glistening with sweat. It took him a half hour to recover every time he waited on her.

When the door opened again a few minutes later, it almost seemed as if he would not be able to get up, but Mrs. Gibbs's bellow brought him immediately to his feet. "Coming," he called with a sudden frog in his throat and hurried inside. Then Herm heard her yelling about something, but her voice was so powerful the sound blurred. He got up and stood at the door.

It was her, all right, a tub of a woman with a large hat, a meaty face, and a thick rump covered in mink.

"You stupid dope," she shouted at the butcher, "you don't even know how to wrap a package. You let the liver blood run all over my fur. My coat is ruined."

The anguished butcher attempted to apologize, but her voice beat him down. He tried to apologize with his hands and his rolling eyes and with his yellow straw hat, but she would have none of it. When he went forth with a clean rag and tried to wipe the mink, she drove him back with an angry yelp. The door shut with a bang. On the counter stood her dripping bag. Herm could see his father had tried to save paper.

He went back to the table. About a half hour later the butcher came in. His face was deathly white and he looked like a white scarecrow with a yellow straw hat. He sat in the rocker without rocking. The cat tried to jump into his lap but he wouldn't let it and sat there looking into the back yard and far away.

Herm too was looking into the back yard. He was thinking of all the places he could go where there were horses. He wanted to be where there were many and he could ride them all.

But then he got up and reached for the blood-smeared apron hanging on a hook. He looped the loop over his head and tied the strings around him. They covered where the riding pants had been, but he felt as though he still had them on.

1953

A Confession of Murder

WITH THE DOING of the deed embedded in his mind like a child's grave in the earth, Farr shut the door and walked heavy-hearted down the stairs. At the third-floor landing he stopped to look out the small dirty window, across the harbor. The late-winter day was sullen, but Farr could see the ocean in the distance. Although he was carrying the weapon, a stone sash weight in a brown paper bag, heedless of the danger he set it down on the window ledge and stared at the water. It seemed to Farr that he had never loved the sea as he did now. Although he had not crossed it—he thought he would during the war but didn't—and had never gone any of the different ways it led, he felt he someday ought to. As he gazed, the water seemed to come alive in sunlight, flowing with slanted white sails. Moved to grief at the lovely sight he remained at the window with unseeing eyes until he remembered to go.

He went down the creaking stairs to the black, airless cellar. Farr pulled the rasping chain above the electric bulb and, when the dim light fell on him, searched around for a hiding place. As his hand uncoiled he realized with horror that he had forgotten the sash weight. He bounded up three flights of stairs, coming to a halt as he saw through the banister that an old woman was standing at the window, resting her bundle on the ledge—on the sash weight itself! Agitated, Farr watched to see whether she would discover the bloody thing, but she too was looking at the water and made no move to go. When she finally left, Farr, who had been lurking on the landing below, ran up, seized the package, and fled down to the cellar.

There he was tempted to draw the weapon out of the paper to inspect it but did not dare. He hunted for a place to bury it but felt secure nowhere. At last he tore open the asbestos covering of an insulated water pipe overhead and shoved the sash weight into the wool. As he was smoothing the asbestos he heard footsteps above and broke into a chilling sweat at the fear he was being followed. Stealthily he put out the light, sneaked close to the wall, and crouched in the pitch dark behind a dusty dresser abandoned there. He waited with indrawn breath for whoever he was to come limping down. Farr planned to yell into his face, escape up the stairs.

No one came down. Farr was afraid to abandon the hiding place, stricken at the thought that it was not a stranger but his father, miraculously recovered from his wound, who sought him there, as he had in the past, shouting in drunken rage against his son, stalking him in the dark, threatening to beat his head off with his belt buckle if he did not reveal himself. The memory of this so deeply affected Farr that he groaned aloud. It did not console him that his father had at last paid a terrible price for all the misery he had inflicted on him.

Farr trudged up the steps out of the cellar. In the street he felt unspeakable relief to be out of the grimy tenement house. He brushed the cobwebs off his brown hat and spanked a whitewash smear off the back of his long overcoat. Then he went down the block to where the houses ended and stood at the water's edge. The wind, whipping whitecaps along the surface of the harbor water, struck him with force. He held tightly to his hat. A flight of sparrows sprang across the sky, flying over the ships at anchor and disappearing in the distance. The aroma of roasting coffee filled Farr's hungry nostrils, but just then he saw some eggshells bobbing in the water and a dead rat floating. Surfeited, he turned away.

A skinny man in a green suit was standing at his elbow. "Sure looks like snow." The man wore no overcoat and his soiled shirt was open at the collar. His face and hands were tinged blue. Farr cupped a match to his cigarette, puffing quickly. He would have walked away but was afraid of being followed, so he stayed.

"Just a whiff of a butt makes me hungry to the bottom of my belly," said the man.

Farr listened, looking away.

After a minute the man, staring absently at the water, said, "The chill bites deep when there's no food between it and the marrow."

Suspecting him of planning to trick him, Farr warned himself to confess nothing. They'd have to ram a crowbar through his teeth to pry his jaws open.

"You wouldn't know it from the look of me," said the man, "but I'm a gentleman at heart." He wore a strained smile and held forth a trembling hand. Farr reached into his pants pocket, where he had five crumpled dollars plus a large assortment of coins. He pulled out a fistful of change, selected a nickel and five pennies, and dropped them into the man's outstretched hand.

Without thanking Farr, he drew back his arm and pitched the money into the water. Farr's suspicions awoke. He hurried up the block, glancing back from time to time to see if he was being followed, but the man had dropped out of sight.

He turned on the half run up the treeless avenue, angered with the bum for spoiling his view of the harbor. Yet though Farr was now passing the pawnshops, which reminded him of things he did not like to remember, his spirits rose. He accounted for this strange and unexpected change in him by his having done the deed. For an age he had been tormented by the desire to do it, had grown silent, lonely, sullen, until the decision came that the doing was the only way out. Much too long the plan had festered in his mind, waiting for an action, but now that it was done he at last felt free of the rank desire, the suppressed rage and fear that had embittered and thwarted his existence. It was done; he was content. As he walked, the vista of the narrow avenue, a street he had lived his life along, broadened, and he could see miles ahead, down to the suspension bridge in the distance, and was aware of people walking along as separate beings, not part of the mass he remembered avoiding so often as he'd trudged along here at various times of day and night.

* * *

One of the pawnshop windows caught his eye. Farr reluctantly stopped, yet he scanned it eagerly. There among the wedding bands, watches, knives, crucifixes, and the rest, among the stringed musical instruments and brasses hanging on pegs on the wall, he found what his eye sought—his mandolin—and felt a throb of pity for it. But Farr had not been working for more than a year—had left the place one rainy day in the fall—and the only way, thereafter, that he could keep himself in cigarette, newspaper, and movie money was to part, one by one, with the things he had bought for himself in a better time: a portable typewriter, used perhaps now and then to peck out a letter ordering a magazine; a pair of ice skates worn twice; a fine wristwatch he had bought on his birthday; and lately, with everything else gone, he had sold this little mandolin he'd liked so well, which he had taught himself to strum as he sang, and it was this bit of self-made music that he missed most. He considered redeeming it with the same five one-dollar bills he had got for it a month ago, but didn't relish the thought of strumming alone in his room; so sighing, Farr tore himself away from the window.

* * *

At the next corner stood Gus's Tavern. Farr, who had not gone in in an age, after a struggle entered, gazing around as if in a cathedral. Gus, older, with a folded apron around his paunch and an open vest over his white shirt, was standing behind the bar polishing beer glasses. When he saw Farr he put down the glass he was shining and observed him in astonishment.

"Well, throw me for a jackass if 'tisn't the old Punch-Ball King of South Second!"

Farr grunted awkwardly at the old appellation. "Surprised, Gus?"

"That's the least of it. Where in the name of mud have you been these many months—or is it years?"

"In the house mostly," Farr answered huskily.

Gus continued to regard him closely, to Farr's discomfort. "You've changed a lot, Eddie, haven't you now? I ask everybody whatever has become of the old Punch-Ball King and nobody says they ever see you. You used to haunt the streets when you were a kid."

Farr blinked but didn't reply.

"Married?" Gus winked.

"No," Farr said, embarrassed. He stole a glance at the door. It was still there.

Gus clucked. "How well I remember standing on the curbstone watching you play. *Flippo* with his left hand and the ball spins up. *Biffo* with his right, a tremendous sock lifting it far over the heads of all the fielders. How old were you then, Eddie?"

Farr made no attempt to think. "Fifteen, I guess."

An expression of sorrow lit Gus's eyes. "It comes back to me now. You were the same age as my Marty."

Farr's tongue tightened. It was beyond him to speak of the dead.

Himself again after a while, Gus sighed, "Ah yes, Eddie, you missed your true calling."

"One beer," Farr said, digging into his pocket for the change.

Gus drew a beer, shaved it, and set it before him.

"Put your pennies away. Any old friend of my Marty's needn't be thirsty here."

Farr gulped through the froth. A cold beer went with how good he now felt. He thought he might even break into a jig step or two.

Gus was still watching him. Farr, finding he couldn't drink, set the glass down.

After a pause Gus asked, "Do you still ever sing, Eddie?"

"Not so much anymore."

"Do me a favor and sing some old-time tune."

Farr looked around, but they were alone. Pretending to be strumming his mandolin, he sang, "In the good old summertime, in the good old summertime."

"Your voice has changed, Eddie," said Gus, "but it's still pleasing to the ear."

Farr then sang, "Ah, sweet mystery of life, at last I've found you."

Gus's eyes went wet and he blew his nose. "A fine little singer was lost to the world somewhere along the line."

Farr hung his head.

"What are your plans now, Eddie?"

The question scared him. Luckily, two customers came in and stood at the bar. Gus went to them, and Farr did not have to answer.

He picked up the beer and pointed with one finger to a booth in the rear.

Gus nodded. "Only don't leave without saying goodbye."

Farr promised.

*   *   *

He sat in the booth, thinking of Marty. Farr often thought and dreamed about him, but though he knew him best as a boy he dreamed of him as a man, mostly as he was during the days and nights they stood on street corners, waiting to be called into the army. There didn't seem anything to do then but wait till they were called in, so they spent most of their time smoking, throwing the bull, and making wisecracks at the girls who passed by. Marty, strangely inactive for the wild kid he had been—never knowing what wild thing to do next—was a blond fellow whose good looks the girls liked, but he never stopped wisecracking at them, whether he knew them or not. One day he said something dirty to this Jewish girl who passed by and she burst into tears. Gus, who had happened to be watching out of the upstairs window, heard what Marty said, ran down in his slippers, and smacked him hard across the teeth. Marty spat blood. Farr went sick to the pit of his stomach at the sound of the sock. He later threw up. And that was the last any of them had ever seen of Marty, because he enlisted in the army and never came out again. Gus got a telegram one day saying that he was killed in action, and he never really got over it.

*   *   *

Farr was whispering to himself about Marty when he gazed up and saw this dark-haired woman standing by his table, looking as if she had slyly watched his startled eyes find her. Half rising, he remembered to remove his hat.

"Remember me, Ed? Helen Melisatos—Gus told me to say hello."

He knew she was this Greek girl—only she'd been very pretty then—who had once lived in the same tenement house with him. One summer night they had gone together up to the roof.

"Sure," said Farr. "Sure I remember you."

Her body had broadened but her face and hair were not bad, and her dark brown eyes seemed still to be expecting something that she would never get.

She sat down, telling him to sit.

He did, placing his hat next to him on the seat.

She lit a cigarette and smoked for a long time. A man called her from the bar but she shook her head. He left without her.

Her lips moved hungrily. Although he could at first hear no voice, she seemed, against his will, to be telling him a story he didn't want to hear. It was about this boy and a girl, a slim dark girl with soft eyes, seventeen then, wearing this nice white dress on a hot summer night. They'd been kissing. Then she had slipped off her undergarment and lain back, uncovered, on the tar-papered roof. With heart thudding he watched her, and when she said to kneel he kneeled, and then she said it was hot and why didn't he take off his pants. He wanted to love her with their clothes on. When he got his pants off he stopped and couldn't go on. What do you think of a guy who would do a thing like that to a girl? He wasn't much of a lover, was he? She was smiling broadly now, and she spoke in an older, disillusioned voice, "You're different, Ed." And she said, "You used to talk a lot."

He listened intently but said nothing.

"But you still ain't a bad-looking guy. How old are you, anyway?"

"Twenty-eight, going on twenty-nine."

"Married?"

"Not yet," he said quickly. "How about you?"

"I had enough," Helen said.

He cagily asked her another question to keep her talking about herself. "How's your brother George?"

"He lives in Athens now. He went back with my mother after the war. My father died here."

Farr put on his hat.

"Going someplace, Ed?"

"No." He whispered to himself that he must say nothing about his own father.

She shrugged.

"Drink?" he asked.

She lifted her half-full whiskey glass. "Order yourself."

"I got my beer." But when he took up the glass it was empty.

"Still absentminded?" She smiled.

"My mind's okay," Farr said.

"I bet you're still a virgin?"

"I bet you're not." Farr grinned and drained a drop from the glass.

"Remember that night on the roof?"

He harshly said he didn't want to hear about it.

"I couldn't believe in myself for a long time after that," Helen said.

"I don't want to hear about it."

She sat silent, not looking at him. She sat silent so long his confidence finally ebbed back.

"Remember," he said, "when you had that sweet-sixteen party in your house, your mother gave us that Greek coffee that had jelly in the bottom of the little cup?"

She said she remembered.

"Let me buy you a drink." Farr reached into his pocket. He was smoking and squinted as he counted the coins.

He caught Gus's eye and ordered whiskey for her, but Gus wouldn't take anything for it. Farr then slid a coin into the jukebox.

"Dance?" he said, fighting a panicky feeling.

"No."

Vastly relieved, he went to the bar and ordered another beer. This time Gus let him pay. Farr cashed one of his dollar bills.

"Nothing like old friends, eh, Eddie?"

"Yeah," said Farr happily. He lit a cigarette and steered the beer over to the table. Helen had another whiskey and Farr another beer. He got used to the way her eyes looked at him over her glass.

After a time Helen asked him if he had had supper.

A violent hunger seized him as he remembered his last meal had been breakfast.

He said no.

"Come on up to my place. I'll fix you something good."

Farr whispered to himself that he ought to go. He ought to, and later talk her into going up to the roof with him. If he did it to her now, maybe he would feel better and then things that had gone wrong would go right. You could never tell.

Her face was flushed, and all the time she was grinning at him in a dirty way.

Farr whispered something and she strained to catch it but couldn't. "What the hell are you saying?"

"Nothing."

"Come on up with me, kid," she urged. "After, I'll show you how to make a man out of yourself."

His head fell with a bang against the tabletop. His eyes were shut, and he wouldn't move.

"Imagine a guy your age who never made love," Helen taunted.

He answered nothing and she began cursing him, her face lit in livid anger. Finally she got up, a little unsteady on her feet. "Why don't you go and drop dead?"

He said he would.

*   *   *

Farr walked again in the darkened streets. He stopped at the heavy wooden doors of the Catholic church. Pulling one open, he glanced hastily inside and saw the holy-water basin. He wondered what would happen if he went in and gargled a mouthful. A girl in a brown coat and purple bandanna came out of the church and Farr asked her when was confession.

She looked up at him in fright and quickly said, "Saturday."

He thanked her and walked away. It was Monday.

She ran after him and said she could arrange for him to see the priest if he wanted to.

He said no, that he was not a Catholic.

Though his coat reached to his ankles, his legs were cold. So were the soles of his feet. He walked as if he were dragging a burden. The burden was the way he felt. The good feeling had gone and this old one was heavier now than anything he remembered. He would not mind the cold so much if he could only get rid of this dismal heaviness. His brain felt like a rock. Still it grew heavier. That was the unaccountable thing. He wondered how heavy it could get. If it got any heavier, he would keel over in the street and nobody'd be able to lift him. They would all give up and leave him lying with his head sunk in asphalt.

On the next street shone two green lamps on both sides of some stone steps leading into a dark and dirty building. It was a police station. Farr stood across the street from it, but nobody went in or came out. Finally it grew freezing cold. He blew into his fists, looked around to see if he was being followed, and then went in.

He was grateful for the warmth. The sergeant sat at the desk writing. He was a bald-headed man with a bulbous nose, which he frequently scratched with his little finger. His second and third fingers had ink stains on them from a leaky fountain pen. The sergeant glanced up in surprise, and Farr did not care for his face.

"What's yours?" he said.

Farr's tongue was like a sash weight. Unable to speak, he hung his head.

"Remove your hat."

Farr took it off.

"Come to the point," said the sergeant, scratching his nose.

Farr at last confessed to a crime.

"Such as what?" said the sergeant.

Farr's lips twitched and assumed odd shapes. "I killed somebody."

"Who, for instance?"

"My father."

The sergeant's incredulous look vanished. "Ah, that's too bad."

He wrote Farr's name down in a large ledger, blotted it, and told him to wait on a bench by the wall.

"I got to locate a detective to talk to you, but as it happens nobody's around just now. You picked suppertime to come in."

Farr sat on the bench with his hat on. After a while a heavyset man came through the door, carrying a paper bag and a pint container of coffee.

"Say, Wolff," called the sergeant.

Wolff slowly turned around. He had broad, bent shoulders and a thick mustache. His large black hat was broad-brimmed.

The sergeant pointed his pen at Farr. "A confession of murder."

Wolff's eyebrows went up slightly. "Where's Burns or Newman?"

"Supper. You're the only one that's around right now."

The detective glanced uneasily at Farr. "Come on," he said.

Farr got up and followed him. The detective walked heavily up the wooden stairs. Halfway up he stopped, sighed inaudibly, and went up more slowly.

"Hold this," he said at the top of the stairs.

Farr held the bag of food and the coffee. The hot container warmed his cold hand. Wolff unlocked a door with a key, then took his supper from Farr, and they went inside. The church bell in the neighborhood bonged seven times.

Wolff routinely frisked Farr. He sat down heavily at his desk, tore open the paper bag, and unwrapped his food. He had three meat-and-cheese sandwiches and a paper dish of cabbage salad which he ate with a small plastic fork that annoyed him. As he was eating he remembered the coffee and twisted the top off the container. His hand shook a little as he poured the steaming coffee into a white cup without a handle.

He ate with his hat on. Farr held his in his lap. He enjoyed the warmth of the room and the peaceful sight of someone eating.

"My first square today," said Wolff. "Busy from morning."

Farr nodded.

"One thing after another."

"I know."

Wolff, as he ate, kept his eyes fastened on Farr. "Take your coat off. It's hot here."

"No, thanks." He was now sorry he had come.

The detective finished up quickly. He rolled the papers on his desk and what remained of the food into a ball and dumped it into the wastebasket. Then he got up and washed his hands in a closet sink. At his desk he lit a cigar, puffed with pleasure two or three times, put it to the side in an ashtray, and said, "What's this confession?"

Although Farr struggled with himself to speak, he couldn't.

Wolff grew restless. "Murder, did somebody say?"

Farr sighed deeply.

"Your mother?" Wolff asked sympathetically.

"No, my father."

"Oh ho," said Wolff.

Farr gazed at the floor.

The detective opened a black pocket notebook and found a pencil stub.

"Name?" he said.

"You mean mine?" asked Farr.

"Yours—who else?"

"My father's."

"First yours."

"Farr, Edward."

"His?"

"Herman J. Farr."

"Age of victim?"

Farr tried to think. "I don't know."

"You don't know your own father's age?"

"No."

"How old are you?"

"Twenty-nine, going on thirty."

"That you know?"

Farr didn't answer.

Wolff wrote down something in the book.

"What was his occupation?"

"Upholsterer."

"And yours?"

"None," Farr said, in embarrassment.

"Unemployed?"

"Yes."

"What's your regular work?"

"I have none in particular."

"A jack of all trades." Wolff broke the ash off in the tray and took another puff of the cigar. "Address?"

"80 South Second."

"Your father too?"

"Yes."

"That where the body is?"

Farr nodded absently.

The detective then slipped the notebook into his pocket.

"What did you use to kill him with?"

Farr paused, wet his dry lips, and said, "A blunt instrument."

"You don't say? What kind of a blunt instrument?"

"A window sash weight."

"What'd you do with it?"

"I hid it."

"Whereabouts?"

"In the cellar where we live."

Wolff carefully tapped his cigar out in the ashtray and leaned forward. "So tell me," he said, "why does a man kill his father?"

Alarmed, Farr half rose from his chair.

"Sit down," said the detective.

Farr sat down.

"I asked you why did you kill him?"

Farr gnawed on his lip till it bled.

"Come on, come on," said Wolff, "we have to have the motive."

"I don't know."

"Who then should know—I?"

Farr tried frantically to think why. Because he had had nothing in his life and what he had done was a way of having something?

"What did you do it for, I said," Wolff asked sternly.

"I had to—" Farr had risen.

"What do you mean 'had to'?"

"I had no love for him. He ruined my life."

"Is that a reason to kill your father?"

"Yes," Farr shouted. "For that and everything else."

"What else?"

"Leave me alone. Can't you see I'm an unhappy man?"

Wolff sat back in his chair. "You don't say?"

"Sarcasm won't get you anyplace," Farr cried angrily. "Be humble with suffering people."

"I don't need any advice on how to run my profession."

"Try to remember a man is not a beast." Trembling, Farr resumed his seat.

"Are you a man?" Wolff asked slyly.

"No, I have failed."

"Then you are a beast?"

"Insofar as I am not a man."

They stared at each other. Wolff flattened his mustache with his fingertips. Suddenly he opened his drawer and took out a picture.

"Do you recognize this woman?"

Farr stared at the wrinkled face of an old crone. "No."

"She was raped and murdered on the top floor of an apartment house in your neighborhood."

Farr covered his ears with his hands.

The detective laid the picture back in the drawer. He fished out another.

"Here's a boy aged about six or seven. He was brutally stabbed to death in an empty lot on South Eighth. Did you ever see him before?"

He thrust the picture close to Farr's face.

When Farr looked into the boy's innocent eyes he burst into tears.

Wolff put the picture away. He pulled on the dead cigar, then examined it and threw it away.

"Come on," he said, tiredly rising.

*   *   *

The cellar was full of violent presences. Farr went fearfully down the steps.

Wolff flashed his light on the crisscrossed pipes overhead. "Which one?"

Farr pointed.

The detective brushed aside some cobwebs and felt along the pipe with his fingers. He found the loose asbestos and from the wool inside plucked forth the sash weight.

Farr audibly sucked in his breath.

In the yellow glow of the hall lamp upstairs the detective took the sash weight out of the bag and examined it. Farr shut his eyes.

"What floor do you live on?"

"Fourth."

Wolff looked up uneasily. They trudged up the stairs, Farr leading.

"Not so fast," said Wolff.

Farr slowed down. As they passed the third-floor window he looked out to sea, but all was dark. On the next floor he stopped before a warped door with a top panel of frosted glass.

"In here," Farr said at last.

"Have you got the key?"

Farr turned the knob and the door fell open, bumping loudly against the wall. The corridor to the kitchen was black. The detective's light pierced it, lighting up a wooden table and two wooden chairs.

"Go on in."

"I'm afraid," whispered Farr.

"Go on, I said."

He stepped reluctantly forward.

"Where is he?" said the detective.

"In the bedroom." He spoke hoarsely.

"Show me."

Farr led him through a small windowless room containing a cot and some books and magazines on the floor. Wolff's light shone on him.

"In there." Farr pointed to the door.

"Open it."

"No."

"Open, I said."

"For godsake, don't make me."

"Open."

Farr thought quickly: in the dark there he would upset the detective and make a hasty escape into the street.

"For the last time I said open."

Farr pushed the door and it squeaked open on its hinges. The long narrow bedroom was heavy with darkness. Wolff's light hit the metal headboard of an old double bed, sunken in the middle.

A groan rose from the bed. Farr groaned too, his hair on end.

"Murder," said the groan, "terrible, terrible."

A white bloodless face rose into the light, old and staring.

"Who's there?" cried Wolff.

"Oh, my dreams, my dreams," wept the old man, "I dreamed I was bein murdered."

Flinging aside the worn quilt, he slid out of bed and hopped in bare feet on the cold floor, skinny in his long underwear. He groped toward them.

Farr whispered wild things to himself.

The detective found the light chain and pulled it.

The old man saw the stranger in the room. "And who are you, might I ask?"

"Theodore Wolff, detective from the Sixty-second Precinct." He flashed his shield.

Herman Farr blinked in surprise and shame. He hastily got into the pants that had been draped across a chair and, stepping into misshapen slippers, raised suspenders over his shoulders.

"I must've overslept my nap. I usually have supper cookin at six and we eat half past six, him and I." He suddenly asked, "What are you doin here if you're a detective?"

"I came here with your son."

"He didn't do anything wrong?" asked the old man, frightened.

"I don't know. That's what I came to find out."

"Come into the kitchen," said Herman Farr. "The light's better."

They went into the kitchen. Herman Farr got a third chair from the bedroom and they sat around the wooden table, Farr waxen and fatigued, his father gaunt and bony-faced, with loose skin sprouting gray stubble, and on the long side of the table, the heavyset Wolff, wearing his black hat.

"Where are my glasses?" complained Herman Farr. He got up and found them on a shelf above the gas stove. The lenses were thick and magnified his watery eyes.

"Until now I couldn't tell the nature of your face," he said to the detective.

Wolff grunted.

"Now what's the trouble here?" said Herman Farr, staring at his son.

Farr sneered at him.

The detective removed the sash weight from the paper bag and laid it on the table. Farr gazed at it as if it were a snake uncoiling.

"Ever see this before?"

Herman Farr stared stupidly at the sash weight, one hand clawing the back of the other.

"Where'd you get it?" he cried in a quavering voice.

"Answer my question first."

"Yes. It belongs to me, though I wish to Christ I had never seen it."

"It's yours?" said Wolff.

"That's right. I had it hid in my trunk."

"What's this stain on it here?"

Farr gazed in fascination where the detective pointed.

Herman Farr said he didn't know.

"It's a bloodstain," Wolff said.

"Ah, so it is," sighed Herman Farr, his mouth trembling. "I'll tell you the truth. My wife—may God rest her soul—once tried to hit me with it."

Farr laughed out loud.

"Is this your blood?" asked Wolff.

"No, by the livin mercy. It's hers."

They were all astonished.

"Are you telling the truth?" said Wolff sternly.

"I'd give my soul if I only wasn't."

"Did you hit her with it?"

Herman Farr lifted his glasses and with a clotted yellow handkerchief wiped the tears from his flowing eyes.

"A sin is never lost. Once in a drunken fit, enraged as I was by my long-lastin poverty, I swung it at her and opened a wound on her head. The blood is hers. I could never blame her for wantin to kill me with it. She tried it one night when I was at my supper, but the thing fell out of her hand and smashed the plate. I nearly jumped out of my shoes. Seein it fall I realized the extent of my wickedness and kept the sash weight hid away at the bottom of my trunk as a memory of my sins."

Wolff scratched a match under the table, paused, and shook it out. Farr smoked the last cigarette in his crushed pack. The old man wept into his dirty handkerchief.

"I have deserved a violent endin of my life if anybody ever did. In my younger days I was a beast—cruel, and a weaklin. I treated them both very badly." He nodded to Farr. "As he more than once said it, I killed her a little every day. Many times—may the livin God keep torturin me for it—I beat her black and blue, once bloodyin her nose on a frosty morning when she complained of the cold, and another time pushin her down a flight of stairs. As for him, I more than once skinned his back with my belt buckle."

Farr crushed his cigarette and snapped it into the sink.

Wolff then lit a cigar and puffed slowly.

The old man wept openly. "This young man is the livin witness of my terrible deeds, but he don't know half the depths of my sufferin since that poor soul left this world, or the terrible nature of my nightly dreams."

"When did she die?" the detective asked.

"Sixteen years ago, and he has never forgiven me, carryin his hatred like a fire in his heart, although she, good soul, forgave me in his presence at the time of her last illness. 'Herman,' she said, 'I'm goin to a place where I would be ill at ease if I didn't forgive you,' and with that she went to her peace. But my son has hated me throughout the years, and I can't look at him without seein it in his eyes. 'Tis true, he has sometimes been kind to a helpless old man, and when my arthritis was so bad that I couldn't move, he more than once brought a plate of soup to my bed and fed me with a spoon, but in the depths of his soul my change has made no difference to him and he hates me now as he did then, though I've repented on sore knees a thousand times. I have often said to him, 'What's done is done, and judge me for what I have since become'—for he is an intelligent man and reads books you and I never heard of—but on this thing he won't yield or be reasoned with."

"Did he ever try to hurt you?"

"No more than to nag or snarl at me. No, for all he does nowadays is to sit alone in his room and read and reflect, although his learnin doesn't in the least unbend his mind to me. Of course I don't approve him givin up his job, because with these puffed and crippled hands I am lucky when I can work half time, but there are all sorts in the world and some have greater need for reflection than others. He has been inclined in that direction since he was a lad, although I did not notice his quiet and solitary ways until after he had returned from the army."

"What did he do then?" said Wolff.

"He worked for a year at his old job, then gave it up and became a hospital orderly. But he couldn't stand it long and he quit and stayed home."

Farr looked out the dark fire-escape window and saw himself walking along the dreary edge of a desolate beach, the wind wailing at his feet, driftwood taking on frightening shapes, and his footsteps fading behind, to appear on the ground before him as he walked along the vast, silent shore . . .

Wolff rubbed the cigar out against the sole of his shoe. "You want to know why I'm here?" he said to Herman Farr.

"Yes."

"He came to the station house around suppertime and made a statement that he had murdered you with this sash weight."

The old man groaned. "Not that I don't deserve the fate."

"He thought he actually did it," Wolff said.

"It's his overactive imagination on account of not gettin any exercise to speak of. I've told him that many times but he don't listen to what I say. I can't describe to you the things he talks about in his sleep. Many a night they keep me awake."

"Do you see this sash weight?" Wolff asked Farr.

"I do," he said, with eyes shut.

"Do you still maintain that you hit or attempted to hit your father with it?"

Farr stared rigidly at the wall. He thought, If I answer I'll go crazy. *I mustn't. I mustn't.*

"He thinks he did," Wolff said. "You can see he's insane."

Herman Farr cried out as though he had been stabbed in the throat.

Farr shouted, "What about that boy I killed? You showed me his picture."

"That boy was my son," Wolff said. "He died ten years ago of terrible sickness."

Farr rose and thrust forth his wrists.

The detective shook his head. "No cuffs. We'll just call the ambulance."

Farr wildly swung his fist, catching the detective on the jaw. Wolff's chair toppled and he fell heavily to the floor. Amid the confusion and shouting by Herman Farr that he was the one who deserved hanging, Farr fled down the ill-lighted stairs with murder in his heart. In the street he flung his coins into the sky.

1953

The Elevator

ELEONORA WAS an Umbrian girl whom the portiere's wife had
brought up to the Agostinis' first-floor apartment after their two
unhappy experiences with Italian maids, not long after they had
arrived in Rome from Chicago. She was about twenty-three, thin,
and with bent bony shoulders which she embarrassedly characterized as gobbo—hunchbacked. But she was not unattractive and
had an interesting profile, George Agostini thought. Her full face
was not so interesting; like the portinaia's, also an Umbrian, it was
too broad and round, and her left brown eye was slightly wider
than her right. It also looked sadder than her right eye.

She was an active girl, always moving in her noisy slippers at a
half trot across the marble floors of the furnished two-bedroom
apartment, getting things done without having to be told, and
handling the two children very well. After the second girl was let
go, George had wished they didn't have to be bothered with a full-
time live-in maid. He had suggested that maybe Grace ought to
go back to sharing the signora's maid—their landlady across the
hall—for three hours a day, paying her on an hourly basis, as they
had when they first moved in after a rough month of apartment
hunting. But when George mentioned this, Grace made a gesture
of tearing her red hair, so he said nothing more. It wasn't that he
didn't want her to have the girl—she certainly needed one with
all the time it took to shop in six or seven stores instead of one
supermarket, and she was even without a washing machine, with
all the kids' things to do; but George felt he wasn't comfortable

with a maid always around. He didn't like people waiting on him, or watching him eat. George was heavy, and sensitive about it. He also didn't like her standing back to let him enter a room first. He didn't want her saying "Comanda" the minute he spoke her name. Furthermore he wasn't happy about the tiny maid's room the girl lived in, or her sinkless bathroom, with its cramped sitzbath and no water heater. Grace, whose people had always been much better off than his, said everybody in Italy had maids and he would get used to it. George hadn't got used to the first two girls, but he did find that Eleonora bothered him less. He liked her more as a person and felt sorry for her. She looked as though she had more on her back than her bent shoulders.

One afternoon about a week and a half after Eleonora had come to them, when George arrived home from the FAO office where he worked, during the long lunch break, Grace said the maid was in her room crying.

"What for?" George said, worried.

"I don't know."

"Didn't you ask her?"

"Sure I did, but all I could gather was that she's had a sad life. You're the linguist around here, why don't you ask her?"

"What are you so annoyed about?"

"Because I feel like a fool, frankly, not knowing what it's all about."

"Tell me what happened."

"She came out of the hall crying, about an hour ago," Grace said. "I had sent her up to the roof with a bundle of wash to do in one of the tubs up there instead of our bathtub, so she doesn't have to lug the heavy wet stuff up to the lines on the roof but can hang it out right away. Anyway, she wasn't gone five minutes before she was back crying, and that was when she answered me about her sad life. I wanted to tell her I have a sad life too. We've been in Rome close to two months and I haven't even been able to see St. Peter's. When will I ever see anything?"

"Let's talk about her," George said. "Do you know what happened in the hall?"

"I told you I didn't. After she came back, I went down to the ground floor to talk to the portinaia—she has some smattering of English—and she told me that Eleonora had been married but had lost her husband. He died or something when she was eighteen. Then she had a baby by another guy who didn't stay around long enough to see if he recognized it, and that, I suppose, is why she finds life so sad."

"Did the portinaia say whether the kid is still alive?" George asked.

"Yes. She keeps it in a convent school."

"Maybe that's what got her down," he suggested. "She thinks of her kid being away from her and then feels bad."

"So she starts to cry in the hall?"

"Why not in the hall? Why not anywhere so long as you feel like crying? Maybe I ought to talk to her."

Grace nodded. Her face was flushed, and George knew she was troubled.

He went into the corridor and knocked on the door of the maid's room. "Permesso," George said.

"Prego." Eleonora had been lying on the bed but was respectfully on her feet when George entered. He could see she had been crying. Her eyes were red and her face pale. She looked scared, and George's throat went dry.

"Eleonora, I am sorry to see you like this," he said in Italian. "Is there something either my wife or I can do to help you?"

"No, Signore," she said quietly.

"What happened to you out in the hall?"

Her eyes glistened but she held back the tears. "Nothing. One feels like crying, so she cries. Do these things have a reason?"

"Are you satisfied with conditions here?" George asked her. "Yes."

"If there is something we can do for you, I want you to tell us."

"Please don't trouble yourself about me." She lifted the bottom of her skirt, at the same time bending her head to dry her eyes on it. Her bare legs were hairy but shapely.

"No trouble at all," George said. He closed the door softly.

"Let her rest," he said to Grace.

"Damn! Just when I have to go out."

But in a few minutes Eleonora came out and went on with her work in the kitchen. They said nothing more and neither did she. Then at three George left for the office, and Grace put on her hat and went off to her Italian class and then to St. Peter's.

That night when George got home from work, Grace called him into their bedroom and said she now knew what had created all the commotion that afternoon. First the signora, after returning from an appointment with her doctor, had bounded in from across the hall, and Grace had gathered from the hot stew the old woman was in that she was complaining about their maid. The portinaia then happened to come up with the six o'clock mail, and the signora laced into her for bringing an inferior type of maid into the house. Finally, when the signora had left, the portinaia told Grace that the old lady had been the one who had made Eleonora cry. She had apparently forbidden the girl to use the elevator. She would listen behind the door, and as soon as she heard someone putting the key into the elevator lock, she would fling open her door, and if it was Eleonora, as she had suspected, she would cry out, "The key is not for you. The key is not for you." She would stand in front of the elevator, waving her arms to prevent her from entering. "Use the stairs," she cried, "the stairs are for walking. There is no need to fly, or God would have given you wings."

"Anyway," Grace went on, "Eleonora must have been outwitting her or something, because what she would do, according to the portinaia, was go upstairs to the next floor and call the elevator from there. But today the signora got suspicious and followed Eleonora up the stairs. She gave her a bad time up there. When she blew in here before, Eleonora got so scared that she ran to her room and locked the door. The signora said she would have to ask us not to give our girl the key anymore. She shook her keys at me."

"What did you say after that?" George asked.

"Nothing. I wasn't going to pick a fight with her even if I could speak the language. A month of hunting apartments was enough for me."

"We have a lease," said George.

"Leases have been broken."

"She wouldn't do it—she needs the money."

"I wouldn't bet on it," said Grace.

"It burns me up," George said. "Why shouldn't the girl use the elevator to lug the clothes up to the roof? Five floors is a long haul."

"Apparently none of the other girls does," Grace said. "I saw one of them carrying a basket of wash up the stairs on her head."

"They ought to join the acrobats' union."

"We have to stick to their customs."

"I'd still like to tell the old dame off."

"This is Rome, George, not Chicago. You came here of your own free will."

"Where's Eleonora?" George asked.

"In the kitchen."

George went into the kitchen. Eleonora was washing the children's supper dishes in a pan of hot water. When George came in she looked up with fear, the fear in her left eye shining more brightly than in her right.

"I'm sorry about the business in the hall," George said with sympathy, "but why didn't you tell me about it this afternoon?"

"I don't want to make trouble."

"Would you like me to talk to the signora?"

"No, no."

"I want you to ride in the elevator if you want to."

"Thank you, but it doesn't matter."

"Then why are you crying?"

"I'm always crying, Signore. Don't bother to notice it."

"Have it your own way," George said.

He thought that ended it, but a week later as he came into the building at lunchtime he saw Eleonora getting into the elevator with a laundry bundle. The portinaia had just opened the door for her with her key, but when she saw George she quickly ducked down the stairs to the basement. George got on the elevator with Eleonora. Her face was crimson.

"I see you don't mind using the elevator," he said.

"Ah, Signore"—she shrugged—"we must all try to improve ourselves."

"Are you no longer afraid of the signora?"

"Her girl told me the signora is sick," Eleonora said happily.

Eleonora's luck held, George learned, because the signora stayed too sick to be watching the elevator, and one day after the maid rode up in it to the roof, she met a plumber's helper working on the washtubs, Fabrizio Occhiogrosso, who asked her to go out with him on her next afternoon off. Eleonora, who had been doing little on her Thursday and Sunday afternoons off, mostly spending her time with the portinaia, readily accepted. Fabrizio, a short man with pointed shoes, a thick trunk, hairy arms, and the swarthy face of a Spaniard, came for her on his motorbike and away they would go together, she sitting on the seat behind him, holding both arms around his belly. She sat astride the seat, and when Fabrizio, after impatiently revving the Vespa, roared up the narrow street, the wind fluttered her skirt and her bare legs were exposed above the knees.

"Where do they go?" George once asked Grace.

"She says he has a room on the Via della Purificazióne."

"Do they always go to his room?"

"She says they sometimes ride to the Borghese Gardens or go to the movies."

One night in early December, after the maid had mentioned that Fabrizio was her fiancé now, George and Grace stood at their living-room window looking down into the street as Eleonora got on the motorbike and it raced off out of sight.

"I hope she knows what she's doing," he muttered in a worried tone. "I don't much take to Fabrizio."

"So long as she doesn't get pregnant too soon. I'd hate to lose her."

George was silent for a time, then remarked, "How responsible do you suppose we are for her morals?"

"Her morals?" laughed Grace. "Are you batty?"

"I never had a maid before," George said.

"This is our third."

"I mean in principle."

"Stop mothering the world," said Grace.

Then one Sunday after midnight Eleonora came home on the verge of fainting. What George had thought might happen had. Fabrizio had taken off into the night on his motorbike. When they had arrived at his room early that evening, a girl from Perugia was sitting on his bed. The portiere had let her in after she had showed him an engagement ring and a snapshot of her and Fabrizio in a rowboat. When Eleonora demanded to know who this one was, the plumber's helper did not bother to explain but ran down the stairs, mounted his Vespa, and drove away. The girl disappeared. Eleonora wandered the streets for hours, then returned to Fabrizio's room. The portiere told her that he had been back, packed his valise, and left for Perugia, the young lady riding on the back seat.

Eleonora dragged herself home. When she got up the next morning to make breakfast she was a skeleton of herself and the gobbo looked like a hill. She said nothing and they asked nothing. What Grace wanted to know she later got from the portinaia. Eleonora no longer ran through her chores but did everything wearily, each movement like flowing stone. Afraid she would collapse, George advised her to take a week off and go home. He would pay her salary and give her something extra for the bus.

"No, Signore," she said dully, "it is better for me to work." She said, "I have been through so much, more is not noticeable."

But then she had to notice it. One afternoon she absentmindedly picked up Grace's keys and got on the elevator with a bag of clothes to be washed. The signora, having recovered her health, was waiting for her. She flung open the door, grabbed Eleonora by the arm as she was about to close the elevator door, and dragged her out.

"Whore," she cried, "don't steal the privileges of your betters. Use the stairs."

Grace opened the apartment door to see what the shouting was about, and Eleonora, with a yowl, rushed past her. She locked herself in her room and sat there all afternoon without moving. She wept copiously. Grace, on the verge of exhaustion, could do nothing with her. When George came home from work that evening he tried to coax her out, but she shouted at him to leave her alone.

George was thoroughly fed up. "I've had enough," he said. He thought out how he would handle the signora, then told Grace he was going across the hall.

"Don't do it," she shouted, but he was already on his way.

George knocked on the signora's door. She was a woman of past sixty-five, a widow, always dressed in black. Her face was long and gray, but her eyes were bright black. Her husband had left her these two apartments across the hall from each other that he had owned outright. She lived in the smaller and rented the other, furnished, at a good rent. George knew that this was her only source of income. She had once been a schoolteacher.

"Scusi, Signora," said George, "I have come with a request."

"Prego." She asked him to sit.

George took a chair near the terrace window. "I would really appreciate it, Signora, if you will let our girl go into the elevator with the laundry when my wife sends her up to the tubs. She is not a fortunate person and we would like to make her life a little easier for her."

"I am sorry," answered the signora with dignity, "but I can't permit her to enter the elevator."

"She's a good girl and you have upset her very much."

"Good," said the signora, "I am glad. She must remember her place, even if you don't. This is Italy, not America. You must understand that we have to live with these people long after you, who come to stay for a year or two, return to your own country."

"Signora, she does no harm in the elevator. We are not asking you to ride with her. After all, the elevators are a convenience for all who live in this house and therefore ought to be open for those who work for us here."

"No," said the signora.

"Why not think it over and let me know your answer tomorrow? I assure you I wouldn't ask this if I didn't think it was important."

"I have thought it over," she said stiffly, "and I have given you the same answer I will give tomorrow."

George got up. "In that case," he said, "if you won't listen to reason, I consider my lease with you ended. You have had your last month's rent. We will move on the first of February."

The signora looked as if she had just swallowed a fork.

"The lease is a sacred contract," she said, trembling. "It is against the law to break it."

"I consider that you have already broken it," George said quietly, "by creating conditions that make it very hard for my family to function in this apartment. I am simply acknowledging a situation that already exists."

"If you move out, I will take a lawyer and make you pay for the whole year."

"A lawyer will cost you half the rent he might collect," George answered. "And if my lawyer is better than yours, you will get nothing and owe your lawyer besides."

"Oh, you Americans," said the signora bitterly. "How well I understand you. Your money is your dirty foot with which you kick the world. Who wants you here," she cried, "with your soaps and toothpastes and your dirty gangster movies!"

"I would like to remind you that my origin is Italian," George said.

"You have long ago forgotten your origin," she shouted.

George left the apartment and went back to his own.

"I'll bet you did it," Grace greeted him. Her face was ashen.

"I did," said George.

"I'll bet you fixed us good. Oh, you ought to be proud. How will we ever find another apartment in the dead of winter with two kids?"

She left George and locked herself in the children's bedroom. They were both awake and got out of bed to be with her.

George sat in the living room in the dark. I did it, he was thinking.

After a while the doorbell rang. He got up and put on the light. It was the signora and she looked unwell. She entered the living room at George's invitation and sat there with great dignity.

"I am sorry I raised my voice to a guest in my house," she said. Her mouth was loose and her eyes glistened.

"I am sorry I offended you," George said.

She did not speak for a while, then said, "Let the girl use the elevator." The signora broke into tears.

When she had dried her eyes, she said, "You have no idea how bad things have become since the war. The girls are disrespectful. Their demands are endless, it is impossible to keep up with them. They talk back, they take every advantage. They crown themselves with privileges. It is a struggle to keep them in their place. After all, what have we left when we lose our self-respect?" The signora wept heartbrokenly.

After she had gone, George stood at the window. Across the street a beggar played a flute.

I didn't do it well, George thought. He felt depressed.

On her afternoon off Eleonora rode up and down on the elevator.

1957

An Exorcism

FOGEL, a writer, had had another letter from Gary Simson, the would-be writer, a request as usual. He wrote fiction but hadn't jelled. Fogel, out of respect, saved letters from writers but was tempted not to include Simson although he had begun to publish. I am not his mentor, though he calls himself my student. If so what have I taught him? In the end he placed the letter in his files. I have his others, he thought.

Eli Fogel was a better than ordinary writer but not especially "successful." He disliked the word. His productivity was limited by his pace which, for reasons of having to breathe hard to enjoy life, was slow. Two and a half books in fifteen years, the half a paperback of undistinguished verse. My limp is symbolic, he thought. His leg had been injured in a bicycle accident as a youth, though with the built-up shoe the limp was less noticeable than when he hobbled around barefoot. He limped for his lacks. Fogel, for instance, regretted never having married, blaming this on his devotion to work. It's not that it has to be one or the other, but for me it's one or none. He was, mildly, a monomaniac. That simplified life but reduced it—what else? Still, he did not pity himself. It amused Fogel rather than not that the protagonists of his two published novels were married men with families, their wounds deriving from sources other than hurt members and primal loneliness. Imagination saves me, he thought.

Both his novels had received praise, though not much else; and Fogel had for the past six years labored on a third, about half completed. Since he declined to write reviews, lecture, or teach regularly, he ran into money problems. Fortunately he had from his father a small inheritance that came to five thousand annually, a shrinking sum in an inflated world; so Fogel reluctantly accepted summer-school invitations, or taught, somewhat on the prickly side, at writers' conferences, one or two a summer. With what he had he made do.

It was at one of these conferences in Buffalo, in June, and at another in mid-August of the same summer, on the campus of a small college in the White Mountains, that the writer had met, and later renewed a friendship with, Gary Simson, then less than half Fogel's age; a friendship of sorts, mild, fallible, but for a while satisfying; that is to say, possessing some of the attributes and possibilities of friendship.

Gary, a slight glaze in his eyes as he listened to Fogel talk about writing, wanted, he seriously confessed with a worried brow, "more than anything," even "desperately," to be a writer—the desperation inciting goose bumps on Fogel's flesh, putting him off for a full fifteen minutes. He sat in depressed silence in his office as the youth fidgeted. "What's the rush?" the writer ultimately asked. "I've got to get there," the youth replied. "Get where?" "I want to be a good writer someday, Mr. Fogel." "It's a long haul, my boy," Eli Fogel said. "Make a friend of time. And steer clear of desperation. Desperate people tend to be bad writers, increasing desperation." He laughed a little, not unkindly. Gary sat nodding as though he had learned the lesson of his life. He was twenty-two, a curly-haired senior in college, with a broad fleshy face and frame. On his appearance at the Buffalo conference he wore a full reddish mustache drooping down the sides of his thick-lipped mouth. He shaved it off on meeting Fogel and then grew it again later in the summer. He was six feet tall and his height and breadth made him look older than he was, if not wiser. For a while after his talk with Fogel he pretended to be more casual about his work, one who skirted excess and got it right. He pretended to be Fogel a bit, amusing Fogel. He had never had a disciple before and felt affection for the boy. Gary livened things up for the writer. One could see him in the distance, coming with his yellow guitar. He strummed without distinction but sang fairly well, a tenor aspiring, related to art. "Sing me 'Ochi Chornye,' Gary," Fogel said, and the youth obliged as the older man became pleasantly melancholic, thinking what if he'd had a son. Touch a hand to a guitar and Fogel had a wet eye. And Gary offered services as well as devoted attention: got books Fogel needed from the library; drove him into town when he had errands to do; could be depended on to retrieve forgotten lecture notes in his room—as if it were in compensation, though Fogel required none, for the privilege of sitting at his feet and plying him with questions about the art of fiction. Fogel, touched by his amiability, all he had yet to learn, by his own knowledge of the sadnesses of a writer's life, invited him, usually with one or another of his friends, to his room for a drink before dinner. Gary brought along a thick notebook to jot down Fogel's table talk. He showed him the first sentence he had copied down: "Imagination is not necessarily Id," causing the writer when he read it to laugh uncomfortably. Gary laughed too. Fogel thought the note taking silly but didn't object when Gary scribbled down long passages, although he doubted he had wisdom of any serious sort to offer. He was wiser in his work—one would be who revised often enough. He wished Gary would go to his books for answers to some of the questions he asked and stop treating poor Fogel like a guru.

"You can't dissect a writer to learn what writing is or entails. One learns from experience, or should. I can't teach anyone to be a writer, Gary—I've said that in my lectures. All I do here is talk about some things I've learned and hope somebody talented is listening. I always regret coming to these conferences."

"You can give insights, can't you?"

"Insights you can get from your mother."

"More specifically, if I might ask, what do you think of my writing thus far, sir?"

Fogel reflected. "Promise you have—that's all I can say now, but keep working."

"What should I work most for?"

"Search possibility in and out and beyond the fact. I have the impression when I read your stories—the two in Buffalo and the one you've given me here—that you remember or research too much. Memory is an ingredient, Gary, not the whole stew; and don't make the error some do of living life as though it were a future fiction. Invent, my boy."

"I'll certainly try, Mr. Fogel." He seemed worried.

Fogel lectured four mornings a week at eight-thirty so he could spend the rest of the day at work. His large bright room in a guest house close to a pine grove, whose fragrance he breathed as he wrote on a cracked table by a curtained window, was comfortable even on hot afternoons. He worked every day, half day on Sundays, quitting as a rule around four; then soaked in a smallish stained tub, dressed leisurely, whistling through his teeth, in a white flannel suit fifteen years in service, and waited, holding a book before his nose, for someone to come for a drink. During the last week of the White Mountain conference he saw Gary each night. Sometimes they drove to a movie in town, or walked after supper along a path by a stream, the youth stopping to jot down in his notebook sentences given off by Fogel, chaff as well as grain. They went on until the mosquitoes thickened or Fogel's limp began to limp. He wore a Panama hat, slightly yellowed, and white shoes he whitened daily, one with a higher heel than the other. Fogel's pouched dark eyes, even as he spoke animatedly, were contemplative, and he listened with care to Gary though he didn't always hear. In the last year or two he had lost weight and his white suit hung on his shoulders. He looked small by Gary's side, although he was shorter by only three inches. And once the youth, in a burst of vitality or affection, his one imaginative act of the summer, lifted Fogel at the hips and held him breathless in the air. The writer gazed into Gary's gold-flecked eyes; that he found them doorless to the self filled him with remorse.

Or Gary drove them in his noisy Peugeot to a small piano-playing bar by a crossroads several miles the other side of town, sometimes in the company of one or two students, occasionally a colleague but usually students; and this made it a fuller pleasure because Fogel enjoyed being with women. Gary, who had a talent for acquiring pretty girls, one night brought along one of the loveliest Fogel had ever seen. The girl, about twenty-five, with streaked dyed-blond and dark hair wore a red dress on her long-waisted body, the breasts ample, loose, her buttocks shapely, sweet. A rare find indeed; but the youth, senseless, sullen, or stoned, gave her scant attention. He glanced at her once in a while as if trying to remember where he had met her. Sad-eyed, she drank Scotch on the rocks, gnawing her lip as she watched his eyes roving over the dancers on the floor. Too bad she doesn't know how much I appreciate her, Fogel mused.

Where does he get so many attractive girls—he had been equally effective in Buffalo—and why doesn't he bring the same one two nights running? This blessed creature in red would last me half a lifetime. The youth's taste in women could not be faulted—but he seemed, after a short time, unmoved by them and yawned openly, although it was rumored he enjoyed an active heterosexual life. He has so many and goes through them so quickly—where does he think one learns longing? Where does poetry come from? She's too good for him, he thought, not knowing exactly why, unless she was good for *him*. Ah youth, ah summer. Once again he seriously considered the possibility of marriage. After all, how old is forty-six—not, in any case, *old*. A good twenty-five or thirty years to go, enough to raise a family.

On what?

For his companion Fogel had asked along a schoolteacher from his class, a Miss Rudel from Manhattan, unmarried but not lacking a sense of humor; nor did she take her dabbling in fiction seriously, a pleasant change from the desperate ladies who haunted the conference. But he looked her over and found her wanting, then found himself wanting.

Perhaps because the evening had acquired a sexual tone he remembered Lucy Matthews, a desperate writer presently attending his lectures. About a week ago, after going through a shoe box full of exasperating stories she had left with him, representing the past year's work, he had told her bluntly, "Miss Matthews, let's not pretend that writing is a substitute for talent." And when she quietly gasped, cracking the knuckles of one hand, then of the other, he went on: "If you are out to save your soul, there are better ways."

The lady gazed bleakly at Fogel; a slim woman with fair figure, tense neck, and anxious eyes.

"But, Mr. Fogel, how does one go about finding out the extent of her talent? Some of my former professors told me I write capable stories, yet you seem to think I'm hopeless." Tears brimmed in her eyes.

Fogel was about to soften his judgment but warned himself it would be less than honest to encourage her. She was from Cedar Falls and this was her fourth conference of the summer. He vowed again to give them up forever.

Lucy Matthews plucked a Kleenex out of her handbag and quietly cried, waiting for perhaps a good word, but the writer, sitting in silence, had none to offer. She got up and hurriedly left the office.

But at ten o'clock that night, dressed in a taffeta party dress, her hair brushed into a bright sheen, briskly perfumed, Lucy tapped on Fogel's house door. Accepting his surprised invitation to enter, after three silent sips of bourbon and water, she lifted her noisy dress over her head and stood there naked.

"Mr. Fogel," she whispered passionately, "you aren't afraid to tell the truth. Your work represents art. I feel that if I could hold you in my arms I would be close to both—art and truth."

"It just isn't so," Fogel replied as he fought off the feeling that he had stepped into a Sherwood Anderson story. "I would like to sleep with you, frankly, but not for the reasons stated. If you had said, 'Fogel, you may be an odd duck but you've aroused me tonight and I would gladly go to bed with you'—could you say that?"

"If you prefer fellation—" Lucy whispered tensely.

"Thank you kindly," he said with tenderness, "I prefer the embrace of a woman. Would you care to answer my question?"

Shivering around the shoulders, Lucy Matthews came to her finest moment at writing conferences.

"I can't truly say so."

"Ah, too bad," Fogel sighed. "Anyway, I'm privileged you saw fit to undress in my presence."

She slipped on the dress at her feet and departed. Fogel especially regretted the loss because the only woman he had slept with that summer, a young chambermaid in a Buffalo hotel he had stayed at in June, had hurt him dreadfully.

"Are you dreaming about something, Mr. Fogel?" Gary asked.

"Only vaguely," Fogel replied.

"An idea for a story, I bet?"

"It may come to that."

When the conference ended, Gary, waiting outside the lecture barn to take Fogel to the train, asked him, "Will I ever be a good writer, do you think, Mr. Fogel?"

"It depends on commitment. You'll have to prove yourself."

"I will if you have faith in me."

"Even if I have no faith in you. Who is Eli Fogel, after all, but a man trying to make his own way through the woods."

Fogel smiled at the youth and, though not knowing exactly why, felt he had to say, "One must grow spirit, Gary."

The youth blinked in the strong sunlight.

"I'm glad we're both writers, Mr. Fogel."

*   *   *

The next spring, a wet springtime, Fogel, wandering in a damp hat and coat in the periodical room of the New York Public Library, without forethought plucked off the shelf a college magazine and came upon Gary Simson in the table of contents, as the author of a story called "Travails of a Writer." He was surprised because they were in correspondence and Gary hadn't told him he had published his first story. Maybe it wasn't such a good one? Reading it quickly Fogel found it wasn't; but that wasn't why Gary hadn't mentioned it. The reason depressed him.

The story concerned a Mr. L. E. Vogel, a sarcastic, self-centered, although not thoroughly bad-natured middle-aged writer with a clubfoot, who wore in summertime a white suit, the pants of which dripped over his heels, an old-fashioned straw hat, and the same yellow knitted necktie, day after day. He was a short man with a loud laugh that embarrassed him, and he walked a good deal though he limped. One summer he had taught at a writers' conference in Syracuse, New York. There the writer had fallen for a college girl chambermaid at the hotel he had lived in during his two weeks of lecturing. She had slept with him for kicks after learning he had published two novels. Once was enough for her, but Vogel, having tasted young flesh, was hooked hard. He fell in love with the girl, constantly sought her presence—a blond tease of twenty—with solemn offers of marriage, until she became sick of him. To get him off her back she arranged with a boyfriend to enter his room with a passkey and give him a bad time. Vogel, soaking in his afternoon tub, heard someone shout, "Fire, everybody out!" He climbed out of the bath, was grabbed by the arm and shoved into the hall by the boyfriend, who pulled the door shut after him and disappeared down the stairs. The naked writer wandered like a half-drowned animal in the huge hotel hall, knocking at doors that were slammed in his face, until he found an elderly lady who handed him a blanket to cover himself and phoned the manager for a key to his room. Vogel, heartbroken that the girl had done this to him—he understood at once she had contrived the plot and for what reason—packed and left Syracuse a full week before the conference had ended.

"Poor Vogel swore off love to keep on writing."

End of "Travails of a Writer."

Arriving home, Eli Fogel dashed a white pitcher of daffodils to the kitchen floor, and kicked with his bad leg at the shards and flowers.

"Swine! Have I taught you nothing?"

Incensed, humiliated to the hilt (the story revived the memory; he suffered from both), Fogel, in a rare rage, cursed out Gary, wished on him a terrifying punishment. But reason prevailed and he wrote him, instead, a scalding letter.

Where had he got the story? Probably it was rife as gossip. He pictured the girl and her friend regaling all who would hear, screaming over the part where the hairy-chested satyr wanders in a wet daze in the hotel hallway. Gary might easily have heard it from them or friends of theirs. Or perhaps he had slept with the girl and she had confided it directly. Good God, had *he* put her up to it? No, probably not.

Why, then, had he written it? Why hadn't he spared Fogel this mortification, though it was obvious he had not expected him to find the story and read it? That wasn't the point; the point was he had not refrained—out of friendship—from writing it. So much for friendship. He detested the thought that the boy had sucked up to him all summer to collect facts for the piece. Or possibly he had heard the story and been tempted by it, Fogel hoped, *after* the White Mountain conference. He had probably harbored the "idea" during the summer but did not decide to write it until he got back to San Francisco, where he went to college. All he had to do was salt the anecdote with some details of appearance, a few mannerisms, and the tale was as good as written, acceptable at once for publication in the college quarterly. Maybe Gary had thought of it as a sort of homage: this good writer I know portrayed as human being. He hadn't been able to resist. After a summer of too much talk of writing he had felt the necessity of having something immediately in print, no matter what. He had got it down on paper almost wholly as received. It invented nothing, in essence a memoir once removed.

When he felt he had regained objectivity, Fogel sat at his desk facing the landlady's garden behind the house and, dipping his fountain pen into black ink, began a letter to Gary: "I congratulate you on the publication of your first story although I cannot rejoice in it."

He tore that up and on another sheet wrote:

> Your story, as is, signified little and one wonders why it was written. Perhaps it represents the desperate act of one determined to break into print without the patience, the art—ultimately—to transmute a piece of gossip into a fiction; and in the process, incidentally, betraying a friend. If this poor thing indicates the force and depth of your imagination, I suggest you give up writing.
> L. E. Vogel, indeed! Yours truly, Eli Fogel.
> P.S. Look up "travail." It's an experience not easy to come by.

After sealing the letter he didn't send it. We all have our hang-ups, Fogel thought. Besides, life isn't that long. He tore it up and sent a Picasso postcard instead, a woman with six faces sitting on a chamber pot.

Dear Gary, I read your story in *SF Unicorn*. I wish I could say it was a good story, but it isn't, not so good as the ones I read last summer that you couldn't get published. I wish I had had your opportunity to write about L. E. Vogel; I would have done him justice.

He received, airmail, a four-page, single-spaced letter from Gary.

To tell the honest truth I *was* kind of anxious about my writing. I couldn't finish a story for months after the W.M. conference, and without doubt took the easy way out. All I can say is I hope you will forgive and forget. Once I reread the story in the *Unicorn* I prayed that you wouldn't see it. If I have hurt our friendship, which I truly hope I haven't, I am willing to try to do better if you have the patience. I would like to be a better friend.

Also I recently read in an article about Thomas Wolfe that he said it was all right to write about other people you might know, but it's wrong to include their address and phone number. As you know, Mr. Fogel, I have a lot to learn about writing, that's for sure. As for what you could have done with the same material, please don't compare your magnificent powers with my poor ones.

I enclose a picture of my latest bride as well as one of myself.

In the envelope was an underexposed snapshot of a long-haired brunette in briefest bikini, sitting on a blanket by Gary's yellow guitar, on a California beach. Resting back on her arms, she stared distantly, certainly not happily, at the birdie; lost, as it were, to time and tide. She looked worn, cheerless, as though she had been had, and was, in her own mind, past having. She seemed to understand what she had experienced. She was, for Fogel, so true, lovely, possible, present, so beautifully formed, that he thought of her as a work of art and audibly sighed.

Gary, the hero himself of the other, overexposed colored snap, probably taken by the discontented lady herself, wore white bathing trunks, prominent genitals, and a handsome sunburned body; spare, dark, leaner than he was when Fogel had seen him last. His eyes staring blankly at the camera contradicted the smile on his face. Perhaps he was not looking at the unhappy lady but through her. The youth darkened in bright sunlight as the beholder beheld, or was Fogel prejudiced?

On the back of his picture Gary had scrawled, "You may not recognize me so well. I've changed, I've lost weight."

"What do you mean 'bride'?" Fogel wrote in the postscript of his reply forgiving Gary. He had urged patience in writing. "If you push time, time pushes you. One has less control."

"Not in the married sense," Gary explained when he appeared in person in Fogel's flat, in dungaree jacket and field boots, wearing a six-day growth of beard after driving practically nonstop across the country in a new secondhand station wagon, during the winter recess. He had brought his guitar and played "Ochi Chornye" for Fogel.

They were at first stiff with each other. Fogel, despite goodwill, felt distaste for the youth, but by degrees relented and they talked exhaustively. The older man had, more than once, to set aside the image of himself dripping along the hotel hallway before he could renew affection for Gary. The guitar helped. His singing sometimes brought tears to the eyes. Ah, the human voice, nothing like it for celebrating or lamenting life. I must have misjudged his capacity to relate, or else he does it better. And why should I bear him a grudge for his errors, considering those I make myself?

It was therefore freer talk than they had engaged in last summer, as though between equals, about many more interesting matters than when Gary was hastily taking it down to preserve for humanity. Yet as they conversed, particularly when Fogel spoke of writing, the youth's fingers twitched as though he were recording the older man's remarks in an invisible notebook, causing him later to say, "Don't worry if you can't remember word for word, Gary. Have you read Proust? Even when he remembers he invents."

"Not as of yet, but he's on my list."

There was still something naïve about him, though he was bright enough and gave the impression that he had experienced more than one ordinarily would have at his age. Possibly this was an effect of the size of his corpus, plenty of room to stuff in experience. Fogel was at the point of asking what women meant to him, but it was a foolish question so he refrained; Gary was young, let him find his way. Fogel would not want to be that young again.

The youth remained for three days in the small guest room in

Fogel's rent-controlled flat in the three-story brick house on West Ninth Street. Gary one night invited over some friends, Fogel adding two or three former students, including Miss Rudel. A noisy crowded party flowered, especially pleasurable to Fogel when Gary sang, strumming his guitar, and a young man with a thin beard and hair to his shoulders accompanied him on a recorder. Marvelous combinations, inventions, the new youth dreamed up. The guests played records they had brought along and danced. A girl who smelled heavily of pot, dancing barefoot, kissed Fogel and drew him into the circle of her gyrations. The steps weren't so hard, he decided, really they were no steps, so he pulled off his shoes and danced in his black socks, his limp as though choreographed in. At any rate, no one seemed to notice and Fogel had an enjoyable time. He again felt grateful to the youth for lifting him, almost against his will, out of his solitude.

On the morning he left, Gary, bathed, shaved, fragrantly lotioned, in white T-shirt and clean cords, tossed a duffel bag into the station wagon and stood talking on the lowest stoop step with Fogel, who had come out to see him off. The writer sensed Gary was leading up to something, although he was ostensibly saying goodbye. After some introductory noises the youth apologized for bringing "this" up but he had a request to make, if Fogel didn't mind. Fogel, after momentary hesitation, didn't mind. Gary said he was applying for admission to one or two writing centers in universities on the West Coast and he sort of hoped Fogel would write him a letter of recommendation. Maybe two.

"I don't see why not."

"Hey thanks, Mr. Fogel, and I don't want to bug you but I hope you won't mind if I put your name down as a reference on other applications now and then?"

"What for, Gary? Remember, I'm a working writer." He felt momentarily uneasy, as though he were being asked to extend credit beyond credit earned.

"I promise I'll keep it to the barest minimum. Just if I apply for a fellowship to help me out financially, or something like that."

"That seems all right. I'll consider each request on its merits."

"That's exactly what I want you to do, Mr. Fogel."

Before the youth drove off, Fogel was moved to ask him why he wanted to be a writer.

"To express myself as I am and also create art," Gary quickly replied. "To convey my experience so that I become part of my readers' experience, so, as you might say, neither of us is alone."

Fogel nodded.

"Why are you writing?"

"Because it's in me to write. Because I can't not write." Fogel laughed embarrassedly.

"That doesn't contradict what I said."

"I wouldn't want to contradict it." He did not say Gary remembered his summer notes perhaps better than he knew.

The youth thrust forth his hand impulsively. "I'm grateful for your friendship as well as hospitality, Mr. Fogel."

"Call me Eli if you like."

"I'll certainly try," Gary said huskily.

Several months later he wrote from the Coast: "Is morality a necessary part of fiction? I mean, does it have to be? A girl I go with here said it does. I would like to have your opinion. Fondly, Gary."

"It is as it becomes aesthetic," Fogel replied, wondering if the girl was the brunette in the bikini. "Another way to put it is that nothing that is art is merely moral."

"I guess what I meant to ask," Gary wrote, "is does the artist *have* to be moral?"

"Neither the artist nor his work."

"Thanks for being so frank, Mr. Fogel."

In rereading these letters before filing them, Fogel noticed that Gary always addressed him by his last name.

Better that way.

In two years Fogel lost four pounds and wrote seventy more pages of his novel. He had hoped to write one hundred and fifty pages but had slowed down. Perfection comes hard to an imperfectionist. He had visions of himself dying before the book was completed. It was a terrible thought: Fogel seated at the table, staring at his manuscript, pen in hand, the page ending in a blot. He had been blocked several months last fall and winter but slowly wrote himself out of it. Afterward he loved the world a bit better.

He hadn't seen Gary during this time, though they still corre-
sponded. Fogel left his letters lying around unopened for months
before answering them. The youth had written in November that
he was driving East before Christmas and could he call on Fogel?
He had answered better not until the writing was going well once
more. Gary then wrote, "We must have some kind of mutual ESP,
because the same thing has happened to me. I mean it's mostly
because I have been uptight about future worries after I get my
M.F.A. in June, especially money worries. Otherwise I've had two
stories published, as you know, in the last year." (Both troubled
Fogel: unrisen loaves. Gary said they had been "definitely invented." One was about a sex-starved man and the other about a
sex-starved woman.) "And I've been thinking ahead because I want
to get to work on a novel and wonder if you would like to rec-
ommend me to the MacDowell Colony for a six months' stay so I
can get started on it?"

Fogel wrote: "Gary, I've recommended you for everything in
sight because I thought you ought to have a chance to prove yourself. But I'd be less than honest if I didn't admit I've been doing
it uneasily the last one or two times because there's such a thing
as overextending goodwill. I'll think it over if you can send me
something really good in the way of a fiction, either a new story
or chapter or two of your novel."

He got in reply, hastily, Gary. The youth appeared several days
later, as Fogel was in the street on his way to the liquor store on
the corner. He heard the bleat of a horn, a dark green microbus
drew up to the curb, and Gary Simson hopped out of the door and
pumped the writer's hand.

"I have this new story for you." He held up a black dispatch
case.

Though he smiled broadly he looked as though he hadn't slept
for a week. His face was worn, eyes hardened, as if something in
his nature had deepened. He was on the verge of desperate, Fogel
thought.

"I'm sorry I couldn't warn you but I came up from the Coast
suddenly, and as you know, you have no phone." He paused,

suffering his usual opening stiffness although Fogel returned his smile.

"Have you had supper, Gary?"

"Not as of yet."

"We'll go upstairs and have a bit."

"Fantastic," Gary said. "And it's a pleasure to see you after all this time gone. You're looking swell but a little thin and pasty-faced."

"Vicissitudes, Gary. Not to mention endless labor, which is the only way I seem able to survive. One ought to be careful how he creates his life's order."

He was about to suggest calling a few people for a party but thought it premature.

They ate a simple meal. Fogel cooked a tasty soufflé. There was salad, Italian bread, and wine. Both ate hungrily and smoked Gary's cigars over coffee.

In Fogel's study the youth snapped open the dispatch case lock he had been fiddling with—too bad it wasn't the guitar—and they were at once alertly attentive to each other. Fogel detected an odor of sweat and Gary proved it by wiping his face, then twice around the flushed neck with his handkerchief.

"This is the first draft of a story I did the other day, my first in months. As I wrote you in my letter, I just wasn't making the scene for a while. I got the idea for this story the night before last. I was planning to drop in on you yesterday but instead spent the day on twenty cups of coffee in this girl's room while she was out working, and finally knocked off the story. It feels good to me. Would you care to hear it, Mr. Fogel?"

"A first draft?" asked Fogel in disappointment. "Why don't you finish it and let me read it then?"

"I would certainly do that if the closing date for my application wasn't hitting me in the eye this coming Monday. I'd really like to work on it another week at the very least, and the only reason I suggest reading it to you now is so you will have a quick idea of the merits of what I've done with it so far."

"Well, then let me read it myself," Fogel said. "I get more out of it that way."

"My typing isn't so hot, as you well know, and it'll be hard for you to make out the corrections in my lousy handwriting. I'd better read it to you."

Fogel nodded, removing his shoes to ease his feet. So did Gary. He sat cross-legged on the couch in tennis socks, holding his papers. Fogel, rocking slowly in his rocker, gazed melancholically at the pile of his own manuscript on the writing table. Remembering his youthful aspirations, the writer wanted Gary's story to be good.

The youth brushed his lips with a wet thumb. "I haven't got a sure title yet but I was thinking of calling it 'Three Go Down.'" He began to read and Fogel's rocker stopped creaking.

The narrator of the story was George, a graduate student at Stanford who had driven to New York and, having nothing to do one spring day, had looked up Connie, who had been in love with him last summer. She lived in the West Village, in an apartment with two friends, Grace and Buffy, pretty girls; and soon George, while eating with them, on learning that none of the girls was going out that night, had decided to sleep with each of them, one after the other. He wanted it to be a test of himself. Connie, he figured, he had been in before and knew the way back. Grace was uneasy when he looked her over, which he thought of as an advantage. Buffy, the best looking of the lot, seemed a cool drink of water, aloof or pretending it, maybe impossible, but he wouldn't think of her as yet. It was a long night and there was no hurry.

George invited Connie for a walk and later bought her a drink in a bar on Sullivan Street. While they were at the bar he told her he hadn't forgotten last summer in Bloomington, Indiana. Connie called him a shit for bringing it up. George, after saying nothing, said it had been one of the best summers of his life. He then became deeply silent. They had a second drink and in the street she softened to him and walked close by his side.

It was a warm airy evening and they wandered in the Village streets. George said it was his impression that Buffy was a pothead, but Connie said it was ridiculous, Buffy was the really stable one of them. She worked for a youth opportunity program as secretary in charge of anything. Her father had been killed in the Korean

War and she was devoted to her widowed mother and two younger sisters in Spokane.

"What about Grace?"

Connie admitted that Buffy had a lot more patience with Grace than she had. Grace's problems, though she didn't say what they were, were more than Connie cared to contend with. "Even when she has a good time she comes home in a funk and pulls out some more of her eyelashes, one by one, while sitting at the mirror."

After a while George told Connie that he had loved her last summer but hadn't been willing to admit it to himself. His father had been hooked into an early marriage and he didn't want that to happen to him; the old man had regretted it all his life. Connie again called him a shit but let him kiss her when he wanted to.

When she said she would sleep with him George said there was a mattress in his bus and why bother going upstairs? Connie laughed and said she had never made love in a microbus but was willing to try if he parked in a quiet, private place.

In the bus he gave it to her the way he remembered she liked it.

Connie went to bed with a headache. She had said he could stay in the living room till morning and no later. "That's our rule and Buffy doesn't like it if we break it." George sat on the sofa, reading a magazine for a while, then looked into Grace's room. Her door was open and he went in without knocking. Most of Grace's eyelashes were gone. She wore a terry-cloth robe and said she didn't mind talking to George so long as he kept his machismo in his pants. She wasn't careful with her robe and he saw her large bruised breasts through the nightgown.

That's her bag, George thought.

He started talking sex with her and told her about some girlfriends he had in California who had given it to him in various interesting ways. She listened with slack mouth and uneasy eyes while drying her hair with a large towel.

George asked her where the gin was, he would make the drinks. She said she didn't want a drink. He asked her if she wanted to split a joint.

"I'm not interested," Grace said.

"What interests you?" George said.

"I'll bet you slept with Connie."

"Why don't you ask her?"

He then said he knew what interested her. George got up, and though she grabbed his hands, he freed one, forced her chin up, and French-kissed her. She shoved him away, her robe falling open. George, pretending he was a prizefighter, went into a crouch, ducked, then feinted with his left. With his right hand he grabbed her breast and twisted hard. Grace gasped and was about to cry. Instead, after wavering hesitations, searching his face, she swung to him, her eyes unfocused, grinning. When they kissed she bit his lip. George punched her between the legs. Grace came close again with a quiet moan. He began to pull off her robe but she caught his hands, then shut the door.

"Not here," Grace whispered.

"Put on your dress and meet me downstairs."

She came down in a green dress, wearing nothing underneath but her bruises. Grace stepped into the bus. "I love you," she said.

George handed her his belt and said she could hit him a few whacks but not too hard.

Buffy had been reading in bed. She said come in when he knocked but, seeing who it was, drew up her legs and asked him not to since it was late and she had to go to work in the morning. George offered her one of the joints he had got from Grace but Buffy said to cool it. He asked her if she would mind talking for a few minutes, then he'd go. She said she would mind. George then told her he was leaving for the war in the morning.

She asked him why was that, they were sending few draftees in.

"My draft board was saving me up. They were sore at all the postponements I had requested."

"Why don't you refuse to serve?"

He said he had been a physical coward all his life and it was time to get over it. She called it a useless, unjust war, but George said you only died once. He offered her the joint again and she lit up. Buffy smoked for a few minutes, then said it wasn't turning her on.

"Nor me either," George admitted. "Why don't you get dressed and come out for a walk? It's a nice night."

When she asked him hadn't he done enough walking with Connie and Grace, he told her she was the one who really aroused him.

"Before I left I wanted to tell you."

"I must be five years older than you."

"That doesn't change my feelings."

"What malarkey," she said.

George said goodbye. He thanked her for the supper and for talking to him. "See you after the war."

"Connie said you were staying here tonight."

He said he would be sleeping in his bus downstairs. He had to be at Fort Dix at seven, and before that had to deliver the bus to a friend who would drive him to Jersey, then keep it for him while he was away. He was leaving at 5:00 a.m., and no sense waking everybody in the house.

"Are you afraid of death?" Buffy asked him.

"Who wouldn't be?"

He shut her door and went down the stairs. In the bus George, plugging in the shaver, began to shave for the morning. There was a tap on the door. It was Buffy in skirt and sweater, ready for a walk. Her hair in a coil at the neck fell over her right breast. She wore a golden bracelet high up on her left arm.

When they returned it was still a warm breezy night. After talking quietly awhile they entered the microbus. George plowed her three times and the third time she finally came.

As they lay on the narrow mattress, smoking, she asked him whether he had also had Connie and Grace that night, and George admitted it.

"Three go down."

That was the story.

What have I fostered? Fogel thought.

*   *   *

"Ah," said the writer, his bad leg trembling. He stepped into his slippers to pour himself a drink and was angered by the empty bourbon bottle. He drank a long unsatisfactory glass of water.

Gary had finished strong and was at the edge of the couch, his feet turned inward. He was observing his tennis socks, occasionally darting glances at Fogel.

"You like?" he finally had to ask. "I don't mind if you slog it to me so long as it's the truth."

"I guess Connie's right in characterizing George as a shit?"

"Up to a point, an anti-hero is an anti-hero," George explained defensively. "What the story means is that's how the crow flies, or words of that effect. In other words, c'est la vie. But how do you like it is what I want to know."

Fogel sat motionless in his rocker.

"I wish you were more than a walking tape recorder of your personal experiences, Gary."

He did not accuse him of having lived the experience to record it, though the thought was distastefully on his mind.

Gary laced up his shoes, a glaze of annoyance in his eyes.

"I don't see what's so bad about that. You yourself once said that story material has no pedigree of any kind. You told me it depends on what the writer does with it."

"That's right," said Fogel. "To be honest, I would have to say that, all in all, this story seems an improvement over your last two. It's a compelling narrative."

"Well, that's a lot better, Mr. Fogel."

"As for the recommendation, I want to think about it. I'm not sure."

Gary rose, waving both arms. "Jesus, Mr. Fogel, give me a break. What am I going to live on for the next year? I have no father who left *me* a trust fund of five thousand bucks a year as you told me your father did for you."

"You have me there," said Fogel, rising from the rocker. "I've got to have a drink. I was on my way to the liquor store when you drove up."

Gary offered to go for the bottle but Fogel wouldn't hear of it.

The writer limped down the stairs in his slippers. At the curb stood the green bus. The sight of it nauseated him.

He's no friend of mine.

He went to the corner and on an impulse returned to the bus

to try the door handle. The door was open. The back seats had been removed and on the floor lay a battered pink-and-gray thin-striped mattress.

In the liquor store Fogel bought a fifth of bourbon. Stepping into Gary's bus he pulled the door shut. The curtains were drawn. He did not flick on the light.

As he opened the whiskey bottle, Fogel, as though surprised by what he was about to do, told himself, "I have the better imagination."

On his knees, using a small silver penknife he kept to sharpen pencils, the writer thoroughly slashed the mattress and sloshed whiskey over it. He lit the soaked cotton batting with several matches. The mattress stank as it burned with a blue flame.

Fogel then went upstairs and told Gary he had entered his story to give it a more judicious ending.

After the firemen had extinguished the blaze and the youth had driven off in his smoky bus, the writer took his letters out of the folder in his files and tore them up.

He got one last communication from Gary, enclosing a magazine with the published "Three Go Down" much as he had written it in the first draft. Amid the pages he had inserted some leaves of poison ivy.

1968

A Wig

IDA WAS AN ENERGETIC, competent woman of fifty, healthy, still attractive. Thinking of herself, she touched her short hair. What's fifty? One more than forty-nine. She had been married at twenty and had a daughter, Amy, who was twenty-eight and not a satisfied person. Of satisfying, Ida thought: she has no serious commitment. She wanders in her life. From childhood she has wandered off the track, where I can't begin to predict. Amy had recently left the man she was living with, in his apartment, and was again back at home. "He doesn't connect," Amy said. "Why should it take you two years to learn such a basic thing?" Ida asked. "I'm a slow learner," Amy said. "I learn slowly." She worked for an importer who thought highly of her though she wouldn't sleep with him.

As Amy walked out of the room where she had stood talking with her mother, she stopped to arrange some flowers in a vase, six tight roses a woman friend had sent her on her birthday, a week ago. Amy deeply breathed in the decaying fragrance, then shut her door. Ida was a widow who worked three days a week in a sweater boutique. While talking to Amy she had been thinking about her hair. She doubted that Amy noticed how seriously she was worried; or if she did, that it moved her.

When she was a young woman, Ida, for many years, had worn a tight bun held together by three celluloid hairpins. Martin, her husband, who was later to fall dead of a heart attack, liked buns and topknots. "They are sane yet sexy," he said. Ida wore her bun until she began to lose hair in her mid-forties. She noticed the hair coming loose when she brushed it with her ivory-topped brush. One day the increasing number of long hairs left in the comb frightened her. And when she examined her hairline in the mirror, it seemed to Ida that her temples were practically bare.

"I think the tight bun contributes to my loss of hair," she told Martin. "Maybe I ought to get rid of it?"

"Nonsense," he had said. "If anything, the cause would be hormonal."

"So what would you advise me to do?" Ida looked up at him uneasily. He was a wiry man with wavy, graying hair and a strong neck.

"In the first place, don't wash it so often. You wash it too often."

"My hair has always been oily. I have to shampoo it at least twice a week."

"Less often," Martin advised, "take my tip."

"Martin, I am very afraid."

"You don't have to be," he said, "it's a common occurrence."

One day, while walking on Third Avenue, Ida had passed a wigmaker's shop and peered into the window. There were men's and women's wigs on abstract, elegant wooden heads. One or two were reasonably attractive; most were not.

How artificial they are, Ida thought. I could never wear such a thing.

She felt for the wigs a mild hatred she tied up with the fear of losing her hair. If I buy a wig, people will know why. It's none of their business.

Ida continued her brisk walk on Third Avenue. Although it was midsummer, she stepped into a hat shop and bought herself a fall hat, a wide-brimmed felt with a narrow, bright green ribbon. Amy had green eyes.

*   *   *

One morning after Ida had washed her hair in the bathroom sink, and a wet, coiled mass of it slid down the drain, she was shocked and felt faint. After she had dried her hair, as she gently combed it, close to the mirror, she was greatly concerned by the sight of her pink scalp more than ever visible on top of her head. But Martin, after inspecting it, had doubted it was all that noticeable. Of course her hair was thinner than it had been—whose wasn't?—but he said he noticed nothing unusual, especially now that she had cut her hair and was wearing bangs. Ida wore a short, swirled haircut. She shampooed her hair less frequently.

And she went to a dermatologist, who prescribed an emulsion he had concocted, with alcohol, distilled water, and some drops of castor oil, which she was to shake well before applying. He instructed her to rub the mixture into her scalp with a piece of cotton. "That'll stir it up." The dermatologist had first suggested an estrogen salve applied topically, but Ida said she didn't care for estrogen.

"This salve does no harm to women," the doctor said, "although I understand it might shrink a man's testicles."

"If it can shrink a man's testicles, I'd rather not try it," she said. He gave her the emulsion.

Ida would part a strand of hair and gently brush her scalp with the emulsion-soaked cotton; then she would part another strand and gently brush there. Whatever she tried didn't do much good, and her scalp shone through her thinning hair like a dim moon in a stringy dark cloud. She hated to look at herself, she hated to think.

"Martin, if I lose my hair I will lose my femininity."

"Since when?"

"What shall I do?" she begged.

Martin thought. "Why don't you consider another doctor? This guy is too much a salesman. I still think it could be caused by a scalp ailment or some such condition. Cure the scalp and it slows down the loss of hair."

"No matter how I treat the scalp, with or without medication, nothing gets better."

"What do you think caused it?" Martin said. "Some kind of trauma either psychic or physical?"

"It could be hereditary," Ida answered. "I might have my father's scalp."

"Your father had a full head of hair when I first met him—a shock of hair, I would call it."

"Not when he was my age, he was already losing it."

"He was catting around at that age," Martin said. "He was some boy. Nothing could stop him, hair or no hair."

"I'll bet you envy him," Ida said, "or you wouldn't bring that up at this particular time."

"Who I envy or don't envy let's not talk about," he replied. "Let's not get into that realm of experience, or it becomes a different card game."

"I bet you wish you were in that realm of experience. I sometimes feel you envy Amy her odd life."

"Let's not get into that either," Martin insisted. "It doesn't pay."

"What *can* we talk about?" Ida complained.

"We talk about your hair, don't we?"

"I would rather not," she said.

The next day she visited another skin man, who advised her to give up brushing her hair or rubbing anything into her scalp. "Don't stress your hair," he advised. "At the most, you could have it puffed up once in a while, or maybe take a permanent to give it body, but don't as a rule stress it. Also put away your brush and use only a wide-toothed comb, and I will prescribe some moderate doses of vitamins that might help. I can't guarantee it."

"I doubt if that's going to do much good," Ida said when she arrived home.

"How would you know until you've tried it?" Amy asked.

"Nobody has to try everything," Ida said. "Some things you know about without having to try them. You have common sense."

"Look," said Martin, "let's not kid ourselves. If the vitamins don't do anything for you, then you ought to have yourself fitted for a wig or wiglet. It's no sin. They're popular with a lot of people nowadays. If I can wear false teeth, you can wear a wig."

"I hate to," she confessed. "I've tried some on and they burden my head."

"You burden your head," Amy said.

"Amy," said her mother, "if nothing else, then at least mercy."

Amy wandered out of the room, stopping first at the mirror to look at herself.

Martin, that evening, fell dead of a heart attack. He died on the kitchen floor. Ida wailed. Amy made choked noises of grief. Both women mourned him deeply.

*   *   *

For weeks after the funeral, Ida thought of herself vaguely. Her mind was befogged. Alternatively, she reflected intensely on her life, her eyes stinging, thinking of herself as a widow of fifty. "I am terribly worried about my life," she said aloud. Amy was not present. Ida knew she was staying in her room. "What have I done to that child?"

One morning, after studying herself in the full-length looking glass, she hurried to the wigmaker's on Third Avenue. Ida walked with dignity along the busy, sunlit street. The wig shop was called Norman: Perukier. She examined the window, wig by wig, then went determinedly inside. The wigmaker had seen her before and greeted her casually.

"Might I try on a wig or two?"

"Suit yourself."

Ida pointed to a blond wig in the window and to another, chestnut brown, on a dummy's head on a shelf, and Norman brought both to her as she sat at a three-paneled mirror.

Ida's breathing was audible. She tried on the first wig, a light, frizzy, young one. Norman fitted it on her head as if he were drawing on a cloche hat. "There," he said, stepping back. He drew a light blue comb out of his inside pocket and touched the wig here and there before stopping to admire it. "It's a charming wig."

"It feels like a tight hat," Ida said.

"It's not at all tight," Norman said. "But try this."

He handed her the other wig, a brown affair that looked like a haircut Amy used to wear before she had adopted a modified afro in college.

Norman flicked his comb at the wig, then stepped back. He too was breathing heavily, his eyes intent on hers, but Ida would not let his catch hers in the mirror; she kept her gaze on the wig.

"What is the material of this wig?" Ida asked. "It doesn't seem human hair."

"Not this particular one. It's made of Dynel fiber and doesn't frizz in heat or humidity."

"How does a person take care of it?"

"She can wash it with a mild soap in warm water and then either let it dry or blow it dry. Or if she prefers, she can give it to her hairdresser, who will wash, dry, and style it."

"Will my head perspire?"

"Not in this wig."

Ida removed the wig. "What about that black one?" she asked hesitantly. "I like the style of it."

"It's made of Korean hair."

"Real hair?"

"Yes."

"Oh," said Ida. "I don't think I'd care for Oriental hair."

"Why not, if I may ask?" Norman said.

"I can't really explain it, but I think I would feel like a stranger to myself."

"I think you are a stranger to yourself," said the wigmaker, as though he was determined to say it. "I also don't think you are interested in a wig at all. This is the third time you've come into this shop, and you make it an ordeal for all concerned. Buying a wig isn't exactly like shopping for a coffin, don't you know? Some people take a good deal of pleasure in selecting a wig, as if they were choosing a beautiful garment or a piece of jewelry."

"I am not a stranger to myself," Ida replied irritably. "All we're concerned about is a wig. I didn't come here for an amateur psychoanalysis of my personality." Her color had heightened.

"Frankly, I'd rather not do business with you," said the wigmaker. "I wouldn't care for you among my clientele."

"Tant pis pour vous," Ida said, walking out of Norman's shop.

In the street she was deeply angered. It took her five minutes to begin walking. Although the day was not cool she knotted a kerchief on her head. Ida entered a hat shop close by and bought a fuzzy purple hat.

That evening she and Amy quarreled. Amy said, as they were eating fish at supper, that she had met this guy and would be moving out in a week or two, when he returned from California.

"What guy?" snapped Ida. "Somebody that you picked up in a bar?"

"I happened to meet this man in the importing office where I work, if you must know."

Ida's voice grew softer. "Mustn't I know?"

Amy was staring above her mother's head, although there was nothing on the wall to stare at, the whites of her eyes intensely white. Ida knew this sign of Amy's disaffection but continued talking.

"Why don't you find an apartment of your own? You earn a good salary, and your father left you five thousand dollars."

"I want to save that in case of emergency."

"Tell me, Amy, what sort of future do you foresee for yourself?"

"The usual. Neither black nor white."

"How will you protect yourself alone?"

"Not necessarily by getting married. I will protect myself, myself."

"Do you ever expect to marry?"

"When it becomes a viable option."

"What do you mean option, don't you want to have children?"

"I may someday want to."

"You are now twenty-eight. How much longer have you got?"

"I'm twenty-eight and should have at least ten years. Some women bear children at forty."

"I hope," said Ida, "I hope you have ten years, Amy, I am afraid for you. My heart eats me up."

"After you it eats me up. It's an eating heart."

Ida called her daughter a nasty name, and Amy, rising, her face grim, quickly left the room. Ida felt like chasing after her with a stick, or fainting. She went to her room, her head aching, and lay on the double bed. For a while she wept.

She lay there, at length wanting to forget their quarrel. Ida rose and looked in an old photograph album to try to forget how bad she felt. Here was a picture of Martin as a young father, with a black mustache, tossing Amy as a baby in the air. Here she was as a pudgy girl of twelve, never out of jeans. Yet not till she was eighteen had she wanted her long hair cut.

Among these photographs Ida found a picture of her own mother, Mrs. Feitelson, surely no more than forty then, in her horsehair sheitel. The wig looked like a round loaf of dark bread lying on her head. Once a man had tried to mug her on the street. In the scuffle he had pulled her wig off and, when he saw her fuzzy skull, had run off without her purse. They wore those wigs, the Orthodox women, once they were married, not to attract, or distract, men other than their husbands. Sometimes they had trouble attracting their husbands.

Oh, Mama, Ida thought, did I know you? Did you know me?

What am I afraid of? she asked herself, and she thought, I am a widow and losing my looks. I am afraid of the future.

After a while she went barefoot to Amy's room and knocked on her door. I will tell her that my hair has made me very nervous. When there was no answer she opened the door a crack and said she would like to apologize. Though Amy did not respond, the light was on and Ida entered the room.

Her daughter, a slender woman in long green pajamas, lay in bed reading in the light of the wall lamp. Ida wanted to sit on the bed but felt she had no right to.

"Good night, dear Amy."

Amy did not lower her book. Ida, standing by the bedside looking at Amy, saw something she long ago had put out of her mind: that the girl's hair on top of her head was thinning and a fairly large circle of cobwebbed scalp was visible.

Amy turned a page and went on reading.

Ida, although tormented by the sight of Amy's thinning hair, did not speak of it. In the morning she left the house early and bought herself an attractive wig.

1980

Zora's Noise

HERE'S THIS UNHAPPY NOISE that upsets Zora.

She had once been Sarah. Dworkin, when he married her not long after the death of Ella, his first wife, had talked her into changing her name. She eventually forgave him. Now she felt she had always been Zora.

"Zora, we have to hurry."

"I'm coming, for godsake. I am looking for my brown gloves."

He was fifty-one, she ten years younger, an energetic, plump person with an engaging laugh and a tendency to diet unsuccessfully. She called him Dworky: an animated, reflective man, impassioned cellist—and, on inspiration, composer—with an arthritic left shoulder. He referred to it as "the shoulder I hurt when I fell in the cellar." When she was angry with him, or feeling insecure, she called him Zworkin.

*   *   *

I hear something, whatever do I hear? Zora blew her nose and listened to her ear. Is my bad ear worse? If it isn't, what are those nagging noises I've been hearing all spring? Because I listen, I hear. But what makes me listen?

The really bothersome noise had begun in April when the storm windows came off and the screens went up; yet it seemed to Zora she hadn't become conscious of its relentless quality until June, after being two months on a diet that didn't work. She was heavier

than she cared to be. She had never had children and held that
against herself too.

*   *   *

Zora settled on the day after her forty-first birthday, at the end
of June, as the time when the noise began seriously to affect her.
Maybe I wasn't listening with both my ears up to then. I had my
mind elsewhere. They say the universe exploded and we still hear
the roar and hiss of all that gas. She asked Dworky about that,
forgetting to notice—Oh, my God—that he was practicing his cello,
a darkly varnished, mellow Montagnana, "the best thing that ever
happened to me," he had once said.

No response from him but an expression of despair: as though
he had said, "I practice in the living room to keep you company,
and the next thing I know you're interfering with my music."
"Please pardon me," Zora said.

"The cello," he had defined it shortly after they met, "is an
independent small Jewish animal." And Zora had laughed as though
her heart were broken. There were two streams to her laughter—
a full-blown humorous response, plus something reserved. You
expected one and maybe got the other. Sometimes you weren't
sure what she was laughing at, if laughing. Dworkin, as he seesawed
his rosin-scented bow across the four steel strings, sometimes sang
to his cello, and the cello throatily responded. Zora and Dworkin
had met many years ago after a concert in L.A., the night he was
the guest of the Los Angeles Philharmonic.

"My cello deepens me," he had told her.

"In that case I'll marry you both."

That was how she had proposed, he told friends at their dinner
table, and everyone laughed.

*   *   *

"Do you hear that grating, sickening sound?" she had asked as
they were undressing late one summer's night in their high-
ceilinged bedroom. The wallpaper was Zora's, spread through with
white cosmos pasted over the thickly woven cerise paper selected
by Ella many years ago when she and Dworkin had first moved

into this spacious, comfortable house. "Do you like it?" he had asked Zora. "Love it." She immediately had the upstairs sun deck built, and the French doors leading to it, giving her, she said, "access to the sky."

"What sickening sound?" he asked.

"You don't hear it?"

"Not as of right now."

"Well, it isn't exactly the music of the spheres," Zora responded. She had in her twenties worked in a chemistry laboratory, though her other interests tended to be artistic.

Zora was plump, in high heels about Dworkin's height; she had firm features and almost a contralto speaking voice. She had once, at his suggestion, taken singing lessons that hadn't come to much. She was not very musical, though she loved to listen and had her own record collection. When they were first married she had worked in an art gallery in Stockbridge. They lived in Elmsville, a nearby town, in a clapboard house painted iron-gray, with marine-blue shutters. The colors were Zora's own good colors. For Ella it had been a white house with black shutters. They were both effective with their colors.

Dworkin taught the cello to students in the vicinity and at a master class in the New England Conservatory of Music at Lenox. He had stopped concertizing a year after his fall in the cellar. Zora, who was not much tempted by travel, liked to have him home regularly. "It's better for your arthritis. It's better for me."

She said, referring to the noise, "I would describe it as absolutely ongoing, with a wobbly, enervating, stinky kind of whine."

That was in July. He honestly couldn't hear it.

*   *   *

At night she woke in slow fear, intently listening.

"Suppose it goes on forever?" She felt herself shudder. It was an ugly thrumming sound shot through with a sickly whine. She listened into the distance, where it seemed to begin, and then slowly drew in her listening as though it were a line she had cast out; and now she listened closer to shore. Far or near, it amounted to the same thing. The invasive noise seemed to enter the house by way of their bedroom, even when the windows were tightly shut, as if it had seeped through the clapboard and the walls, and once or twice frighteningly seemed to metamorphose into a stranger sitting in the dark, breathing audibly and evenly, pausing between breaths.

In the near distance there was a rumble of light traffic, though she knew no traffic was going through town at this time of night. Maybe an occasional truck, changing gears. The nearer sound was Dworkin sleeping, breathing heavily, sometimes shifting into a snore.

"Dworky," she said patiently, "snoring." And Dworkin, with a rasping sigh of contrition, subsided. When she had first taken to waking him out of a sound sleep to break his snoring, he had resented it. "But your snore woke *me* out of sound sleep," Zora said. "It isn't as though I had *planned* to wake you up." He saw the justice of her remark and permitted her to wake him if he was snoring. He would stir for a minute, break his galloping rumble, then more quietly slumber.

Anyway, if someone sat there, it wasn't Dworkin making dream noises. This was a quiet presence, perhaps somebody in the Queen Anne chair by the long stained-glass window in their bedroom, Ella's invention. Someone contemplating them as they slept? Zora rose on her elbow and peered in the dark. Nothing glowed or stank, laughed madly or assaulted her. And she was once more conscious of the unhappy sound she was contending with, a vibrato hum touched with a complaining, drawn-out wail that frightened her because it made her think of the past, perhaps her childhood oozing out of the dark. Zora felt she had had such a childhood.

"Zworkin," she said in a tense whisper, "do you hear this wretched noise I've been referring to?"

"Is that a reason to wake me again, Zora, to ask such a goddamn question? Is that what we've come to at this time in our lives? Let me sleep, I beg you. I have my arthritis to think of."

"You're my husband—who else will I ask? I've already spoken to the people next door. Mrs. Duvivier says the noise originates in a paint factory across town, but of that I'm not so sure."

She spoke in hesitation and doubt. She had been an uncertain young woman when he met her. She wasn't heavy then but had always been solid, she called it, yet with a figure and a lovely face, not fat. Ella, on the other hand, who could be a restless type, was always on the slim side of slender. Both had been good wives, yet neither would have guessed the other as his wife. As Zora gained weight her uneasiness seemed to grow. Sometimes she aroused in Dworkin an anguished affection.

He leaned on his arm and strained to listen, wanting to hear what she heard. The Milky Way crackling? A great wash of cosmic static filled his ears and diminished to a hush of silence. As he listened the hum renewed itself, seeming to become an earthly buzz—a bouquet of mosquitoes and grasshoppers on the lawn, rasping away. Occasionally he heard the call of a night bird. Then the insects vanished, and he heard nothing: no more than the sound of both ears listening.

That was all, though Dworkin sometimes heard music when he woke at night—the music woke him. Lately he had heard Rostropovich, as though he were a living element of a ghostly constellation in the sky, sawing away on the D-major Haydn cello concerto. His rich cello sound might be conceived of as a pineapple, if fruit was your metaphor. Dworkin lived on fruit, but his own playing sounded more like small bittersweet apples. Listening now, he only heard the town asleep.

"I don't hear anything that could be characterized as the whining or wailing you mention," he said. "Nothing of that particular quality."

"No steady, prolonged, hateful, complaining noise?"

He listened until his ears ached. "Nothing that I hear or have heard," he confessed.

"Thank you, and good night, my dear."

"Good night," Dworkin said. "I hope we both sleep now."

"I hope so." She was still assiduously listening.

*　　*　　*

One night she rose out of dizzying sleep, seemed to contemplate her blanket in the dark, and then hopped out of bed and ran to the bathroom, where she threw up. Dworkin heard her crying as she stepped into the shower.

"Anything wrong?" he asked, popping his head into the steaming room.

"I'll be all right."

"Something I can do for you?"

"Not just now."

He returned to bed and after a few troubled minutes drew on his trousers and a shirt, and in sneakers descended into the street. Except for a barking dog at the end of the block he heard only summer night sounds, and in the distance a rumble that sounded like traffic and might be. But if he concentrated, he could make out the whomp-whomp of machinery, indeed from the direction of the paint factory on the eastern edge of town. Zora and Dworkin hadn't been inconvenienced by the factory or its legendary smells until she began to hear her noise. Still, what she said she heard she no doubt heard, though it was hard to explain anything like a whine.

He circled the house to hear if one or another noise, by some freak of acoustics, was louder on the back lawn, but it wasn't. In the rear he saw Zora on the upstairs deck, pudgy in her short nightdress, staring into the moonlit distance.

"What are you doing outside in a nightgown at this time of night, Zora?" Dworkin asked in a loud whisper.

"Listening," she said vaguely.

"At least why don't you put on a robe after your hot shower? The night air is chilly."

"Dworkin, do you hear the awful whining that I do? That's what made me puke."

"It's not whining I hear, Zora. What I hear is more like a rumble that could be originating in the paint factory. Sometimes it throbs, or whomps, or clanks a little. Maybe there's a kind of a hum, but I can't make out anything else or anything more unusual."

"No, I'm talking about a different sound than you mention. How I hate factories in neighborhoods that should be residential."

Dworkin trotted up the stairs to bed. "It would be interesting to know what some of the other people on this street besides the Duviviers have to say about the sounds you are hearing."

"I've talked to them all," said Zora, "and also to the Cunliffes and the Spinkers."

Dworkin hadn't known. "What did they say?"

"Some hear something"—she hesitated—"but different things than I do. Mrs. Spinker hears a sort of drone. Mrs. Cunliffe hears something else, but not what I hear."

"I wish I did."

"I wouldn't want to afflict you."

"Just to hear it," he said.

"Don't you believe me, Dworky?"

He nodded seriously.

"It might have to come to our moving someday," Zora reflected. "Not only is there that zonky noise I have to contend with, which made me throw up, but the price of heating oil is way up. On the other hand, the real estate market is good, and maybe we ought to put the house up for sale."

"To live where?" Dworkin asked.

She said she might like to get back to city life sometime.

"That's news to me. I assumed you didn't care for city life anymore."

"I do and I don't. I'm forty-one and have been thinking I ought to be making changes. I think I'd like to get back into the art world. I'd like to be near a neighborhood of museums and galleries. That appalling noise all summer has made me honestly wonder if we shouldn't seriously be looking into the possibility of selling this house."

"Over my dead body. I love this house," Dworkin shouted.

*   *   *

As she was preparing a salmon soufflé for supper, the newsboy came to collect for the paper. After she had glanced at the first page, Zora uttered a short cry of surprise and sat down. Dworkin, who had been practicing in the living room, quickly laid down his cello and went to her.

"Here it is in cold print," Zora, her hand on her bosom, said. "Now I know I'm not going crazy."

Dworkin took the newspaper. An article described a class-action suit organized by several citizens in the eastern part of town against the D-R Paints Company "for pollution of the atmosphere." They cited "a persistent harrowing noise," and one of the women interviewed complained of "a sneaky sound that goes up and down like a broken boat whistle. I hear it at night, but I sometimes hear it during the day."

"I feel as though I have been reprieved from being thought mad," Zora said bitterly.

"Not by me," Dworkin insisted.

"But you never seemed to hear the whine I've been hearing."

"In good faith."

Zora began slowly to waltz on the rug in the living room. Dworkin's cello was resting on the floor, and he sat down and plucked strings to her dancing.

*   *   *

One rainy night, Dworkin in pajamas, vigorously brushing his teeth, heard an insistent, weird, thrumming whistle. "What have we here?" he asked himself uneasily. He had been attempting to develop a melody that eluded him, when a keen breeze blowing from afar seemed to invade his ears. It was as though he were lying in bed and someone had poured a pitcher full of whistling wind into both ears. Dworkin forcefully shook his head to dispel the uncomfortable sound, but it refused to disappear.

As Zora lay in bed perusing the paper—she complained she couldn't concentrate well enough to read a book—Dworkin went downstairs for a coat and rain hat and stepped out-of-doors. Facing toward the D-R Paints Company, he listened intently. Though he could not see the factory in the rainy dark, a few foggy, bluish lights were visible in the east, and he felt certain the plant was in operation. The low, thrumming wind in his ears persisted. It was possible that a machine had gone haywire in the factory and was squealing like a dying animal. Possible, but not highly likely—they surely would have found some means to shut it off, he thought irritably. Could it be that the experience was, on his part, a form of autosuggestion out of empathy for Zora? He waited for the droning whine to thin out and crawl off, but nothing happened. Dworkin shook his fist at the foggy blue lights and hurried inside.

"Zora, has your noise been sounding different lately?"

"It isn't only mine," she responded. "It's other people's too. You read that yourself in the *Courier*."

"Granted, but would you say it has increased in volume lately— or otherwise changed?"

"It stays more or less the same but is still with me. I hear it plainly enough. I hear it this very minute."

"In this room, or throughout the house?"

"There's no one place. I used to feel snug here and enjoyed reading in bed. Now I'm afraid to come up at night."

Listening affirmed it overwhelmingly—the ongoing intrusive sound—her keen wail, his thrumming whine.

Dworkin then told his wife about his own unsettling experience. He described what he was presently hearing in both ears. "It's an insult, to say the least."

But Zora responded jubilantly. "At least you've heard it. Thank God."

He was about to ask why that should make her so gay but didn't.

As if he had asked, she said, "If I seem relieved, it's simply because I feel that you can now confirm that what I heard, and was trying to get you to hear, last summer, was substantial and real."

"Whoever said it wasn't?"

Her lips trembled. Dworkin observed her watching him. When he coughed she cleared her throat.

*   *   *

In the morning he went to the music room and got his cello out of its case. It was like lifting a girl gently out of bed. The music room—Ella's name for it; she had named all the rooms in the house—was a large, white-walled room with a mellow pine floor. The eastern wall was rounded, containing four windows through which the morning sun shone warmly. It was a cold room in winter, but Dworkin had installed a wood stove. Here he practiced, composed, sometimes taught. After nervously tuning up he began the first bars of the Prelude to the Bach Unaccompanied D-minor Suite. He had played it in his sleep last night.

Dworkin crouched over the cello, playing somberly, slowly, drawing the sensuous melody out of his instrument. He played the Bach as though pleading with God. He speaks as a man stating his fate. He says it quietly and, as he plays, deepens the argument. He sings now, almost basso, as though he were someone imprisoned in a well singing to a circle of blue sky.

The music ceased. Dworkin, with bowed head, listened. He had been struggling to obliterate the whirling whistle in his head but it had effectively dirtied every note. He could not keep the Bach pure. He could not, past the opening measures, hear himself play. Gripping the cello by its neck, he rose from the chair with a cry.

"Zora," he called.

She arrived at once.

"What's happening?"

He said he could not go on with the suite. It was curdled by the disgusting whine in his ears.

"Something drastic has to be done."

She said they had already joined the class-action suit.

He threatened to abandon the accursed town if there was no quick improvement in the situation; and Zora, observing him, said that was entirely on his own head.

*　　*　　*

Away from home there was some measure of relief. Driving to Lenox for a class, he escaped the sound in his ears—certainly it diminished outside of Elmsville, but it worried him that he seemed still to be listening for its return. He couldn't be sure he was entirely rid of it. Yet just as he thought he had begun taking the noise with him wherever he went, the situation seemed to change.

One night in winter the *Courier* announced that the malfunctioning ventilation system at the plant had been replaced by a noiseless apparatus. Zora and Dworkin, as they lay in bed bundled in blankets, listened with two of the three windows wide open. She heard the same unhappy sound, he only the delicious country silence. But the noise had diminished a little, Zora admitted, and possibly she could stand it now.

* * *

In the spring, as she approached her forty-second birthday, she was restless again. She had gone back to the gallery where she had formerly worked and was in the process of arranging a show of two women painters and a male sculptor. During the day Zora wasn't home; Dworkin was—practicing and teaching. He was at work on a sonata for four cellos that was developing well. Four cellos gave it an organlike choral quality.

But Zora, after the gallery day, was impatient with herself, self-critical, "not with it."

"Why don't you tell me what's on your mind," Dworkin said one evening after they had had dinner out.

"Nothing much."

"Or is it the usual thing?"

"I can't burden you with my every worry."

She wiped her eyes but was not crying.

That night she woke Dworkin and, in a hushed, hesitant voice, begged him to listen. "I mean, just listen to what you hear in this room. What do you hear?"

He listened until he heard the cosmos, the rush of stars; otherwise he heard nothing.

"Not much, I'm afraid. Nothing I can lay a finger on."

On earth he heard nothing.

"Don't you hear," she asked, slowly sitting up, "a sort of eerie whine? This is drawn out as though at the far end of someone crying. I would call it a ghostly sound."

She held Dworkin tightly.

"Ghostly?" he said, trying to see her in the dark.

She listened keenly. "It has that quality."

"No," Dworkin replied after a good two minutes. "I don't hear any wail, whine, or whatever. I emphatically don't."

In the morning she firmly asked, "Would you move out of this house if it came to that, Dworkin? I mean if I asked you to?"

He said he would once he felt certain he heard the noise she was hearing. She seemed to accept that as fair.

*   *   *

Dworkin waited by the D-R factory fence in every wind and weather. He had talked to the owner, who promised him the problem was already solved. Zora said she didn't think so. They listened together on the bedroom deck, and Zora, pale-faced, raised a pale finger when she heard the noise especially clearly. "As though it were directly in front of our faces."

He wondered whether what she was hearing might be psychologically inspired. Zora had wanted a child but had never had one. Might she who can't conceive begin to hear a ghostly wailing?

Too simple, thought Dworkin.

Ella had taken her troubles in stride. Their baby was born dead, and she had not wanted another. But Zora could never conceive, though she had wanted to very much.

She agreed to have her ears tested when Dworkin suggested it. He reminded her that years ago she had had a disease of the middle ear, and she consented to see her former ear doctor.

Then Dworkin privately telephoned two of his neighbors and confirmed they no longer heard the noise Zora said she still heard.

"It's been solved for my husband and me with the new ventilation system they put in," Mrs. Spinker explained. "So we dropped the suit because nobody hears those noises anymore."

"Or echo thereof?"

"Not anymore."

Dworkin said he too would drop it.

Zora said she would try a new diet before visiting the ear doctor; but she promised to go.

*   *   *

The diet, after several weeks, appeared not to be working, and she was still hearing the quavering, eerie noise. "It comes up like a flute that hangs still in the air and then flows back to its source. Then it begins to take on the quality of a moaning or mystical sound, if that's what you can call it. Suppose it's some distant civilization calling in, trying to get in touch with us, and for some reason I am the one person who can hear this signal, yet I can't translate the message?"

"We all get signals we don't necessarily pick up," Dworkin said.

She woke him that night and said in a hushed voice, "There it goes again, a steady, clear sound, ending in a rising wail. Don't you hear it now?"

"I tell you I don't. Why do you still wake me?"

"I can't help wishing you would hear it too."

"I don't want to. Leave me the hell out of it."

"I hate you, Zworkin. You are a selfish beast."

"You want to poison my ears."

"I want you to confirm whether something I hear is real or unreal. Is that so much to ask somebody you are married to?"

"It's your noise, Zora—don't bang it on my head. How am I going to support us if I can't play my cello?"

"Suppose I go deaf," she said, but Dworkin was snoring.

*   *   *

"La la, la la," she sang to herself in the looking glass. She had been gaining weight and resembled, she said, an ascending balloon.

Dworkin, returning from Lenox that evening, complained he'd had trouble in his master class because the arthritis in his shoulder was taking a harder bite.

When he came upstairs before midnight, she was reading a magazine in bed, both ears plugged with wads of cotton. Her legs snapped together when he entered the room.

"The bedroom is virtually a sound box," Zora said. "It captures every earthly sound, not to speak of the unearthly."

I'd better stop listening, he thought. If I hear what she does, that is the end of my music.

*   *   *

Zora drove off in a station wagon for three days, traveling into Vermont and New Hampshire. She had not asked Dworkin to come along. Each night she called from a different motel or country inn and sounded fine.

"How's it coming?" he asked.

"Just fine, I suppose. I confess I haven't heard anything greatly unusual in my ears."

"No noises from outer space?"

"Nor from inner."

He said that was a good sign.

"What do you think we ought to do?" she asked.

"Concerning what?"

"About the house. About our lives. If I go on hearing noises when I get back."

He said after a minute, "Zora, I would like to help you extricate yourself from this misery. I speak with love."

"Don't make me feel like a crippled pigeon," she said. "I know I hear a real enough noise when I am in that house."

"I warn you, I love this house," he said.

＊　　　＊　　　＊

On the night after her return from her trip alone, Dworkin, awakened by a burst of cello music in the sky, stood in yellow pajamas and woolen navy robe on the deck, staring at the clustered stars.

Spanning the knotted strings of glowing small fires across the night sky, he beheld, after its slow coming into sight, like a lighted ship out of fog, his personal constellation: the Cellist. Dworkin had observed it in childhood, and often since then, a seated figure playing his cello—somewhere between Cassiopeia and Lyra. Tonight he beheld Casals sitting in a chair constructed of six jeweled stars, playing gorgeously as he hoarsely sang. Dworkin watched engrossed, trying to identify the music; like Bach but not Bach. He was not able to. Casals was playing a prelude lamenting his fate. Apparently he had—for him—died young. It was hours past midnight and Zora slumbered heavily, exhausted by her lonely journey. After the stars had dimmed and the celestial cellist and his music all but vanished, Dworkin drew on a pair of knee socks under his pajamas, and in tennis shoes he went quietly downstairs to the music room, where he lifted the dark cello out of its hand-carved casket and for a moment held it in his arms.

He dug the end pin into the pockmarked floor—he would not use a puck, he had informed both his wives. Dworkin wanted the floor to move if the cello caused it to. Embracing the instrument between his knees, the delicate curved shell against his breast, he drew his bow across the bridge, his left fingers fluttering as though they were singing. Dworkin felt the vibrations of the cello rise in his flesh to his head. He tried to clear his throat. Despite the time of night and the live pain in his shoulder, he played from the andante of Schubert's B-flat major trio, imagining the music of the piano and violin. Schubert breaks the heart and calls it *un poco mosso*. That is the art of it. The longing heart forever breaks yet is gravely contained. The cello Dworkin passionately played played him.

He played for the space and solidity and shape of his house, the way it fitted together. He played for the long years of music here, and for the room in which he had practiced and composed for a quarter of a century, often looking up from his score to glance at the elms through the window of the arched wall. Here were his scores, records, books. Above his head hung portraits of Piatigorsky and Boccherini, who seemed to watch him when he entered the room.

Dworkin played for his gabled dark-gray, blue-shuttered house, built early in the century, where he had lived with both of his wives. Ella had a warm singing voice excellently placed and sup-ported. Had she been braver she would have been a professional singer. "Ah," she said, "if I were a brave person." "Try," Dworkin urged. "But I'm not," said Ella. She had never dared. In the house she sang wherever she happened to be. She was the one who had thought of putting in the stained-glass windows of beasts and flow-ers. Dworkin played the allegro, and once more the andante of the heart-laden Schubert. He sang to Ella. In her house.

As he played, Zora, in a black nightgown, stood at the closed door of the music room.

After listening a moment she returned quickly to the bedroom.

When he left the music room, Dworkin detected his wife's perfume and knew she had been standing at the door.

He searched his heart and thought he understood what she had expected to hear.

*   *   *

As he went along the hallway, he caught a glimpse of a fleeting figure.

"Zora," he called.

She paused, but it was not Zora.

"Ella," Dworkin sobbed. "My dearest wife, I have loved you always."

She was not there to assent or ask why.

*   *   *

When Dworkin got back to bed, Zora was awake. "Why should I diet? It's an unnatural act."

"Have you been lying there thinking of dieting?"

"I've been listening to myself."

"You hear something again, after being absolved in your travels?"

"I believe I am slowly going deaf," Zora said.

"Are you still hearing the whine or wail?"

"Oho, do I hear it."

"Is it like the sound of someone singing?"

"I would call it the sound of my utter misery."

Dworkin then told her he was ready to move.

"I guess we ought to sell the house."

"Why ought we?"

"It comes to me at this late date that it's never been yours."

"Better late than later." Zora laughed. "It is true, I have never loved this house."

"Because it was Ella's?"

"Because I never loved it."

"Is that what caused your noises, do you think?"

"The noises cause the noises," Zora said.

*   *   *

Dworkin, the next day, telephoned the real estate agents, who came that night, a man and his amiable wife in their sixties.

They inspected the house from basement to attic. The man offered to buy a child's fiddle he had seen in the attic, but Dworkin wouldn't sell.

"You'll get a good price for this place," the woman said to Zora. "It's been kept in first-rate shape."

When they were moving out in the early spring, Dworkin said he had always loved this house, and Zora said she had never really cared for it.

1985

A Lost Grave

HECHT WAS a born late bloomer.

One night he woke hearing rain on his windows and thought of his young wife in her wet grave. This was something new, because he hadn't thought of her in too many years to be comfortable about. He saw her in her uncovered grave, rivulets of water streaming in every direction, and Celia, whom he had married when they were of unequal ages, lying alone in the deepening wet. Not so much as a flower grew on her grave, though he could have sworn he had arranged perpetual care.

He stepped into his thoughts perhaps to cover her with a plastic sheet, and though he searched in the cemetery under dripping trees and among many wet plots, he was unable to locate her. The dream he was into offered no tombstone name, row, or plot number, and though he searched for hours, he had nothing to show for it but his wet self. The grave had taken off. How can you cover a woman who isn't where she is supposed to be? That's Celia.

The next morning, Hecht eventually got himself out of bed and into a subway train to Jamaica to see where she was buried. He hadn't been to the cemetery in many years, no particular surprise to anybody considering past circumstances. Life with Celia wasn't exactly predictable. Yet things change in a lifetime, or seem to. Hecht had lately been remembering his life more vividly, for whatever reason. After you hit sixty-five, some things that have two distinguishable sides seem to pick up another that complicates the picture as you look or count. Hecht counted.

Now, though Hecht had been more or less in business all his life, he kept few personal papers, and though he had riffled through a small pile of them that morning, he had found nothing to help him establish Celia's present whereabouts; and after a random looking at gravestones for an hour he felt the need to call it off and spend another hour with a young secretary in the main office, who fruitlessly tapped his name and Celia's into a computer and came up with a scramble of interment dates, grave plots and counter plots, that exasperated him.

"Look, my dear," Hecht said to the flustered young secretary, "if that's how far you can go on this machine, we have to find another way to go further, or I will run out of patience. This grave is lost territory as far as I am concerned, and we have to do something practical to find it."

"What do you think I'm doing, if I might ask?"

"Whatever you are doing doesn't seem to be much help. This computer is supposed to have a good mechanical memory, but it's either out of order or rusty in its parts. I admit I didn't bring any papers with me, but so far the only thing your computer has informed us is that it has nothing much to inform us."

"It has informed us it is having trouble locating the information you want."

"Which adds up to zero minus zero," Hecht said. "I wish to remind you that a lost grave isn't a missing wedding ring we are talking about. It is a lost cemetery plot of the lady who was once my wife that I wish to recover."

The pretty young woman he was dealing with had a tight-lipped conversation with an unknown person, then the buzzer on her desk sounded and Hecht was given permission to go into the director's office.

"Mr. Goodman will now see you."

He resisted "Good for Mr. Goodman." Hecht only nodded, and followed the young woman to an inner office. She knocked once and disappeared, as a friendly voice talked through the door.

"Come in, come in."

"Why should I worry if it's not my fault?" Hecht told himself.

Mr. Goodman pointed to a chair in front of his desk and Hecht was soon seated, watching him pour orange juice from a quart container into a small green glass.

"Will you join me in a sweet mouthful?" he asked, nodding at the container. "I usually take refreshment this time of the morning. It keeps me balanced."

"Thanks," said Hecht, meaning he had more serious problems. "Why I am here is that I am looking for my wife's grave, so far with no success." He cleared his throat, surprised at the emotion that had gathered there.

Mr. Goodman observed Hecht with interest.

"Your outside secretary couldn't find it," Hecht went on, regretting he hadn't found the necessary documents that would identify the grave site. "Your young lady tried her computer in every combination but couldn't produce anything. What was lost is still lost, in other words, a woman's grave."

"*Lost* is premature," Goodman offered. "*Displaced* might be better. In my twenty-eight years in my present capacity, I don't believe we have lost a single grave."

The director tapped lightly on the keys of his desk computer, studied the screen with a squint, and shrugged. "I am afraid that we now draw a blank. The letter *H* volume of our ledgers that we used before we were computerized seems to be missing. I assure you this can't be more than a temporary condition."

"That's what your young lady already informed me."

"She's not my young lady, she's my secretarial assistant."

"I stand corrected," Hecht said. "This meant no offense."

"Likewise," said Goodman. "But we will go on looking. Could you kindly tell me, if you don't mind, what was the status of your relationship to your wife at the time of her death?" He peered over half-moon glasses to check the computer reading.

"There was no status. We were separated. What has that got to do with her burial plot?"

"The reason I inquire is, I thought it might refresh your memory. For example, is this the correct cemetery, the one you are looking in—Mount Jereboam? Some people confuse us with Mount Hebron."

"I guarantee you it was Mount Jereboam."

Hecht, after a hesitant moment, gave these facts: "My wife wasn't the most stable woman. She left me twice and disappeared for months. Although I took her back twice, we weren't together at the time of her death. Once she threatened to take her life, though eventually she didn't. In the end she died of a normal sickness, not cancer. This was years later, when we weren't living together anymore, but I carried out her burial, to the best of my knowledge, in this exact cemetery. I also heard she had lived for a short time with some guy she met somewhere, but when she died, I was the one who buried her. Now I am sixty-five and lately I have had this urge to visit the grave of someone who lived with me when I was a young man. This is a grave which everybody now tells me they can't locate."

Goodman rose at his desk, a short man, five feet tall. "I will institute a careful research."

"The quicker, the better," Hecht replied. "I am still curious what happened to her grave."

Goodman almost guffawed, but caught himself and thrust out his hand. "I will keep you well informed, don't worry."

Hecht left, irritated. On the train back to the city he thought of Celia and her various unhappinesses. He wished he had told Goodman she had spoiled his life.

That night it rained. To his surprise he found a wet spot on his pillow.

The next day Hecht again went to the graveyard. "What did I forget that I ought to remember?" he asked himself. Obviously the grave plot, row, and number. Though he sought it diligently he could not find it. Who can remember something he has once and for all put out of his mind? It's like trying to grow beans out of a bag of birdseed.

"But I must be patient and I will find out. As time goes by I am bound to recall. When my memory says yes I won't argue no."

But weeks passed and Hecht still could not remember what he was trying to. "Maybe I have reached a dead end?"

Another month went by and at last the cemetery called him. It was Mr. Goodman, clearing his throat. Hecht pictured him at his desk sipping orange juice.

"Mr. Hecht?"

"The same."

"This is Mr. Goodman. A happy Rosh Hashanah."

"A happy Rosh Hashanah to you."

"Mr. Hecht, I wish to report progress. Are you prepared for an insight?"

"You name it," Hecht said.

"So let me use a better word. We have tracked your wife and it turns out she isn't in the grave there where the computer couldn't find her. To be frank, we found her in a grave with another gentleman."

"What kind of gentleman? Who in God's name is he? I am her legal husband."

"This one, if you will pardon me, is the man who lived with your wife after she left you. They lived together on and off, so don't blame yourself too much. After she died he got a court order, and they removed her to a different grave, where we also laid him after his death. The judge gave him the court order because he convinced him that he had loved her for many years."

Hecht was embarrassed. "What are you talking about? How could he transfer her grave anywhere if it wasn't his legal property? Her grave belonged to me. I paid cash for it."

"That grave is still there," Goodman explained, "but the names were mixed up. His name was Kaplan but the workmen buried her under Caplan. Your grave is still in the cemetery, though we had it under Kaplan and not Hecht. I apologize to you for this inconvenience but I think we now have got the mystery cleared up."

"So thanks," said Hecht. He felt he had lost a wife but was no longer a widower.

"Also," Goodman reminded him, "don't forget you gained an

empty grave for future use. Nobody is there and you own the plot."

Hecht said that was obviously true.

The story had astounded him. Yet whenever he thought of telling it to someone he knew, or had just met, he wasn't sure he wanted to.

1984

In Kew Gardens

ONCE, as they walked in the gardens, Virginia felt her knickers come loose and slip down her ankles. She grabbed at her maiden-hair as the garment eluded her frantic grasp and formed a puddle of cloth at her feet. Swooping up her underpants, with a cry of dismay she plunged into the bushes, shrilly singing "The Last Rose of Summer." As she stood up, the elastic knot she had tied snapped, and the knickers again lay limp at her feet.

"Christ, goddamn!"

Vanessa listened at the bushes.

"Don't be hysterical. No one will see through your dress."

"How can you be certain?"

"No one would want to."

She shrieked slowly.

"Forgive me, dear goat," Vanessa told her. "I meant no harm."

"Oh, never, no, never."

Insofar as I was ever in love I loved Vanessa.

George Duckworth, affectionate stepbrother, carried his tormented amours from the parlor to the night nursery. He nuzzled, he fondled, he fiddled with his finger. To his sisters he was obscenity incarnate. He touched without looking.

"I meant no harm. I meant to comfort you."

Virginia lost her underpants and wondered where she had been.

Her erotic life rarely interested her. It seemed unimportant compared with what went on in the world.

I was born in 1882 with rosy cheeks and green eyes. Not enough was made of my coloring.

When her mother died she tore the pillow with her teeth. She spat bleeding feathers.

Her father cried and raged. He beat his chest and groaned aloud, "I am ruined."

The mother had said, "Everyone needed me but he needed me most."

"Unquenchable seems to me such presence": H. James.

The father moaned, "Why won't my whiskers grow?"

As Virginia lay mourning her mother, dreadful voices cried in the night. They whispered, they clucked, they howled. She suffered piercing occipital headaches.

King Edward cursed her foully in the azalea garden. He called her filthy names, reading aloud dreadful reviews of books she had yet to write.

The king sang of madness, rage, incest.

Years later she agreed to marry Mr. Leonard Woolf, who had offered to be her Jewish mother.

"I am mad," she confessed to him.

"I am marrying a penniless Jew," Virginia wrote Violet Dickinson. She wondered who had possessed her.

"He thinks my writing the best part of me."

"His Jewishness is qualified."

His mother disgusted her.

She grew darkly enraged.

In fact, I dislike the quality of masculinity. I always have.

Lytton said he had no use for it whatever. "Semen?" he asked when he saw a stain on Vanessa's dress.

Vanessa loved a man who found it difficult to love a woman.

She loved Duncan Grant until he loved her.

She had loved Clive Bell, who loved Virginia, who would not love him. Virginia loved Leonard, who loved her. She swore she loved him.

When Julia, the mother, died, the goat threw herself out of a first-story window and lay on the ground with Warren Septimus

Smith. "He did not want to die till the very last minute." Neither had she.

The old king emerged from the wood, strumming a lyre. A silver bird flew over his head, screeching in Greek.

A dead woman stalked her.

Janet Case, her teacher of Greek, loved her. She loved her teacher of Greek.

She loved Violet Dickinson.

She loved Vita Nicolson.

Leonard and she had no children. They lay in bed and had no children. She would have liked a little girl.

"Possibly my great age makes it less a catastrophe but certainly I find the climax greatly exaggerated."

Vanessa wrote Clive: "Apparently she gets no pleasure from the act, which I think is curious. She and Leonard were anxious to know when I had had an orgasm. I couldn't remember, do you?"

"Yet I dare say we are the happiest couple in England. Aren't we, Leonard?"

"My dear."

Leonard and Virginia set up the Hogarth Press but they would not print Mr. James Joyce's *Ulysses*. "He is impudent and coarse."

Mrs. Dalloway loved Warren Septimus Smith though she never met him.

"He had committed an appalling crime and had been condemned by human nature."

"The whole world was clamoring, Kill yourself, kill yourself for our sakes."

(He sat on the windowsill.)

He jumped. Virginia fell from the window.

As for *To the Lighthouse*, I have no idea what it means, if it has a meaning. That's no business of mine.

"[Lily Briscoe] could have wept. It was bad, it was bad, it was infinitely bad! She could have done it differently of course; the colour could have been thinned and faded; the shapes etherealised; that was how Paunceforte would have seen it. But then she did not see it like that. She saw the colour burning on a framework of steel; the light of a butterfly's wing lying upon the arches of a cathedral. Of all that only a few random marks scrawled upon the canvas remained. And it would never be seen; never be hung even, and there was Mr. Tansley whispering in her ear, 'Women can't paint, women can't write . . .'

". . . She looked at the steps; they were empty; she looked at her canvas; it was blurred. With a sudden intensity, as if she saw it clear for a second, she drew a line there, in the centre. It was done; it was finished. Yes, she thought, laying down her brush in extreme fatigue, I have had my vision."

All I need is a room of my own.

"I hate to see so many women's lives wasted simply because they have not been trained well enough to take an independent interest in any study or to be able to work efficiently in any profession": Leslie Stephen to Julia Duckworth.

"There has fallen a splendid tear/From the passion-flower at the gate." —Alfred, Lord Tennyson

"There was something so ludicrous in thinking of people singing such things under their breath that I burst out laughing."

The Waves.

The Years. The bloody years.

The acts among *Between the Acts.*

No one she knew inspired her to more than momentary erotic excitement throughout her life. She loved Shakespeare's sister.

Leonard gave up that ghost.

"They also serve."

She felt a daily numbness, nervous tension. "What a born melancholic I am."

They had called her the goat in the nursery, against which she tore at their faces with her tiny nails.

They had never found Thoby her dead brother's lost portrait. Vanessa had painted and forever lost it.

Her mother died.

My father is not my mother. Leonard is my mother. We shall never conceive a living child.

"I shall never grow my whiskers again."

She heard voices, or words to that effect.

"Maiden, there's turd in your blood," King Edward chanted in ancient Greece.

Her scream blew the bird off its one-legged perch and it flapped into the burning wood.

An old king strode among the orange azaleas.

For years she simply went mad.

She spoke in soft shrieks.

She wrote twenty-one books whose reviews frightened her.

"That was not my doing," said Leonard Woolf.

"Nor mine," sobbed her Greek tutor.

Perhaps it was mine, Vita Nicolson said. "She was so frail a creature. One had to be most careful not to shock her."

I loved Vita. She loved *Orlando*.

Virginia wrote a biography of Roger Fry. She did not want to write a biography of Roger Fry.

Leonard served her a single soft-boiled egg when she was ill. "Now, Virginia, open your mouth and swallow your egg. Only if you eat will you regain the strength to write your novels and essays."

She sucked the tip of his spoon.

"Though you give much I give so little."

"The little you give is a king's domain."

At that time the writing went well and she artfully completed *Between the Acts*, yet felt no joy.

Virginia relapsed into depression and denied herself food.

"Virginia, you must eat to sustain yourself."

"My reviews are dreadful," Virginia said.

"I am afraid of this war," Virginia said.

"I hear clamorous noises in my head," Virginia said.

One morning, to escape the noises of war, she dragged herself to the river Ouse, there removed shoes, stockings, underpants, and waded slowly into the muddy water. The large rock she had forced into her coat pocket pulled her down till she could see the earth in her green eyes.

"I don't think two people could have been happier than we have been."

1984

Alma Redeemed

GUSTAV MAHLER's ghost.

Bruno Walter had seen it as Mahler conducted one of his last concerts. It waxed in music as the conductor waned. The ghost appeared, more or less, to Alma Mahler one or two years after her husband was dead. Alma did not believe in ghosts, but this one troubled her. It had got into her bedsheets but hadn't stayed long.

Can Jews haunt people?

Gustav was a rationalist nonbeliever. "In that clear mind I never detected any trace of superstition," Bruno Walter said. He spoke of Mahler—as Alma clearly remembered—as a "God-struck man," whose religious self flowered in his music, viz., *"Veni, creator spiritus,"* as it flashed in eternity in the Eighth Symphony. Alma felt that Mahler was too subtle a man to have believed simply in God, but that wouldn't mean he might not attempt to disturb her, although she was aware that some of her thoughts of Mahler had caused her more than ordinary fright. Might the fright have produced the ghost? Such things are possible.

In my mind, more than once I betrayed him.

Yet Mahler was a kind man, although an egotist who defined his egotism as a necessity of his genius.

"Gott, how he loved his genius!"

Now, all of Alma's husbands, a collection of a long lifetime including Mahler, Walter Gropius, Franz Werfel—and Oskar Kokoschka, the painter, made it a fourth if you counted in the man she hadn't married, whom Alma conceived to be her most astonishing (if most difficult) lover—they were all artists of unusual merit and accomplishment; yet Alma seemed to favor Mahler, even if she had trouble during her lifetime caring deeply for his music.

When she met Gustav Mahler, Alma stood five feet three inches tall and weighed 144 pounds. She loved her figure. Her deep blue eyes were her best feature. She drew men with half a glance. Alma never wore underpants and thought she knew who might know she wasn't wearing them. When she met him she felt that Mahler didn't know though he may have wanted to.

Alma, a lovely, much-sought-after young woman, one of the prettiest in Vienna in those days, felt Mahler was magnetic, but she wasn't sure she ought to marry him. "He is frightening, nervous, and bounds across the room like an animal. I fear his energy."

She wrote in her diary in purple ink: "At the opera he loves to conduct *Faust.*"

She wanted Gustav. She felt she had snared him in her unconscious.

Yet his demands frightened her. "Is it too late, my dearest Almchi, to ask you to make my music yours? Play as you please but don't attempt to compose. Composition is for heroes."

"How can I make his music mine if I have loved Wagner throughout my life? What passion can I possibly feel for Mahler's music or even for Mahler?" These thoughts concerned her.

"You must understand, my tender girl, that my harmony and polyphony, for all their vivid modernity, which seems to distress you, remain in the realm of pure tonality. Someday your dear ears will open to the glories of my sound."

"Yes, Gustav," said Alma.

"Let us be lovers in a true marriage. I am the composer and you are, in truth, my beloved bride."

Mahler urged her to consult her stepfather and mother. "You must lay to rest your doubts, whatever they are. The matter must be settled before we can contemplate a union for life."

"Say nothing," Carl Moll, her stepfather, advised Alma. "Best get rid of the Jew."

"*Perhaps* get rid of him," said her mother. "I never trusted his conversion to Catholicism though he pleads sincerity. He became Catholic because Cosima Wagner insisted that no Jew be allowed to replace Richard Wagner at the Vienna Opera."

But Alma said she had thought about it and decided she loved Mahler.

She did not say she was already pregnant by him.

Mahler walked in his floppy galoshes to the church on their wedding day.

At breakfast the guests were spirited, although in memoirs she wrote many years later Alma wasn't sure of that. She had trouble defining her mood.

She was twenty-two, Mahler was forty-one.

"If only I could find my own inner balance."

Mahler whispered into her good ear that he loved her more than he had loved anyone except his dear mother, who had died insane.

Alma said she was glad he respected his mother.

"You must give yourself to me unconditionally and desire nothing except my love."

He sounded more like a teacher than a lover.

"Yes, Gustav."

"He is continually talking about preserving his art but that is not allowed to me."

Nothing has come to fruition for me, Alma thought. Neither my beauty, nor my spirit, nor my talent.

Does his genius, by definition, submerge my talent? My ship is in the harbor but has sprung a leak.

He did not lie in bed and make love to her. He preferred to mount her when she was deeply asleep.

His odor was repulsive. "Probably from your cigars," she had informed Mahler. He was a stranger to her, she wrote in her diary, "and much about him will remain strange forever."

She tripped over a paraffin lamp and set the carpet afire.

Mahler dreamed Alma was wearing her hair as she used to in her girlhood. He did not like her to pile her tresses on the top of her head. Gustav said her hairdo was Semitic-looking and he wished to avoid that impression. He assured his friends he was not a practicing Jew. Alma wore her hair long most of the time.

When their daughter, Maria, caught diphtheria and died, Mahler could not stand being alone. Memories of his daughter seared his life. He went from person to person with a new message: "Alma has sacrificed her youth for me. With absolute selflessness she has subordinated her life to my work."

Alma let Ossip Gabrilowitsch hold her hand in a dark room.

"To gain a spiritual center, my Alma, that's the important thing. Then everything takes on another aspect."

Alma found his impersonal preaching repellent and frightening.

Since her youth she had been nervous among strangers and very sensitive about her impaired hearing.

Mahler became frightened at the thought of losing his wife.

Mahler and Freud met in Leiden and walked for four hours along the tree-lined canals. Freud told him a good deal about the life of the psyche and Mahler was astonished though he had guessed much that Freud had told him.

"My darling, my lyre," he wrote his wife, "come exorcise the ghosts of darkness. They claw me, they throw me to the ground. I ask in silence whether I am damned. Rescue me, my dearest."

Mahler suspected that he loved Alma more than she loved him.

He was as strict now about her going back to her music as he had been nine years ago in insisting she give up composing.

One night she woke up and saw him standing by her bed like a ghost.

He dedicated his Eighth Symphony to her.

He feared his Ninth.

"Ah, how lovely it is to love, my dearest Almscherl. And it is only now that I know what love is. Believe me, Tristan sings the truth."

"Alma blossoms, on a splendid diet, and she has given up tippling Benedictine. She looks younger day by day."

One day she had a cold; Mahler invited the doctor who had examined Alma to look him over too.

"Well, you have no cause to be proud of that heart," the doctor said after listening for a minute.

The bacterial tests sealed his doom. Mahler insisted he be told the truth, and he said he wanted to die in Vienna.

He talked to Alma about his grave and tombstone. She listened gravely. He did not want to be cremated. He wanted to be there if people came to the graveyard to see him.

"Mozart," said Mahler, before he died during a thunderstorm. "Boom!"

*   *   *

Alma met the man who later became her second husband in a sanitarium, in Tobelbad when, exhausted by Gustav's pace and striving, she was advised by a country doctor to take the cure.

Gustav displayed an unyielding energy she couldn't keep up with. She was the young one but he made her feel old. That's the trick, she thought. He wants me to match him in age.

At Tobelbad she met a handsome architect, Walter Gropius, age twenty-seven, who lived down the hall and stared at her in astonishment as she walked by. He gazed at Alma with architectural eyes and she was aware she had form.

They began to go for long walks. Gustav usually gave her short lectures in philosophy as they walked together, but this one talked on about nature and architectural masses; he seemed surprised that she did not throw herself into his arms.

Gustav, promoting his conducting career, hurried from city to city, writing to her from where he happened to be, one opera house or philharmonic society after another; but she was in no mood to respond. In his letters to his tender Almscherl he wrote, "I could not bear this depleting routine if it did not end with delicious thoughts of you. Regain your health, my precious dear girl, so that we may again renew our affectionate embraces."

In his letters Mahler tickled her chin and ladled out bits of gossip laced with pious observations. His pace was again frantic; yet wherever he went, he worried about her, though for reasons of scheduling, etc., he found it difficult to visit her at Tobelbad, yet surely she knew the direction of his heart?

He had asked his mother-in-law, Anna Moll, to write Alma a letter requesting news; and soon thereafter she paid her daughter a visit, but there was no news to speak of. "She is responding to her cure, not much more." Gropius was invisible.

Alma had put him out of her mind and returned home. No one knew whether they had become or had been lovers.

"When shall we meet again?" the handsome Gropius had asked. She wasn't sure.

"Seriously, my dearest—"

"Please do not call me 'my dearest,' I am simply Alma."

"Seriously, simply Alma."

"I am a married person, Herr Gropius. Mahler is my legal husband."

"A terrible answer," Gropius replied.

" 'None but the brave deserves the fair.' " He quoted Dryden in English.

When he translated the line, Alma said nothing.

"Mahler met me at the Toblach station and was suddenly more in love with me than ever before."

One night when Mahler and Alma were in Vienna, before returning to their farmhouse in Toblach, Mahler, looking around nervously, whispered, "Alma, I have the feeling that we are being followed."

"Nonsense," said Alma. "Don't be so superstitious." He laughed but it did not sound like a laugh. He did not practice sufficiently, Alma thought.

Gropius then sent Mahler a letter asking his permission to marry his wife. Alma placed her husband's mail on the piano and shivered at lunch as Mahler slowly read the letter, whose writing she had recognized. She had wanted to tear it up but was afraid to.

Mahler read the letter and let out a gasp, then a deep cry.

"Who is this crazy man who asks permission to marry my wife? Am I, then, your father?"

Alma laughed a little hysterically, yet managed to answer calmly.

"This is a foolish young man I met at the sanitarium. I do not love him."

"Who said love?" Mahler shouted.

Alma eventually calmed him, but he felt as though he had been shipwrecked and didn't know why.

That afternoon Alma saw Gropius from her car window as she drove past the village bridge. Gropius didn't see her.

She returned from her errand feeling ill and breathlessly told Mahler whom she had seen walking near the bridge: "That was the young man who was interested in me in Tobelbad although I did nothing to encourage him."

"We shall see." Mahler took along a kerosene lamp and went out searching for Gropius. He found him not far from their farmhouse. "I am Mahler," the composer said. "Perhaps you wish to speak to my wife?"

Gropius, scratching under his arm, confessed that intent. "I am Gropius."

Mahler lit the lamp. It was dark.

He called up the stairs and Alma came down.

"I come," she said.

"You two ought to talk," said Mahler. He withdrew to his study, where he read to himself in the Old Testament.

When Alma, white-faced, came to him in the study, Mahler told her calmly that she was free to decide in whatever way she wanted. "You can do as you feel you must." If he was conducting, no stick was visible.

"Thanks," said Alma. "I want him to go. Please let him stay until morning and then he shall go. I have spoken to him and explained that I will not tolerate bad manners."

Mahler went back to reading the Old Testament. He was thinking of *Das Lied von der Erde* though he had not yet written it.

Gropius stayed overnight and Alma drove him to his train to Berlin in the morning.

Gropius, holding his hat, said he was sorry for the trouble he had caused. Then he said, "When shall we meet again?"

"Never," said Alma. "I am a happy woman. Please stay away from my life."

"Never is *never*."

Gropius said none but the brave deserves the fair.

He got into the train and sent her a worshipful telegram from every station it stopped at.

Gustav, that night, collapsed outside Alma's bedroom. The candle he was holding fell to the floor and the house almost went up in flames.

Alma got him to bed; she put Gropius out of her mind, where he remained until years later, long after Mahler's death, when she felt she could no longer stand Oskar Kokoschka's wild fantasies and burning desires.

*   *   *

Mahler, leaning out of his window at the Hotel Majestic above Central Park, in New York City, heard "boom" in the street below. The boom was for a dead fireman in a horse-drawn funeral cortege.

Mahler wrote the muffled drumbeat into his Tenth Symphony: BOOM!

*   *   *

"I know I am lost if I go any further with the present confusion in my life."—Kokoschka

"May I see you?" he asked.

Alma loved men of genius.

He was worldly, sensuous. He needed love and money.

He came to visit and they went to bed. She woke him and said it was time to go home. When he left her he walked till dawn.

He signed her into his name: Alma Oskar Kokoschka.

"Read this letter in the evening."

He bought the Paris newspapers to check on the weather when she was there.

"Alma, I passed your house at one o'clock and could have cried out in anger because you see the others and leave me in the dirty street."

The women in his paintings resemble Alma.

Remembering Gustav and fearing that she was pregnant by Oskar, Alma worried about any Jew who might see her pregnant.

In view of the Jungfrau he painted her on a balcony.

Oskar's mother railed against his obsession. "She is like a high-society mistress, a whore without garters."

"Shut your black mouth," he told her.

Alma feared pregnancy. It was wrong to have had a child out of wedlock. Maria had died because Alma had become pregnant before her marriage to Mahler.

Oskar's mother threatened to shoot her.

Kokoschka went to Alma's house and found his mother walking around with a gun in her purse.

"Give it here."

She crooked her finger and said, "Boom."

"Those who sin will be punished," Alma said one night to Mahler's ghost.

Oskar: "I am not allowed to see you every day because you want to keep alive the memory of this Jew who is so foreign to me."

"I must have you for my wife or else my talent will perish miserably."

She said she would marry him only after he had created a masterwork.

"Alma, please don't send me any money. I don't want it."

Die Windsbraut is Oskar's painting of Alma and him. She sleeps with her head on his shoulder. He gazes into the distance.

"I dreamed that Gustav was conducting. I was sitting near him and heard the music but it clearly displeased me."

"How far behind me my life with Mahler seems."

"I need my crazy mystique of the artist and from this I always manage to fill my head. The whole world is ultimately a dream that turns bad."

In Kokoschka's painting at Semmering, Alma ascends to heaven in fiery immolation. Oskar is in hell, surrounded by sexy fat serpents.

Alma was pregnant. "She will marry me now": Kokoschka.

Gustav's death mask arrived in the mail. Alma unpacked it and hung it on the wall. She entered the clinic for an abortion.

Austria declared war on Serbia. Alma wrote in her diary: "I imagine I have caused the whole upheaval."

"I would like to break free from Oskar."

"God punished me by sending this man into my life."

"I would give up every man on earth for music."

"Wagner means more to me than anyone. His time will come again."

Mrs. Kokoschka picked up her clay pot and dropped it on the floor. She withdrew a blood-red string of beads she was holding for Kokoschka. Alma had given them to him as a memento of his love for her.

"Yesterday evening I ran away from Oskar."

"What of the Jewish question *now*? They need help and direction—brains and feeling from those of us who are Christians."

She wrote to Gropius.

"I will get him quickly. I feel this is, or will become, something important to me."

Walter's birthday fell on the day Mahler had died.

Alma went to see him. "Finally in the course of an hour he fell in love with me. We were where the wine and good food raised our spirits. I went to the train with him where love overpowered him so that he dragged me onto the moving train, and come what might I had no choice but to travel to Hanover with him."

Walter had the manners of a husband. He was talented, handsome, an Aryan. He was crazily jealous of Kokoschka. Alma married him.

"So married, so free, and yet so bound."

"I wanted to make my own music, or music about which I felt deeply, because Gustav's was foreign to me."

"Jews have given us spirit but have eaten our hearts."

"My husband means nothing to me anymore. Walter has come too late."

She had met Franz Werfel. "Werfel is a rather fat Jew with full lips and watery almond eyes. He says: 'How can I be happy when there is someone who is suffering?' which I have heard verbatim from another egocentric, Gustav Mahler."

*   *   *

Alma married Werfel. He was a Jew who looked like a Jew, yet passable. She had had half a Jew in Mahler, and Werfel made the other half. They had a lot to learn, these Jews. They needed a Christian quality. Gropius was a true Aryan, a fine gentleman, passionate in his way, though she had never loved him. She had given him up for Werfel. She often thought of Kokoschka but hated him. "He wants to annihilate me."

Werfel needed her. He lived in dirty rooms, his clothes uncared for, cigarette butts on the floor. He needed a wife. He already had fathered a son Gropius thought was his child. Walter guessed that out and departed. He had tried to keep their daughter, Manon, but Alma had fought him for her. Gropius retreated like a gentleman. Manon died and was buried next to her half sister, Maria Mahler.

Alma lived with Franz Werfel through her best days. He wrote *Verdi, The Song of Bernadette,* and *The Star of the Unborn.* He made money and they spent it freely. The only really bad time was when they were trying to find their way out of Europe as the Nazis sought them in Spain. Then an American diplomat assisted them and they got out of Portugal on a Portuguese ship and afterward lived in Beverly Hills, U.S.A. Alma was feeling happy again.

But there is no beating out illness and bad health. Werfel died in his sixties. Alma did not attend his funeral though the guests had assembled and were awaiting her. Bruno Walter thrice played a Schubert impromptu as they waited for Alma to appear, but she had had it with funerals of three husbands. She was drinking Benedictine and never got to Werfel's funeral. She often felt that Kokoschka had been her best lover.

*   *   *

"Mahler had a long white face. He sat with his coat buttoned up to his ears. He looked like death masquerading as a monk. I told him this, hoping to exorcise my ghostly pangs of dread."

"Why do I fancy I am free when my character contracts me like a prison?": Mahler.

"Where is *my* truth?": Alma.

"He was always stopping on a walk to feel his pulse. I had always known his heart was diseased."

"The Jews are at once an unprecedented danger and the greatest good luck to humanity."

"I see Hitler as a genuine German idealist, something that is unthinkable to Jews."

"But fortunately he was stupid."

"Oh, my God, my God, why do you *so* love evil?"

"Werfel believed in the world revolution through Bolshevism. I believed that Fascism would solve the problems of the world."

Alma wore long necklaces with earrings and used dark lipstick. She drank Benedictine and ate little.

"Death is a contagious disease. That is the reason," Alma wrote in her diary, "why I will not place a photograph of a living person next to someone who is dead."

She thought she had met Crown Prince Rudolf of Austria on a mountaintop and he asked Alma to bear his child.

One night Mahler's ghost appeared, momentarily freezing her fingers.

"Alma, aren't you yet moved by my classically beautiful music? One can hear eternity in it."

"How can one love Mahler if she best loves Wagner?"

"My time will come."

Mahler diminished as he faded.

Alma felt he had handled her badly in her youth.

Yet there were moments she thought she still loved Mahler. She pictured him in a cemetery surrounded by his grave.

Alma favored cremation.

She was eighty-five when she died in 1964, older than King Lear.

*　　　*　　　*

Alma redeemed.

1984

Sources

"Armistice": Written in Washington in 1940; published here for the first time.

"Spring Rain": Written in 1942 and published here for the first time.

"The Literary Life of Laban Goldman": First published in *Assembly*, vol. 1, no. 1 (November 1943), pp. 24–27.

"The Grocery Store": Written in 1943 and published here for the first time.

"Benefit Performance": First published in *Threshold*, no. 3 (February 1943), pp. 20–22.

"The Place Is Different Now": First published in *American Prefaces*, no. 3 (Spring 1943), pp. 230–42.

"An Apology": First published in *Commentary*, vol. 12, no. 5 (November 1957), pp. 460–64.

"Riding Pants": Written in 1953 and published here for the first time.

"A Confession of Murder": The first section of the unpublished novella *The Man Nobody Could Lift*. See introduction, p. vii. Published here for the first time.

"The Elevator": Written in Italy in 1957; first published in *The Paris Review*, vol. 31, no. 112 (Fall 1989).

"An Exorcism": First published in *Harper's*, vol. 237, no. 1423 (December 1968), pp. 76–89. The text used here was revised by the author for *The Stories of Bernard Malamud* but was not included in that book.

"A Wig": First published in *The Atlantic*, vol. 245, no. 1 (January 1980), pp. 33–36.

"Zora's Noise": First published in *Gentlemen's Quarterly* [GQ] (January 1985), pp. 124–26; 164–68.

"A Lost Grave": First published in *Esquire*, vol. 103, no. 5 (May 1985), pp. 204–6, but written a year or so earlier.

"In Kew Gardens": First published in *Partisan Review*, vol. 51, no. 4 (1984) and vol. 52, no. 1 (1985), pp. 536–40.

"Alma Redeemed": First published in *Commentary*, vol. 78, no. 1 (July 1984), pp. 30–34. See comments on this and the previous story in the introduction, p. vii.

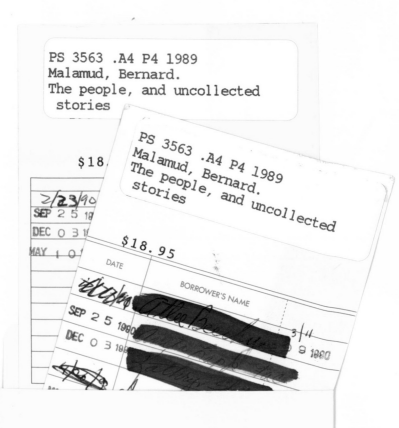